REIGN OF BLOOD SKY

LEIGHTON MOWATT
LEXINGTON MOWATT

1

TORTURE

~

Kristoff Kopensky was groggy when the moldy hood was yanked off. His head reeled in pain as he struggled to concentrate on his surroundings. He tried to rub his temples but found his wrists and ankles were bound to the chair. He heard a man speaking English with a thick foreign accent, but he couldn't understand the words or recognize the accent clearly. He tried to open his eyes several times, but each attempt yielded a bright light that intensified his headache. Fear spiked through his body. He needed to figure out where he was quickly. The last thing he remembered was sitting in the cab of an SUV that was under attack. Then a hood was jammed over his head, followed by unconsciousness. Then he was here, wherever that was.

He looked toward the source of the voice and saw a man speaking while he addressed a camera. Without his glasses, Kopensky couldn't make out the details of the man's face as he moved between what seemed like headlights.

Kopensky turned to his left and saw the beaten faces of two people he recognized: Senator Chadwick Gash and Zara Zogby, their translator, also bound to chairs. They seemed as groggy and as confused as Kopensky. No explanation would come from that side of the room.

He turned to look to his right and saw the disgruntled expression of Jun Li, Gash's personal aide, who was looking at everything around her, quickly assessing her surroundings. That was what Kopensky should have been doing as soon as the hood was removed, but he was not a trained military combatant. Then again, neither was she.

Seated on the opposite side of Jun was Neil Torres, the group's administrative aide. The young man's eyes darted about until they locked on Kopensky's.

Following Jun's example, Kopensky continued to search his surroundings, realizing they were in what looked like a dark, damp basement with a drab stone floor and cement walls.

Walking from behind them to make their presence known were eight sweaty, scruffy, unshaven, angry men holding automatic weapons and wearing dingy clothing and shemaghs. To make the image more frightening, something too large to be a bug skittered between the shadows of the room.

An angry voice from behind him barked an order in a foreign language. Kopensky turned to see who was talking but was hit hard with a blunt object on the back of his head. Now he remembered how his original throbbing headache began.

"Dude, who are you people?" Torres blurted while trying to look at the men behind him. His verbal outburst gained the attention of everyone in the room. This included the large-nosed man who held a commanding presence over the other captors surrounding them. The leader of the insurgent group stepped toward Torres as if he were about to answer his question. Instead, he struck Torres with the butt of his pistol.

Kopensky, Gash, Jun, and Zara exploded with verbal protests.

"Quiet, or you shall receive the same!" The insurgent leader's words exploded with a deep voice. The American prisoners stopped yelling, caught off guard at how loudly the man's voice thundered throughout the room. "Any more comments will be met with equal or greater force." the leader threatened, though with a strangely polite edge to his tone.

"Are you OK, Neil?" Jun whispered from the side of her mouth. The insurgent leader turned to look at her, causing her to stiffen in anticipation of physical retaliation, but their captor chose to ignore her whisper of concern. Torres moaned from the pulsating pain in his head.

Their captors' faces were covered, exposing only their eyes through their grimy scarves. Kopensky looked at Jun once more to see that she was trying hard to maintain control, but it was obvious that she was just as scared as he was, based on the uncontrolled trembling of her hands, which she attempted to hide by grasping the arms of the chair to which she was bound. Unless somebody did something soon, this was not going to end well.

Senior Vice President George Mason walked out of the elevator of the One World Trade Center building, commonly called the Capitol building, flanked by two government Secret Service agents assigned for his safety. He approached the thin, mousy man waiting for him beyond security.

"What's the update, Theodore?" Mason asked as he strode through the lobby. Mason easily towered over him.

"Not much has changed since we last spoke, sir." Theodore said, struggling to keep up with Mason's pace. "Both senators and their travel group are still missing, sir."

"The military escort team that was with them?"

"All Marine protection personnel have been accounted for at the ambushed location, and confirmed dead, sir." Theodore pressed the button that called the elevator to the lobby. "It's been two hours, Mr. Senior Vice President. The covert Navy SEAL team that was first on the scene confirmed that no New American civilians were found in the area, but because it was approximately one hundred miles from hostile territory they were ordered to hold off on any other actions, sir. We should have an update shortly."

Mason adjusted his wire–framed glasses. "This is not good." he mumbled to himself. As senior vice president, he oversaw the Department of Defense. To him the safety of senators and ambassadors was paramount, especially now that resources were scarce. Senators Gash and Kopensky had been sent to Turkey to solidify a trade agreement between the two countries.

Mason and his small entourage hurried down the hallway.

"Who's here?"

"The military representatives that you requested, and Vice President Harp, sir." Theodore huffed, nearly jogging beside Mason.

"No one else?"

At the end of the hallway, two soldiers stepped to opposite sides and opened the double doors.

"No, sir. Everyone else is currently off the island, sir."

"OK." Mason let out a preparatory sigh and then entered the War Room.

The War Room was the site of strategic meetings for the people who controlled New America's armed forces and national security. Each ranking official sat anxiously at the large conference table while their personal aides and assistants scampered around them like worker bees, performing whatever tasks they could to keep their bosses happy. Each department head turned as Mason took his chair at the head of the conference table.

"Senator Gash and Senator Kopensky are missing." he began. "A possible terrorist group has hacked the Global Comtext and will be making a global announcement in a few minutes. What else do we know?"

He eyed the people at the conference table, then looked at the large monitors on the wall showing various still images of the missing government employees.

"Jay?" Mason turned his head in the direction of the only man of color who held the status that allowed him to be seated at the table, Colonel Jay Malo.

"Sir, we confirmed reports that the convoy was ambushed from a ground and air combined assault." Malo reported bluntly, showing only the slightest of hesitation for the fallen troops indirectly under his command. "President Bennet is safe on Air Force One."

"Good Lord!" Mason whispered, turning to the naval fleet admiral. "Admiral Bailey?"

"I have a fleet of my best on standby. Three SEAL teams ready to deploy, George. One on the ground and two offshore."

"What are you waiting for?" Mason blurted, fighting to control his frustration.

"A target, sir. Any intelligence that will give us a location." Bailey responded calmly.

As if on cue, one of the smaller screens on the wall became active, first with the sound of garbled voices, then with the illumination of the screen going from black to blue, signifying that a broadcast was about to begin. Everyone in the room turned to look at the monitor.

"What's that?" Mason asked the technician who was seated at a small desk with several monitors in front of him.

"It's the Global Comtext, sir. It just went live unscheduled. It's being hacked again, Mr. Senior Vice President."

"Put it on the main screen." Mason ordered.

Immediately, the large monitor in the middle of the wall came alive with the motion image of Senators Kopensky, Gash, and their aides bound to individual chairs. Behind each hostage was an armed assailant.

"My God!" Mason said, bracing himself against the table. Recovering from the image on the screen, he turned to the technician. "Can you get their location now?"

"Not in time." he replied, his voice filled with regret.

After the world crisis in 2029, global communication had changed drastically. Military bases and capitol buildings across the world had crumbled into ruins when a mysterious green vapor came into contact with them. The Vapor Incursion, as it was called, corroded specific metals at a molecular level and changed Earth's geography. Continents broke apart, rivers expanded, and mountains flattened. Islands sank beneath the waves, and new ones emerged from the ocean's depths. The cataclysms killed millions in every major nation. The dissolving of metals, earthquakes and tsunamis damaged entire server farms and caused an Internet-wide reset. Emails, cloud data, cryptocurrency, everything digital was disrupted and in many cases wiped out without a trace.

To maintain communications, a new texting system, Comtext, was developed, allowing audio, visual, and text communication across the world. However, there was currently no way for governments to monitor and censor the Internet sufficiently. Hacking Comtext to spread a message was easier than ever before.

They watched helplessly as a distinguished man wearing an emerald-print shemagh over his face, leaving only his eyes visible, stood perfectly still. Those in the War Room were able to see the hostages behind him, but Mason concentrated on the predator's eyes.

"This is to the United Regions of New America." the masked leader said with a heavy Middle Eastern accent while walking toward the hostages.

Mason's fists clenched at the sight of his old friend, Kristoff Kopensky, seated in the center of the hostages with his dark blond hair matted with dirt, blood, and sweat.

"I want to know who that is!" Mason snapped while continuing to watch the screen.

"When the Vapor Incursion destroyed our homes and took our loved ones away from us, you came under the banner of peace and restoration. Your so–called peacekeeping forces took what little resources we had left, then killed our fathers and sons for defending the virtues of our daughters and mothers! You self–righteous thieves and demons brought nothing but evil to the innocents of the world!" the leader said toward the screen and occasionally to the hostages as he walked around them.

"Karen, do we have any way of identifying that man?" Mason turned to Vice President of Homeland Security Karen Harp. Watching Kris bound to a chair helpless and beaten was too much for Mason to bear.

"We're using voice recognition now, sir!" Harp responded, her hazel–green eyes locked on her digital tablet as it ran a voice-recognition program through the international criminal database.

The new Department of Homeland Security had become a combination of the old DHS, branches from the Secret Service, and the Federal Bureau of Investigation. This new merger of departmental resources focused solely on domestic issues unless they flowed past New America's borders. On those few occasions, Harp was given temporary jurisdiction to operate with impunity in foreign affairs with the involvement of the CIA, if it was for the good of the nation.

"Now your country will pay the price for its insolence." the masked leader announced. "We have two of your senators, captured on their way to steal more of our country's resources."

"Answers! Now!" Mason demanded, turning to press the issue with his military personnel.

Harp leapt to her feet. "It's coming through now." she said, a slightly disgruntled edge to her tone. She approached Mason with her tablet in hand. "Voice recognition confirmed, seventy-nine percent! He identifies himself as Batrywt Nayt, which means 'Patriot Knight.' He supports a pure Islam nation and has a history of achieving his goals violently."

Everyone looked at the smaller side monitors, which showed various images of the masked man while the hostage crisis continued playing on the main screen. No matter what the images were, the one constant was the masked man with the large nose and tanned skin leading violent attacks.

"Because I am a man of honor and integrity, I will give you thirty minutes to look upon your comrades and contact their loved ones, so they can tune in and say their goodbyes." the Patriot Knight stated smugly while seemingly staring at his audience.

"I want a full background on him," Mason ordered. "I want everything we have!"

"Sir, shouldn't we concentrate on getting the location of the hostages?" Bailey asked.

"Do both!" Mason snapped.

"We have taken many steps to ensure that by the time you are able to locate the origin of this signal, it will be too late." the Patriot Knight said as if he was listening to the conversation in the War Room.

Mason paused in response to his words and then turned to look at Harp. Her helpless expression was not promising.

"I have all of my resources on this, George, but nothing yet." Harp said in response to his silent question. "We're starting from where they were taken, but somehow they were able to jam our signal, so we couldn't monitor our limited satellite movement for almost an hour in that area. By then they were gone." She dropped her digital tablet on the table and began to pace.

"However . . ." The Patriot Knight walked up to the camera as a rolling table was pushed in front of him. The camera panned down to the table, revealing an array of dental equipment, pliers, power tools, and hammers with differing layers of rust on them. The Patriot Knight picked up a rusted pair of pliers and showed it off to the camera. "I will inflict the pain that your men inflicted on our wives and sisters tenfold!"

Mason turned desperately to Bailey and Malo, who merely shook their heads slowly. He turned back to watch the screens, helpless.

Suddenly, Mason's cell phone rang, filling the silence that had fallen over the room. He allowed it to ring twice, staring at the number flashing on the screen in disbelief. Everyone watched as he answered the call. Harp, Bailey, and Malo looked surprised that he would accept a call during such a critical event. They eyed him intensely, hoping for an update.

"Senior Vice President Mason speaking," he said while staring at the horrific scene on the monitor.

"Sir, is this line secure?" a voice asked.

2

LOLA BRIEFING

~

An old CH–53K King Stallion military chopper flew high above the arid beach. One of the few military aircraft that wasn't stationed on a military base when the Vapor Incursion attack destroyed most metal alloys. The chopper was purchased, salvaged and modified. Three twin-turbine engines, a gun turret controlled from the copilot's seat, and a miniature railgun at the rear door to fend off pursuing adversaries were added. Additional upgrades included extending the aircraft's width and length as well as several hidden technical improvements to flight equipment and interior design.

Her name was *Lola*.

Seated in *Lola's* cockpit was Shana "Swan" Medjinn and Axel "Talon" Medjinn. Standing behind them in the doorway of the cockpit was their father, Alexander "Phoenix" Medjinn. He was a brawny man with an American accent and bronze skin that allowed him to blend into the population of most countries with mixed nationalities.

"Sir, is this line secure?" Phoenix asked while watching a

monitor in the cockpit, which showed the broadcast of the hostages. Swan and Talon focused on the instrument panels but could hear the conversation through their headsets.

"Yes," Mason's voice replied.

"We don't have a lot of time." Phoenix continued, keeping his voice steady and calm. "I'm going to text the coordinates of the hostages to your phone. You won't be able to get a team there in time, but my team is in the vicinity and will begin extraction operations shortly. We'll be at the target location in less than ten minutes. I just wanted to keep you informed, sir."

"I understand." Mason replied, a relieved expression on his face.

The War Room remained quiet as everyone watched him.

"The hostages," Mason asked, "will they be safe?"

Bailey and Malo looked at each other, puzzled, while Harp loomed closer to Mason, hoping to recognize the voice on the other end of the line.

"Sir?" Harp whispered in wonder.

"Who is that?" Malo whispered to Harp. Mason shot Harp a warning look as he took a step away from her. She looked at Malo and shrugged.

"Thank you." Mason disconnected the call, then checked his phone as a text message came through.

"George?" Harp asked again.

"I have the coordinates for their location!" He handed Bailey his phone.

"Who was that?" Harp inquired. Mason looked over her shoulder at the group of low−ranking administrative staff that had all stopped their activity, anxiously awaiting some good news from his call. He refocused his gaze on Harp, staring blankly at her to confirm that he had no intention of answering her question.

"Sir, these coordinates are deep within hostile territory." Bailey said.

"Meaning what, Admiral?" Mason asked.

"Meaning our closest rescue team won't make it before the deadline. They would have to go through hell to get there, then probably fight an army of insurgents to bring the hostages out, sir."

"What can you do?" Mason asked.

"Outside of stall? If they go through with the executions, I can have a squadron of jets destroy the building, then hunt down everyone that was involved for what it's worth, sir." Bailey sounded embarrassed at his limited options.

"Not good enough, Charles!" Harp yelled as her fist banged on the table. "They're Americans, damn it! *Our* Americans! We just can't stand by and allow the entire civilized world to watch them get executed on the Global Comtext!"

"Sir?" Malo turned to address Mason, hoping to get new orders, direction, or a solution. Mason looked at Bailey, Malo, and Harp, then at the screen with an unreadable expression. Harp watched him, puzzled, wondering if he had simply accepted defeat or if there was a glimmer of hope in his eyes.

Phoenix signaled for Swan to disconnect communications while looking at the hostages on the monitor.

"Swan, the ship is yours. Talon, let's go brief the team." Phoenix said. He exited the cockpit, Talon right behind him.

Lola served the team primarily as a transport chopper, but it was still a military vehicle. Per Phoenix's specifications, the helicopter had been rebuilt with advanced acoustic liners so that engine noise was minimized to that of a commercial airliner, allowing a combat team to sit, meet, and prepare their gear and equipment close to the cockpit, allowing the pilots to hear the conversation. Equipment was stored and mounted toward the rear in the cargo hold. The space was tight for combat teams even though the cabin had been extended, but for a helicopter it was practical and efficient.

Phoenix and Talon entered the cabin area. The compartment had room for twenty passengers, but for this mission, only a dozen members of the elite unit were present. The primary combatants were members of SOCIT, the Special Operations Command–Infiltration Team.

"Captain on deck!" Aaron "Warlord" Medjinn announced, causing all chatter to cease as everyone sat up straight and attentive. Warlord was a giant of a man. He trained and commanded SOCIT, sharing tactics that he had learned during his years in the special forces.

"As you were." Phoenix said as Talon stepped to his left and Warlord moved to his right. "You have your assignments. We'll go over the broad strokes one last time. Once we deploy we'll have less than twenty minutes to do the job."

"What happens after twenty minutes, Captain?" asked Andrew "Sandman" Simms, SOCIT's second in command.

"Senator Kopensky, Senator Gash, and their party get executed live over the Comtext." he said bluntly, causing a few members to look at one another with concern. "Warlord will run the briefing, then you can watch the live feed while you finish suiting up." He gave his cousin a slight nod, cuing him to step forward and begin.

"Alright, guys, listen up! We need this clean, quick, and simple." Warlord began, "The enemy is the typical breed of terrorist cockroaches, but they're dug into their hideout deeper than crabs in the crotch of a two–dollar whore, so be careful. SOCIT will be Dozer Team on this mission, so we get to do the intros, break down their defenses, and secure the building. Our focus is neutralizing all enemy combatants. Lola will take us up to fifteen thousand feet where we'll HALO down to the target. "Once we land on the roof, we will engage any hostiles and secure the roof for extraction. Our guardian angels on this mission will be call signed Angel Team. Since they have a reputation for customer service, they will stay close to the principals to assure their safety and cater to their crying and screaming. Our angels will consist of the captain, Hawk, Eagle, and Falcon. Once we've secured the roof, Dozer Team will focus on eliminating any obstacles between the high-value targets and our escape route. Any questions?"

Lawrence "Hawk" Mackenzie and Sean "Eagle" McAllister said nothing as they put on their protective clothing and military gear.

Falcon raised her hand. "Any update on the condition of the HVTs, Commander?" Anthony "Deacon" Bowen, who was standing behind her, nodded in agreement with her inquiry.

"Judging from the live feed, I would say some are worse than others to the point of possibly being critical. We will need your field medic experience on this one. So, you and Deke will handle medical." Phoenix said grimly.

"Yes, Captain." Falcon replied.

"Amen to that, Captain." Deacon nodded with agreement once again.

"From there, Angel Team will take point, reclaim the HVTs, and protect them for the remainder of the mission. Dozer will provide rearguard cover as we all meet back at the extraction point on the roof. Any questions?" Warlord took a moment to look around the cabin before turning to Phoenix.

"Finish gearing up and let's go!" Phoenix ordered before opening his black duffle bag.

∾

The Patriot Knight stared from one hostage to the other before pointing at Torres with the pliers. Two insurgents grabbed the struggling aide, one holding his head steady while the other kept him from pushing back in his chair.

"You remind me of someone," the Patriot Knight said, his voice almost a whisper, "a young American lieutenant during the Blitz War. The things he did to my village . . ." He shook his head slowly before grabbing Torres's jaw and forcing it open as he shoved his rusty pliers into Torres's mouth.

Torres screamed, trying fruitlessly to move away from the invading pliers. "Stop . . . struggling!" the Patriot Knight growled.

Jun discreetly struggled to free herself of her bonds. A shout came from behind her before an insurgent slammed the butt of his rifle into her shoulder. As she screamed in pain, the Patriot Knight briefly turned his attention to Jun before Torres bit his torturer's hand.

The Patriot Knight cursed as he yanked his hand away, eliciting a bloody crunch from Torres's mouth. Chunks of a tooth fell from his bloody pliers. The Patriot Knight kicked Torres in the chest, knocking him and his chair back onto the floor. Before Torres or anyone could scream, the Patriot Knight jumped on the aide, pressing his knee into his chest and pinning his head against the floor with a hand. The Patriot Knight punched Torres in the mouth with the pliers before yanking it open again.

"Bite me again, and you'll lose more than a tooth!" the Patriot Knight growled as he clamped down on the broken molar and began to pull. Kopensky was frozen at the brutal sight but tore his eyes away to look at Jun, who was fighting back tears.

The Patriot Knight stepped back from his handiwork. Clutched between his rusty pliers was a chunk of a broken molar and torn flesh. Zara screamed at the sight of Torres, his lips cut and bruised as he bled from his mouth. At the Patriot

Knight's command, the insurgents picked up Torres, who was crying and moaning, and sat him up in his chair.

The Patriot Knight turned to Zara. "You don't like this, traitor?" he said, looking at the camera before turning back to Zara. "Why is that?"

"I'm not a traitor!" Zara screamed, then broke down in tears.

"Zara, don't cry." Gash said. "Don't give them what they want."

"I can't help it!" Zara sobbed.

"You must be strong, little traitor, like Senator Gash here," the Patriot Knight said to the camera before turning to Gash. "Maybe you should show her how a brave American acts, eh, Senator?" Gash leaned back as the Patriot Knight approached him while unsheathing a large bladed weapon, which had dried blood and rust on the metal.

"Why are you doing this?" Kopensky blurted, causing the insurgents to look at him in surprise. "What do you want?" He asked, fighting to hide the fearful trembling in his throat. "If it's money, then why don't you ask for a ransom?"

"Money?" The Patriot Knight turned to him, insulted. "Do you truly believe that we went through all this detailed, strategic effort to kidnap you in exchange for some pirate's bounty, Senator Kopensky?"

"I don't know. Why don't you tell me?"

The Patriot Knight's eyes smiled, then he turned to face the camera. He took a slow breath to compose himself. "You mean tell *them*, am I right?" He pointed to the camera with his knife. Kopensky shrugged in response.

The Patriot Knight approached the camera. "New America brokered trade with multiple countries in the Middle East. Food, clothes, and supplies in exchange for oil and limestone. The first in a series of trades that would reconcile our countries with yours." The Patriot Knight's voice began to change with a mixture of emotions. "But you dishonest *dogs* took our resources and left us with nothing but starving mouths and a damaged economy! You call yourselves a New America, but you haven't changed at all!"

Kopensky shook his head. "No, no, no. That can't be right. I personally signed the trade agreement. The entire reason we came here was to confirm that the first shipment made it to Saudi Arabia, to see if there was more we could do to help! We're here to help you!"

The Patriot Knight stomped over to Kopensky. "Typical American politician. Pointing fingers in random directions. You are *always* blameless!"

Kopensky took a deep breath. "If the shipment didn't come here, someone must've intercepted it."

"Lies!" the Patriot Knight screamed.

"But that's why we came here." Jun said, her tears welling in her eyes. "We're here to help!"

"Very noble words from a woman!" the Patriot Knight spat. "Typical American culture. Your women speak with comforting words to deceive us while your men take up their weapons and strike us down!"

"Please!" Zara was beginning to regain her composure, drawing strength from her fellow hostages. "That's not the way we are."

She bowed her head and began to speak in Arabic, "Let evil be rewarded with evil. But whosoever forgives and seeks reconcilement shall be recompensed by Allah."

The Patriot Knight stared blankly at nothing as Zara quoted the Quran. Then he scowled in disgust before spinning on his heels and slapping her with the back of his hand, knocking her and her chair to the floor.

"You dare recite holy scripture to me, traitor?" The Patriot Knight kicked her in the stomach while she lay on the floor, still tied to the chair. Kopensky fought against his restraints, ignoring the pain it caused him.

"Stop it!" Jun screamed. "Stop kicking her! She didn't do anything to you!"

"Just tell us what you want from us!" Gash yelled so loudly his voice cracked.

"I want you to suffer!" the Patriot Knight shouted, turning from Zara to Gash. In three strides he crossed the room and grabbed Gash's face, holding him in place while he ran his large knife across Gash's side. Gash cried out in agony as the other hostages screamed.

3

RESCUE

~

Warlord stood by watching as SOCIT and the guardian angels put on their parachutes in preparation for their HALO maneuver. High Altitude Low Opening was a common aerial combat descent that involved freefalling out of an aircraft and waiting until the last moment of descent to open the parachute. Once the entire rescue team was suited up and ready, they joined hands in a brief prayer, a team ritual. Then Warlord moved to the cargo ramp's control unit at the rear of the cabin.

"Time to jump out of a perfectly good chopper again." Warlord winked before opening the rear cargo ramp door. He always took a moment to enjoy the slight gust of fresh air when *Lola's* rear ramp lowered. Many helicopters that he had flown in on missions before joining this team gave a slight push as the air regulated from inside to outside. Some would think that a sudden adjustment needed to be made, but since *Lola* was in flight, not much air rushed in from the rear while moving forward, and *Lola* had been structurally reengineered to regulate cabin pressure during ramp openings, so the change was almost seamless.

The rescue team pulled their black parachutes open a few hundred feet before reaching the roof and opened fire on the combatants with their muzzled rifles. Each rifle was equipped with a customized suppressor, eliminating nearly all sound. The rescue team landed on the roof gently after killing each insurgent during their descent without raising the alarm.

Phoenix detached his parachute from his harness and signaled for the two sub teams to perform their assigned tasks. After folding their parachutes into small bundles and hiding them, the joint team separated.

Remaining on the roof, Hacker broke into the secured box attached to the radio tower while Apache stood guard. The rescue team headed to the roof stairwell.

Swan sat in *Lola's* cockpit watching the digital displays as well as the night sky. The helicopter was hovering thousands of feet above the city. It remained undetected, but it was still in enemy territory. Normally, Swan would read while she waited for the mission teams to return, but because *Lola* was above an unfriendly region, she paid close attention to the monitors and proximity devices that would warn her if any aircraft were flying too close, risking collision or detection. Talon remained in the cabin checking all gun mounts and ammunition in case a fast escape was needed.

"Lola, this is Mother Ship." The female voice coming through Swan's headsets belonged to Athena, the second in command of *Blood Sky*. Talon entered the cockpit at the sound of Athena breaking radio silence, which was against mission protocol unless something unexpected was pending.

"This is Lola. Go with your traffic, Mother Ship," Swan replied nonchalantly.

"Are you watching the broadcast?" Athena asked with a sharp tone that said she already knew the answer to the question.

"No, Mother Ship. There's no reason for me to watch that." Swan responded, repulsed. Talon glared at Swan before reactivating the monitor.

"Well, turn it back on. They're starting to torture the principals. Tell Angel and Dozer to pick up the pace."

Before Athena could finish her sentence, the siblings looked down to see the horrific image of Gash being sliced by the Patriot Knight while he screamed and struggled against his restraints.

"Oh, God!" Swan exclaimed before flicking a few other switches on her control panel. "Angel Leader, Lola! Come in!"

Phoenix led the rescue team through the upper corridor, squatting slightly as he walked.

"Angel Leader, this is Lola. Do you copy?" Phoenix stopped all motion in the corridor upon hearing Swan's voice through his earpiece. He sensed Warlord directly behind him repeat the hand signal and stop the advancing team.

"Go with your traffic, Lola." Phoenix whispered his response.

"Angel Leader, they're torturing the principals," Swan's voice reported into the earpieces of each team member.

"Roger that." he said while studying a three–dimensional wire–frame view of the building displayed on his wrist device, which was the size of a large intelligent phone. He touched the screen, rotating the image. It showed multiple gray-colored bodies standing on the upper floor.

Warlord moved closer to watch the holographic image on Phoenix's forearm.

"Standing by for your orders." Warlord whispered.

Phoenix enlarged the image on the red blip in the center. "Our principals are on the fifth floor, north side, in a room with no windows, dual access from opposite sides."

"Roger that," Warlord confirmed. "Level five, no perimeter access."

"We've run out of time, so change in plans." Phoenix said into his transmitter. "Hacker, don't kill the feed until after we secure the packages."

"Roger that, Angel Leader."

～

The room was filled with screams as the Patriot Knight pulled away from Gash.

"Please don't!"

The Patriot Knight turned in response to the plea, surprised that Torres still had the strength to speak. "Don't hurt them!" Torres said. "Kill me instead. Let them go."

Jun turned to look at Torres. She struggled to contain the tears that came from a combination of helplessness, rage, and uncertainty. She turned and faced the Patriot Knight, hatred burning in her eyes. Kopensky realized she was shedding tears of rage, not fear.

"Is this bravery, or do you just want to die first, so you no longer have to witness your own weakness?" the Patriot Knight asked, grabbing Torres by the throat. "It's so hard to tell with you Americans."

"It's courage." Kopensky said, blood dripping down past his swelling eye.

Torres raised his head to look at Kopensky and Jun as they

watched him with pride and support. Torres struggled and soon found the will to sit up a little taller in his chair. He was only in his mid-twenties, but had decided to show maturity in this time of torture. If he had to die, he was going to die like a man, not a whimpering boy. He was going to follow the leadership of Senator Kopensky and Senator Gash and be strong! After all, the entire nation—no, the entire world—was watching.

The Patriot Knight watched with curiosity as Torres adjusted himself to sit upright.

"Yeah, courage." Torres agreed through blood-soaked lips. With one solid punch, one of the insurgents knocked the manhood clear out of Torres, leaving only the whimpering, hunched-over crying boy once more. The pain was devastating, and his sudden girlish scream was embarrassing.

"Shut up!" the large insurgent said, then laughed with his countrymen.

"Maybe I won't kill you right away." the Patriot Knight said as he approached Gash and Kopensky. "Maybe I should allow you to live long enough to have the world see how poorly you defend your women."

"What are you talking about?" Kopensky asked. "This can easily be fixed if you let us go. I give you my word that your country will receive double what they are owed and that we will find those responsible for taking your shipment."

"I don't want to hear any more of your lies!" the Patriot Knight shouted, then took a moment to compose himself. "I believe I will allow the traitor to bring shame to her family. They will watch her pleasure my men's every sexual desire live over the Global Comtext."

"Nooooo!" Zara cried, struggling against her restraints, trying to escape from her worst nightmare.

"And this one . . ." The Patriot Knight approached Jun and ran his hand along her face. "Maybe I should save her as one of my breeders to make half-breed slave soldiers for our next generation." He touched Jun's long black hair admiringly. She yanked her head away and stared at the far wall, refusing to make eye contact. Jun decided at that moment that she would fight until she died before she allowed any one of these men to rape her. Her tears stopped flowing. She was focused and prepared for the worst. All she needed was an opportunity.

"And you claim to be a holy leader?" Gash spat in disgust, blood running down his side. "You use religion to hide the fact that you're all just a bunch of criminals and rapists!"

"You dare mock me?" The Patriot Knight turned to cut Gash again. "You still find strength to make insulting remarks?" As he passed Kopensky, he stopped, surprised at Kopensky's confident expression.

The next few seconds seemed like minutes in the Patriot Knight's mind as he noticed that Kopensky managed to smiled smugly with his bruised and swollen lips. It was not so much the crooked smile that concerned him but the small flashing light that was shining on Kopensky's face. It was sporadic and blue like a dancing will-o-wisp. The Patriot Knight turned to look behind him, searching for the origin of the strange light.

The lamps in the room shattered simultaneously as pops echoed throughout the room. The Patriot Knight ducked but felt a bullet cut through his shoulder. His yell of anguish was muffled by the screams of his men and the pops of suppressed gunfire. Only one other sound cut through the chaos.

"Kill the feed!"

～

In the War Room, Mason and the others froze in disbelief as the screen filled with chaos.

"What the hell is going on?" Harp yelled, leaping to her feet.

They had heard a man's voice yell "Kill the feed!" before the screen went blue, confirming that their monitors were still on, but the transmission had ended.

"Who said that?" Harp asked, looking to the others at the table for an answer. No one responded, but Mason and Bailey exchanged a glance.

An eerie silence hung over the room, broken only by the sound of a handful of technicians typing, as everyone waited for something, anything, to happen. Harp turned to Bailey and Malo, who had both had the composure to get on their cell phones once the shooting began.

"Did one of your soldiers do that?" Harp asked both military commanders while Mason watched the blank main screen, slowly lowering himself into his chair.

"No, ma'am. My SEAL team is still in international waters, as ordered." Bailey reported.

"I just confirmed that it wasn't Army personnel either." Malo said before turning toward the blank monitor. Harp turned to Mason, who looked from her to the monitors and back again. Finally, he frowned and shrugged. Harp's eyes scanned everyone in the room, her anger rising to the point of explosion.

"What the hell is going on?" Harp yelled.

On the roof of the insurgent building, Hacker finished clipping the wires to the communication tower and antenna, severing the radio repeaters, internet antenna, and broadcast cabling. Apache looked at his watch, then back at Hacker.

"The feed is cut, Angel Leader." Hacker said into his transmitter, his voice tinged with a slight Russian accent. Apache gestured to Hacker before dropping to one knee and pointing his machine gun at the only access door to the roof.

Back in the cell, the insurgents who had not escaped the onslaught lay dead on the floor. Phoenix joined Falcon in freeing the hostages. Eagle and Hawk rushed back into the room, guns at the ready.

"The halls are clear, but asshole number one got away!" Hawk said.

"Figures." Phoenix replied without turning to look at the other two.

"Popped him in the shoulder before he left, though." Eagle added as he stood with Hawk in the doorway facing the adjoining corridors while Falcon, Deacon, and Phoenix helped the wounded hostages to their feet.

"Sit rep?" Phoenix asked.

"Senator Kopensky will need stitches, sir. Senator Gash's wound looks deep." Falcon reported while examining Kopensky's forehead wound and then addressing Jun. "Your shoulder is dislocated. I need to set it before we travel. It's going to hurt. A lot."

"Do it." Jun groaned.

"Some painkillers will help with those two. Senator Gash and Mr. Torres will need antibiotics." Deacon called out as he bandaged Senator Gash's abdomen. Jun screamed in agony as Falcon abruptly shifted her shoulder into place. Gash winced at the sound but hissed in pain as Deacon tightened a clip to apply pressure on his wound.

"Apply as much pressure as you can. It'll slow the bleeding." Deacon said as he took Gash's hand and put it over the bandage.

"We'll need to get these three back to the infirmary ASAP, sir." Falcon said as she tore an insurgent's shirt and used it to make a sling for Jun's arm. Deacon came by, injecting Jun and then the others with a cocktail of antibiotics and morphine.

"Dozer Team?" Phoenix called out while staring at Kopensky, Jun, and Gash.

"Ready when you are, Angel Leader." Warlord announced into their earpieces.

"Hacker, blow it!" Phoenix ordered.

On the roof, an insurgent rushed through the door, only to be shot by Apache. Apache grabbed the insurgent's rifle and fired into an incoming group of insurgents as they approached up the staircase.

Hacker positioned the explosive device on the power grid's main communication box, then tapped Apache on his shoulder. Both men ran for cover before Hacker activated the ignition switch.

At the sound of the explosion and the violent shaking of the building, the hostages turned to their rescuers with panicked expressions.

"What was that?" Kopensky yelled.

"They're going to kill us!" Gash said, his voice strained with pain.

"That was us making sure they can't send for help." Phoenix assured them. Then he turned in response to the distant sound of multiple gunshots. "Time to go!" Phoenix said as they picked up a few of the dead insurgents' rifles and moved toward the exit.

"Zara!" Jun cried out as she rushed to her side, the pain in her own shoulder stopping her for doing more. Zara was barely conscious. Jun looked at Phoenix with a stare that begged for assistance. "Is she going to make it?"

Phoenix looked at Zara and nodded. "Yes, she will," he assured her before he shouldered his rifle and scooped the petite Afghan woman into his arms as if she were a child.

Zara groaned as she drifted in and out of consciousness. Phoenix nodded to Falcon, indicating that he was ready to travel.

"Eagle, Hawk," Phoenix called out while watching Torres and Gash with concern. Eagle repositioned his weapon in one hand as he approached Torres.

"I'll take him." Deacon volunteered, already supporting Torres, who was only semi-conscious, against the wall. Without further conversation, Eagle accepted Deacon's pistol before hoisting Torres over his broad shoulders in a fireman's carry. Once he had Torres's body across his back and balanced on his shoulder for comfort, Deacon extended his hand, and Eagle returned the pistol to the stocky medic.

Gash looked stunned as Hawk's tall, brawny physique towered over him, looking extremely menacing. Gash looked at Zara in Phoenix's arms, then back at Hawk's massive size and muscles.

"You're not going to carry me, are you?" Gash asked.

Hawk glanced at Phoenix, who was cradling Zara, then leaned in closer to Gash. "Do you want me to carry you?" he asked as if he were speaking to a frightened child.

"No." Gash replied.

Hawk wrapped an arm around Gash, pulling him to his feet as the senator hissed in pain. Eagle came around the other side of Gash, balancing him. Falcon made sure that Torres was secure before rushing to the door. Hawk and Eagle kept one hand free to hold their sidearms as they held onto their HVTs.

"Can we go?" Jun asked, frustrated.

"Dozer Leader, you're holding us up!" Phoenix said with controlled urgency.

Suddenly, the remaining members of SOCIT came crashing through the windows in the outer corridor. Most of the hostages ducked behind their rescuers, but Kopensky raised a half smile as the SOCIT members approached. Warlord dusted the broken glass from his clothing. Gash looked at Warlord, who was almost seven feet tall, then back at Hawk, stunned that someone could make Hawk seem average in size.

"Ready," Warlord said. Phoenix watched as Kopensky approached Warlord with a mixture of relief, familiarity, and curiosity. To see Kopensky standing in front of the 300-pound giant was an odd contrast.

"Did you get bigger?" Kopensky asked with sarcasm. Falcon looked at Phoenix, searching for an explanation for the familiarity, but he just shook his head.

"Dozer Team, take point and rearguard positions while we keep the principals safe during transit," Phoenix commanded. The rescue team surrounded the hostages before preparing to move. "Let's go!"

4

HASTY EGRESS

∽

The rescue team made their way through the building one floor at a time, shooting any enemy combatants who crossed their path. Phoenix fired a pistol from under Zara's cradled legs, concentrating on keeping his principals safe and guiding the team back to the roof.

When they reached the end of a hallway, Warlord gave a hand gesture as he looked out the window. Everyone froze, completely silent.

"Why are we stopping?" Gash whispered, panic-stricken at the delay. Warlord turned to the group with a stern expression and gestured for Phoenix to approach.

"Reinforcements are early." Warlord said, looking to Phoenix for instruction. Phoenix looked out the window to see the head-lights of more than twenty vehicles speeding through the dark-ened streets toward them.

Kopensky, Gash, and Jun looked out the window as well, attempting to see what had seized their rescuers' attention.

"Damn!" Kopensky blurted.

"Lola, Angel Leader!" Phoenix said, his voice barely a whisper as the SOCIT team members repositioned themselves in the hallway, creating a defensive posture.

"This is Lola." Swan said.

"Get in position for emergency extraction. We're coming in hot with reinforcements soon to enter the building."

"Roger, Angel Leader. Lola moving into position. We'll drop when we have eyes on you."

As Swan's transmission ended, Phoenix noticed Warlord's troubled expression.

"What?" Phoenix pressed.

"A convoy coming in from the southwest." Warlord looked at his watch. "It's going to be tight."

"Let's move!" Phoenix said. The group rushed to follow Warlord's lead.

Warlord and Falcon were scouting a few meters ahead when the door to their right swung open, and three insurgents ran out with guns drawn. The insurgents took the team by surprise but were too close for accurate fire. Falcon executed a swift double kick, the first kick striking the lead man's throat and the second hurling him through a doorway.

Warlord grabbed the two remaining insurgents' faces and, with an animalistic growl of beastly rage, hoisted the two men off their feet before slamming them through the wall. Kopensky, Gash, and Jun stared, speechless. The torsos of the insurgents rested in the concrete wall, their spines broken and their skulls crushed.

"What the fuck?" Gash blurted, his body trembling from witnessing such a feat of raw power. Jun stared in silence at the legs of the insurgents dangling from the holes in the wall.

Warlord turned to the others, casually brushing plaster dust from his chest, as if the action had required no exertion. "Keep it moving."

Phoenix chuckled to himself as the rescue team proceeded down the corridor behind the behemoth of a man. Jun looked at the faces of these total strangers, noticing that none of them were remotely surprised at what they had just witnessed. Gash and Kopensky stared as they passed the two bodies hanging out the wall. Gash was practically catatonic. If not for Jun pushing him forward, he would have remained immobile indefinitely. Phoenix passed the hostages and moved back to the front of the group.

One by one the rescue team and their principals ran to the southern end of the structure, staying low to avoid detection by those on the street below. Kopensky stopped at the end of the roof to look at the second convoy of vehicles approaching. He lowered Zara from his arms and was surprised, yet grateful, when Jun helped, taking the woman into her right arm that remained functional and relieving him of his burden, so he could focus on their extraction.

Even in the dimness of night, the vehicles headlights revealed that each car and truck had multiple gunmen.

"Dead end?" Kopensky asked with concern while standing at Phoenix's side.

"Not yet." Phoenix glanced down at his watch. "Lola, are you in position?"

"Roger that, Angel Leader." Swan replied.

Phoenix gave them a thumbs-up. Kopensky, Gash, and Jun looked around, confused when they didn't see anything in their immediate vicinity, evidently expecting to see an army of heroic gunmen wearing the same dark-blue tactical attire. The sound of *Lola* descending rapidly from the sky as if in a controlled fall broke the silence. The helicopter was quieter than expected, reducing the chance of detection from the streets below.

"Drop your lines!" Phoenix said, his eyes on Jun in particular.

"I don't see anything," Gash said as a lightweight cable line dropped in front of him from above. Jun, Gash, and Kopensky looked up at the same time, following the cable to its origin at the helicopter's cargo door.

"Hold on!" Hawk instructed Gash as he grabbed the line and tightened his grip around the senator.

Heavily sedated with painkillers and barely able to stand on his own after Deacon lowered him from his shoulders, Torres groggily looked at the cable with his foot in the hoist loop, then stared upward into darkness, not realizing that the black helicopter was above him. It was virtually invisible from below on the moonless night, having no running lights or interior illumination.

"Where does it go?" Torres asked in wonder. "To heaven?" Eagle shook his head as he helped Deacon place a harness around Torres. Deacon connected it to his own body, then tugged on the rescue cable. Seconds later, Deacon and Torres were hoisted into the air, disappearing into the darkness of night while Eagle remained on the roof with his weapon at the ready to protect their position during the extraction.

"Come on, people!" Warlord whispered with urgency while looking over the edge at the insurgent soldiers. They rushed out of their vehicles on the street and were gathering at the front of the building to receive orders from the Patriot Knight, who had exited the building to join his new wave of men.

Phoenix helped Jun slip into her harness and placed one of her feet into the hoist loop at the end of a second cable. She looked at him as if she was about to say something when a movement just over her shoulder caught his attention.

"Move!" Phoenix yelled, spinning Jun to one side and shooting two insurgents who were about to open fire from the window across the street.

As two shots rang out, Warlord instinctively turned to look at the window, then back at the mob forming on the street below. A barrage of bullets whizzed by Warlord's head from below, forcing him to step back.

"We gotta go!" Warlord shouted, returning fire at the gunman across the street. "They know we're on the roof!" The SOCIT crew fired at the gunmen who were attempting to enter the roof. They focused on the immediate threat while Angel Team saw to their escape.

The Patriot Knight watched from the street as the last of the infiltrating mercenaries rose into the night sky. Realizing what was happening, he pulled out his pistol and began shooting at the air above the roof, despite the searing pain in his arm. Every time the insurgents attempted to shine a spotlight on the sky above the roof, one of the infiltrators shot out the light.

The black helicopter rose higher to avoid detection while waiting for all of the passengers to get onboard. The movement caused the Patriot Knight's eyes to focus on the outline of the nearly silent aircraft. He shouted an order, causing his men to start shooting their weapons at the barely visible black helicopter as it veered toward the ocean.

He continued firing until his pistol was empty, ignoring the pain reverberating through his shoulder. Throwing his pistol to the ground, he watched his hostages escape in the distance. A warm wetness made him aware of the blood flowing freely from his gunshot wound, soaking his shirt.

"After them!" he yelled, pulling his shemagh from his face along with his fake large nose. Then he yanked off his expensive toupee, revealing a clean-shaven head. He turned back to the compound. "And someone get me medical attention!"

5

DOGFIGHT

~

I nside *Lola's* cargo hold, Jun sat in one of the passenger seats watching her rescuers remove their gear and taking a moment to relax. After confirming their team had only suffered minor injuries, Phoenix and Warlord moved to the principals to check on their condition.

Jun stared, making sure not to interrupt the activity and concentration as Deacon opened a futuristic-looking red case that was the size of a carry-on luggage bag and passed Falcon everything she needed without a word. Jun glanced at what the pair described as a "medical kit" and saw a range of items from standard first-aid supplies to technology she didn't recognize. Her eyes widened at the sight, but she said nothing and merely watched everyone around her. Gash and Torres were laid out on collapsible wall-mounted gurneys as the two medics cleaned and bandaged their wounds. The rest of the former hostages were seated close by with SOCIT members taking care of their wounds.

"Are you all okay?" Phoenix asked. His tone made it seem as

if everything they had just experienced was routine. It was relaxing and reassuring, almost as if he was mentally projecting his confidence onto her with each word.

"We are, thanks to you." Gash said, extending his hand and then wincing from the pain in his rib cage and stomach. Phoenix looked down at Gash's hand, hesitating before accepting the handshake.

"Will they be okay?" Jun asked, watching Zara and Torres with concern. Phoenix looked at the wounded passengers, then turned back at her with a blank expression. She waited for an answer, a knot forming in her stomach, fearful of his reply. Instead of answering, Phoenix turned to the intercom and activated it. She sighed deeply as she closed her eyes, preparing herself for the worst.

"Nice work, Swan." Phoenix said into the transmitter. "How's Lola?" As Phoenix spoke, he looked at each person in the cabin area in front of him.

"Not good!" a young female voice responded over the speakers. Phoenix turned to Warlord. Jun watched them as they stared at one another, wondering if some sort of unspoken communication was going on. "They got a couple of lucky shots that damaged our propulsion. We have ten aircraft moving toward us, fast, and Lola's acting sluggish." Jun did not show her surprise at the fact that the skilled pilot of the large helicopter was named Swan and was a woman.

"Jets?"

"Too early to tell, but I doubt it." Swan hesitated. "Probably helicopters based on their movement patterns and speed. Either way, they're coming in on our flank fast."

"Can we outrun them?" Phoenix asked, catching Kopensky's reaction as he stiffened in his seat.

"Not for long. If I push the engines, we may blow something

vital. Then we'll go swimming. Our vertical drive is malfunctioning, and we're losing oil from somewhere."

As Swan updated Phoenix, a tall young man in his mid-twenties exited the cockpit and opened one of the engine access hatches.

"What are you going to do?" Kopensky asked Phoenix. Jun could see the effort it was taking Kopensky to hide his panic.

"Time for some support." Phoenix replied.

"Do you think they'll make it in time?" Warlord asked.

"Only one way to find out." Phoenix said, then activated the intercom again. "Swan, deploy the Ravens for rendezvous."

"Roger that!" Swan's voice was filled with urgency.

Phoenix turned to look at what Talon was doing in the ceiling hatch.

"Birds?" Kopensky asked.

"Sort of," Phoenix's expression was flat. Kopensky seemed familiar enough with the man to know there was an unmentioned concern.

Lola cut through the sky over the shores of the enemy landscape, swooping out to the open sea just as the sun broke over the horizon. Tiger gunship helicopters in tight formation were gaining speed on the crippled King Stallion helicopter, five on either side.

The Tiger gunships were originally built to provide advanced air support for ground troops and other aircraft, but after the disaster of 2029, different factions appeared with weapons and vehicles from various countries. Some were legally purchased, others, such as these, were salvaged, and the rest were confiscated by way of raids on crippled military outposts.

As the Tiger helicopters drew closer, their rockets moved into launch position. The insurgents were no longer interested in hostages. Now it was about a high casualty count, and with the rescue team's liberation in progress, this increased the opportunity for more bodies.

With the attack imminent, *Lola* flew straight and true, as if having no concern for the approaching threat. No one knew better than Swan that the shortest distance between two points was a straight line, and when piloting a malfunctioning helicopter, it would not be wise to waste fuel on maneuvering unless as a last resort.

The Tigers maneuvered into an erratic formation, focused on getting in front of *Lola*, moving into missile-lock range.

Inside *Lola's* cabin area, Jun and the former hostages watched the view screens that were mounted on the opposite wall.

"Tee, you have to move faster! Lola is slowing down, and things are about to get hot!" Swan bellowed over the speakers.

"I found one of the leaks! I'm bypassing and patching!" Talon replied.

"How can you work on a helicopter from the inside while it's in flight?" Jun asked, fascinated despite the imminent danger.

"Our engineers redesigned Lola's engines, so we can perform some emergency repairs in mid-flight," Talon explained while grabbing a roll of duct tape and some rubber tubing from the utility bag that was slung over his shoulder.

"Duct tape?" Gash asked in surprise.

"My father always said if you can't fix it with duct tape, then you need more duct tape." Talon responded with a slight smile as he taped the leak with oil–covered fingers.

"That really works?" Jun asked, doubtful.

"Hell no! But it will slow the leak long enough for me to do this." He sprayed a gray foam from a small canister onto the duct-taped area. Within seconds the foam hardened into a plastic–like seal, stopping the leak.

"What's that?" Jun asked as Talon worked with more wires.

"Conduit foam. I call it liquid duct tape." Talon smiled. "Just a quick electrical patch that I created in our lab." As he focused on his repair work, Jun looked at the canister, noticing it had no label.

"Captain, our birds are here!" Swan announced through the speakers. "They must have been on the way before I called."

"Yes!" Talon shouted while patching another leak. "Just in time."

Phoenix rushed past Talon toward the cockpit. Kopensky limped after him. The painkillers numbed the pain if he remained still, but he needed to see.

Once in the cockpit, he saw Phoenix strapping himself into the copilot's chair and putting on a pilot's helmet.

Swan began evasive maneuvers. Kopensky clutched a strap that was mounted to the wall to steady himself. Swan veered suddenly, forcing a groan out of Kopensky as he slammed into the doorway. Phoenix turned at the sound.

"If you're going to stay up here, strap your ass to that chair, and hold on!" he yelled, frustrated that Kopensky had followed him. Kopensky's face flushed with fear when he saw the Tiger helicopters firsthand outside of the windshield, buzzing around like attacking hornets swarming their prey. He scrambled into the jump seat behind Phoenix and locked in his harness.

"Lola, this is Raptor." a smooth, deep baritone voice said into their headsets.

"It's good to hear your voice, Raptor." Swan replied, smiling. Kopensky watched Swan and Phoenix, realizing they were in communication with someone, and grabbed the headset near him, so he could listen.

"We're ten seconds out, and we see you got your hands full, so I want you to head for the deep blue in seven."

"Copy that, Raptor." Swan replied.

Phoenix switched on the intercom. "Everybody, hold on to something!" he yelled into the cabin.

Swan maneuvered *Lola* into a nosedive. Kopensky watched the monitor at his station that showed the camera view of the situation behind *Lola*. The Tiger helicopters had not been ready for the evasive move.

As *Lola* dove, four Enduro Mark Twos flying in tight formation in single file separated and attacked, each launching one of its rockets. The Ravens shot down four of the ten Tiger helicopters before having to break formation.

These newly arriving jetbikes turned, flipped, and spun in mid-flight, avoiding bullets and missiles. Fortunately for the Raven team, the Enduros were far more maneuverable than the Tiger helicopters. Within a few minutes, a fifth Tiger had been shot down, its burning remains falling to the ocean below.

Inside *Lola's* cabin area, Gash was no longer focused on the pain in his body as he watched the SOCIT crew, who had already assumed a defensive posture throughout the cabin. Hawk and Eagle were shooting at the Tiger helicopters using the flanking floor-mounted machine guns. The noise of sporadic heavy gunfire at close proximity from both sides of the cabin was deafening. It made Gash wonder how these people could endure such activity and remain calm. Between the shooting, the helicopter's engine noise, and the voices over the public address system, Gash was fighting not to lose control and scream in panic.

At the rear of the ship, Warlord had the cargo ramp open and was shooting the miniature rail gun at any enemy that was daring enough to get directly behind *Lola*. Apache and Hacker focused on reloading the heavy guns throughout the ship. Gash watched in awe out the open rear ramp as a Tiger helicopter exploded behind *Lola*. Warlord's victory yell, which sounded like a giant prehistoric beast, caused Gash to jump. He was surprised that he felt no remorse for the lives lost, only relief as he looked at the monitors to see that only four Tigers remained. They had become more cautious in their approach.

Meanwhile, Deacon and Falcon concentrated on keeping the seriously injured passengers stable and strapped to their gurneys during the wild ride while Jun sat strapped into one of the seats, holding on to the safety harness to make sure all the tossing about would not yank her out of her seat.

While SOCIT and the Ravens focused on the Tiger helicopters, Gash watched a side monitor that showed *Lola's* scanners detecting more. approaching aircraft.

"All units, be advised we have three additional ships coming in from the west." Swan announced over the intercom speakers. Talon sprayed foam onto the last damaged portion of the oil line before removing the excess oil and closing the ceiling hatch and wiping the oil from his hands while staring at the high-value passengers.

Jun looked at Gash with concern, then at the monitor on the wall that showed the distant blips approaching. She noticed what had caught his attention.

"Lola, you're crippled." Raptor said over the cabin intercom speakers. "We'll finish up these four and distract the new bogies while you get clear."

In the cockpit, Phoenix fired *Lola's* forward guns at the enemy while Swan continued maneuvering the large helicopter through the sky. They were a team in complete sync with one another.

"Roger that, Raptor. Good hunting!" Phoenix said.

Gash stared at the monitors, focusing on the newly approaching aircraft.

"Wait, I know those helicopters!" Kopensky exclaimed from the open cockpit door.

Raptor spiraled his Enduro mid attack before jetting out of enemy target range to address the approaching slate-gray Black Hawk gunship helicopters.

"Unidentified aircraft," a deep, commanding voice bellowed into Raptor's receiver. "This is Major Smythe of the New American Navy. You are over international waters declared neutral by maritime law. State your business, or prepare to be fired upon."

"Jesse?" Phoenix called out over the radio as Raptor's Enduro sped closer to the three oncoming military aircraft. He was prepared to engage in a single–handed battle to defend the passengers but was relieved at the possibility that his captain recognized the lead pilot of the newly arriving combat choppers.

Kopensky looked around the small auxiliary console searching for the communication controls. Once he found them, he activated his radio with a small degree of difficulty.

"How do I talk to them?" he asked.

Phoenix pressed a button on his copilot console and then glanced back at him. "You're clear to talk."

"This is Senator Kopensky," he yelled into his headset. "Major Smythe, stand down! You are interfering in the rescue of myself and the surviving members of the senate party who were abducted last night. Stand down!"

"I hope he believes you." Swan mumbled while continuing to maneuver the chopper.

"Smythe, if you want to help, engage the renegade Tiger gunships and give us a wide berth." Phoenix added.

"Commander?" Smythe asked, his voice filled with surprise.

"Roger that, Smythe." Phoenix replied. "Our Stallion is crippled from enemy fire. Take care of the Tigers, and our jetbikes will provide us safe escort back to my ship and complete the rescue op. Are we clear?"

"Copy that, Commander!" Smythe confirmed.

Kopensky turned to Phoenix with a curious look. "Do you know each other?"

"Jesse Smythe flew under my command . . . before." Phoenix glanced over his shoulder, locking eyes with Kopensky as *Lola* started to level out.

In the War Room, Mason stood staring at the blank monitors, waiting for a change, while Harp paced back and forth, and Bailey talked to a member of his team on the landline. The room was filled with the chatter from the other lower-ranking personnel, who were focused intensely on finding anything to help their superiors. Mason turned away from the blue screen as Theodore approached him.

"Sir, you have a call on line one from someone identifying himself as Senator Kopensky." Everyone stopped talking and turned to Mason. Bailey abruptly ended his call to give Mason his undivided attention.

"Put it through on speaker." Mason said as he sat in his chair, contemplating the conversation he was about to have.

After Theodore keyed up the desk–mounted telephone that was built into the conference table, Mason leaned forward. "This is Senior Vice President Mason speaking."

"George, we're okay." The room exploded with cheering and applause as Kopensky's familiar voice sounded over the speakers.

"Thank God, Kris!" Mason sighed. "When we lost the feed to the broadcast, we assumed the worst."

"Can you take me off speaker please?" Kopensky's voice stated directly.

Mason immediately picked up the handset and disconnected the speaker communication. "Go ahead, Kris."

Kopensky remained in the cockpit's jump seat as he closed the door between the cockpit and the cabin.

"He got us out, George. I don't know how he pulled it off, but he did it. We're safe. Now, I need you to call off the military. I know they're going to want personnel transfer and escort back to New America." Kopensky added, staring at Phoenix.

"You don't want the escort?" Mason asked.

"No. Neil and Zara are pretty bad, and I don't want it public. I think it might be better if we stay with Phoenix and his people until everyone's stable and fit to be transported." Kopensky said, trying to be nonchalant.

"What's wrong, Kris?" Mason asked, concern in his voice.

Kopensky hesitated before answering. Although his brief discussion with Phoenix had confirmed his own suspicions, he and Phoenix agreed that Mason was the only one in the government who could be trusted with their conclusion.

"Phoenix and I think we have a mole."

"Why?"

"The attack on our convoy was too perfect. They had intelligence information that could have only come from inside our government." Kopensky looked at Phoenix, who said nothing.

Mason looked at those in the room around him, his face expressionless. They all stared back with anticipation.

"I understand, Kris. I'll see to it."

After Mason disconnected the call, he turned to Bailey and

Malo. "Charles, Jay, Senators Kopensky and Gash will be taking a couple of days to recover at an undisclosed location. Have your team return to New America after your SEAL team has completed their task."

"But sir, military SOP clearly states . . ." Malo's voice faced when he saw the look on Mason's face and felt Bailey place a hand on his arm.

"Yes, sir." Bailey responded, finishing Malo's sentence for him.

6

SAFE AND SOUND

~

Phoenix exited the cockpit with Kopensky, sighing with relief and satisfaction. Another successful mission with no casualties. Talon took the copilot's chair, so Swan could stretch her legs. Phoenix looked around the cabin and cargo hold, watching each member of the rescued party before approaching them individually.

The former hostages began to relax. Torres was now completely unconscious from the sedatives. The others were standing or seated around the small cargo hold, staring out the windows, privately reflecting.

"What happens now?" Kopensky asked, calmer than Phoenix expected. He looked at Kopensky's trembling hands. When Kopensky realized how much they were shaking, he buried them in his pockets.

"You okay? Do you need to sit down?" Phoenix offered.

"Why won't my hands stop shaking?" Kopensky asked, pulling them out of his pockets again.

"It's just the adrenaline," Deacon said. "It'll calm down soon.

Sit and relax." he suggested, gesturing to the nearest seat.

"We'll be landing on Blood Sky shortly where we can better accommodate your injured." Phoenix assured him.

"I'm confused," Gash said, struggling to sit up on his gurney. He looked around the cabin area. "I thought *this* was Blood Sky."

Swan walked out of the cockpit just in time to hear the tail end of Gash's statement.

"This?" Swan said. "No, this is my ship, Lola." She smiled proudly.

"Lola?" Gash asked, amusement tugging at the corners of his mouth.

"Yes, Lola." Swan said, staring at Gash as if in preparation for an insulting comment about the name. Gash's smile faded, having decided against sharing his opinion. Swan smiled pleasantly at the others. "She's a cargo copter normally. We use her to transport supplies to Blood Sky, but every now and then we use her to rescue politicians." She glared at Gash.

Zara struggled to proper herself up on her gurney. "I thought this team was called Blood Sky." The combat crew looked at Zara in surprise.

"I guess I was farthest from the facts." Jun said, turning to Phoenix. "All the rumors that I heard gave me the impression that Blood Sky was one man: you."

Phoenix watched her for a moment. He was flattered, but he had practiced being stoic for so many decades that it didn't show. Inside, however, he accepted her belief that he alone could have achieved all the things that *Blood Sky* had done over the years as a great compliment.

"Captain Blood Sky?" Eagle chuckled as he continued loading bullets into clips. "Sounds mean."

Swan rolled her eyes. "I'm going back to the cockpit to help Talon prep for landing." Swan said.

As she walked to the front of the ship, Phoenix could tell she was off put by Jun's admiration. She had never been into bravado. An attractive woman giving credit and compliments to her father on such a grand scale was likely more than she cared to witness.

When Swan entered the cockpit, she flipped the switch that activated *Lola's* front camera. This displayed the midnight-black destroyer with a red "X" painted on the side of the hull for all to see on the monitors mounted in *Lola's* cabin area and cargo hold.

"*That's* Blood Sky." Phoenix said.

The passengers who were immobile turned as best as they could to look at the monitors. Those that could move about approached the viewport to see the fully restored, somewhat excessively modified, pre–Vapor Incursion destroyer–class warship on the horizon. Swan did a slow fly–by around their home, providing an aerial tour. The ship's surface was black and charcoal gray, making it uniquely beautiful in daylight and almost invisible at night.

As *Lola* descended, crew members gathered on the primary flight deck at the rear of the destroyer. The King Stallion's powerful rotors blew dust in swirls across the deck.

Doctor Kayla "Kite" Medjinn stood on the flight deck with her medical team. All eight crew members were dressed in matching purple scrubs and had rolling gurneys prepared to receive their patients. Once Lola landed on the flight deck, the rear cargo door lowered, and Kite and her team approached the exiting passengers, joining Falcon and Deacon as they tended to the wounded.

"He needs surgery." Deacon pointed to Torres before motioning to Gash. "Stitches. These two might have bruised or broken ribs." he added, gesturing to Zara and Senator Kopensky.

Falcon pointed to Jun. "Dislocated left shoulder. She'll need a proper sling."

"Got it," Kite replied, then turned to Phoenix. "Any of ours?"

"Falcon and Deke patched us up on Lola. You can check their field dressings after you tend to the vital issues." Phoenix replied, his eyes on Torres. Knowing that was her father's way of saying that the rescue team's injuries were the equivalent of a child skinning their knee on a playground, Kite nodded and then ran after her team as they rushed the former hostages to the infirmary.

Phoenix walked into the infirmary with Warlord and Talon after Kite informed them that all medical procedures and surgeries had been completed. Zara and Torres were sleeping peacefully while Kopensky, Gash, and Jun sat on comfortable reclining chairs as Kite checked their vital signs, helped by her head nurse, Qin Zhang. Jun had a brand-new sling, which kept her left arm and shoulder immobile.

"How are the patients, Doc?" Phoenix asked.

"They'll live. Mr. Torres will have to stay off his feet for a few days and be confined to a wheelchair, at least until we arrive in New America, and probably after we make port." Kite said before looking at Gash. "The cut was shallow, so there were no major organ injuries, only light muscle damage thankfully. Took over a hundred stitches to sew it up, though. Because Falcon said the blade was rusty, we gave him a tetanus shot and antibiotics just to be safe, and we'll monitor daily for any signs of infection."

Kite turned to Zara, softening her expression. "And . . ." Kite looked to Jun for assistance.

"Zara Zogby." Jun said, responding to the unasked question.

"Thank you." Kite nodded to Jun. "Miss Zogby's injuries are minor compared to Mr. Torres, but I think her mental trauma is more severe. She needs a psychological eval before we make port."

"*Before* we make port?" Gash asked. "Do you have a psychologist on this ship?"

Phoenix nodded. "Yes, we do."

"The psychologist is for the pirate attack victims we rescue." Kite explained. "She provides therapy and evaluations, looking for early signs of PTSD, then makes recommendations when we reach the victim's destination."

Phoenix looked at her, grateful she had not mentioned how often the crew used the psychologist for post-traumatic stress as well.

"What kind of warship is this?" Gash asked, looking around in awe.

"It was built as a destroyer, but now I would call it a floating sanctuary." Phoenix said.

"I call it home." Talon added, sharing a grin with Phoenix.

"When can we get the grand tour?" Kopensky asked, smiling in anticipation.

"May I join you?" Jun said.

"Count me in!" Gash added, slowly easing himself off the medical reclining chair.

"Nobody leaves until the doctor clears you." Phoenix announced, looking at Kite.

"We just need their names for our records—in case we ever have to rescue them again." Kite said, turning to Nurse Zhang.

Nurse Zhang went to get the digital tablet that stored their medical records.

"I don't plan on going through anything like that again." Jun grunted.

"How did you find us, anyway?" Gash asked, looking up with realization.

Phoenix remained placid but was surprised it had taken so long for someone to ask that question. Talon stiffened in response. Jun cast a curious look at Talon and then turned to Phoenix, anticipating a response.

"The military didn't even reach us until after you got us out of the country and over neutral waters, which means they would have been too late," Jun said.

"True," Phoenix agreed.

"So, how did you find us when the military couldn't?" Gash pressed.

"That's classified." Phoenix said.

"I'm sorry?" Gash chuckled sarcastically. "I'm a senator from New America."

"That carries very little weight here, Mr. Gash." Warlord said. "We're in international waters. As far as maritime law goes, out here you're just a civilian."

"Chad, you're being rude to the people that saved our lives." Kopensky said. Phoenix locked eyes with Kopensky, who winked, making Phoenix smile. Phoenix's expression eased, Jun noting the familiarity between the two men.

"You're right, Kris," Gash said. "I'm sorry, Captain Phoenix. I didn't mean anything by it. I was just wondering."

"Not a problem, Senator Gash."

Phoenix had read the background on Gash, so he knew that the man was probably not a threat, but Phoenix had been in the business of covert activity and secrets for most of his adult life, so trust had to be earned. Although Gash was an established politician, Phoenix could not rest easy knowing that a spy had leaked information about the group's itinerary. He did not know if that spy was safe back in New America or among the rescued hostages on his ship. Whichever the case, Phoenix did not like a lot of questions, nor did he like to be pressed on issues that he deemed sensitive.

"Please, you saved my life, for Christ's sake. Call me Chad." Gash smiled and bowed slightly in acknowledgment before turning to Kite.

"We just need some information, then you're free to go." Kite said, breaking the tension. "We have Neil Torres, and Zara Zogby." she continued, looking at the electronic tablet in Nurse Zhang's hand as she approached Kopensky.

"Let's get them some clean clothes." Talon suggested to another nurse, noting Gash's bloodstained clothing.

"And your name, sir?" Kite asked politely.

"Kristoff Kopensky." Kopensky replied as the second nurse handed Gash and Jun folded scrubs from the medical supply cabinet.

Kite looked up from the tablet. "Kopensky?" Kite blurted, unable to restrain a smile. Kite turned to Phoenix with a fan—like grin.

"Yes." Kopensky chuckled at her awed response before he turned to Phoenix for an explanation. "I'm guessing you know my name?"

"I'm sorry! I didn't recognize you before when you came in with the bruises and blood on your face, and after you got cleaned up, I was dealing with the other patients." Kite spoke rapidly, as she often did when she became excited.

"It's okay." Kopensky smiled, flattered by the sudden attention,."You were focused on your work. Do you know me?" For Kopensky the chuckle was a momentary yet pleasant distraction from the numbing sensation brought on by the painkillers, which reduced his awareness of the swelling and bruising in his face and body.

"I, uh . . ." Kite turned to Phoenix, not knowing how to respond.

"Your name may have come up in conversation once or twice." Phoenix admitted before signaling for Kite to get a hold of herself. He knew that Warlord and Talon found the exchange entertaining.

Jun watched Phoenix, Kite, Warlord, and Talon, studying their expressions as well as their reactions, then turned to examine the clothing she had been given to wear.

"Okay then." Kopensky pursed his lips, somewhat flushed. He tried to withhold his flattered smile, but within seconds his teeth were showing, rising into a grin. Kite had given him quite the compliment, and it was obvious that Phoenix had talked at length about Kopensky in a positive light, more than he was willing to admit.

Kite sighed deeply as she regained her composure and then turned to Jun, back to business.

"And you are?"

"Jun Li."

"That's different." Kite glanced at him out of the corner of her eye. Jun followed Kite's glance and then looked up at Phoenix. He kept his eyes on the others in the room, but he noticed the smile that Jun was trying to hide.

"Is that L–E–E?"

"No, L–I." Jun replied, returning her attention to Kite. "And Jun, like the month, but no 'E' at the end."

"Thank you." Kite said, then turned to Gash, who was obviously expecting the celebrity recognition that his colleague had received.

"And I take it from the conversation that your last name is Gash and you are a senator, sir?" Kite asked politely.

"You don't know who I am?" Gash asked, disappointed.

"We don't have a lot of time for television and current affairs out here." Warlord commented. "Most of our crew may not know you."

"That's actually good, Chad." Kopensky said. "I'm sure being recognized is what got us into this mess in the first place."

"Yeah, I guess." Gash replied, still a little disappointed. "Senator Chadwick Gash."

After Nurse Zhang typed in his name, she minimized his chart and reopened the last chart on her tablet as Kite approached Phoenix.

"We'll give you a little privacy, so you can change," Phoenix said to the group.

7

TOURING BLOOD SKY

～

P hoenix led the tour of the first New American politicians to board *Blood Sky*. Talon and Warlord accompanied them to ensure that no one strayed. Kopensky, Gash, and Jun, wearing identical purple medical scrubs, were in awe at the fact that they were on the legendary ship.

"We finally get to see all of the gadgets and weapons I've heard so much about." Gash said in anticipation as they left the infirmary.

When they reached an area where they could stand as a group without blocking corridors, Phoenix stopped the procession. "Unfortunately, the only thing you'll see today is what you've already seen, only now you'll just see them up close. The tour will be limited to the non-restricted areas of Blood Sky. The equipment and weapons that we invent are strictly for the crew to use and for occasional product testing. We cannot show civilians everything we're working on."

"Not even to us?" Gash asked, gesturing to himself and

Kopensky, seemingly hoping his status as a senator would convince Phoenix to sway in his decision and expand the tour.

"No, Chad, not even you. We are a functioning ship with classified equipment, not a tourist destination." Warlord said. "Please try to remember that when we pass restricted areas of the ship."

"Product testing?" Jun asked.

Warlord nodded. "Yes. The combat and medical teams field test everything our scientists and engineers make."

"Then what do you do with them?" Kopensky asked.

"Eventually, we sell the designs for cash or make enough to fill an order every now and then, but we're not supplying people with weapons. We only sell our nonlethal inventions." Warlord explained, seeing that Phoenix had become irritated with the direction of the conversation.

"Doesn't sound like you like to share, Captain." Gash teased.

"No," Phoenix said, staring at Gash with a stern expression to drive the message home. "Especially not dangerous things."

Phoenix resumed walking. Kopensky shook his head as he passed Gash, disappointed at his obvious attempt to press for information. Jun passed Gash but said nothing. When Gash turned to look behind him, Warlord was shadowing him uncomfortably close, staring down at him. Gash turned hurried to catch up with the others. Talon chuckled to himself. Warlord enjoyed scaring civilians.

Phoenix spent a large portion of the tour pointing down corridors and stating that they were restricted to crew members only. The tour group, for the most part, understood the need for privacy as well as the potential for injury.

Once they made their way to the ship's rear deck, Phoenix slowed down and gestured to a familiar sight. "This is called the stern or the aft section, depending on who you're talking to." he said. The tour group stared with admiration at *Lola*, which was positioned on the primary flight deck.

"Hi, Swan!" Jun called out, seeing Swan through the cockpit window. Swan looked up, then smiled and waved.

"Swan is the primary pilot of our helicopter." Phoenix said. "As far as we're concerned, it's her ship. We just borrow it from time to time."

"She looks upset." Gash noted.

"You would be too if someone shot up your baby." Warlord said with a grim expression, running his fingers over multiple bullet holes on the side of the helicopter as they walked by.

"Part of *Lola*'s upgrades is that we placed a layer of heavy duty bullet shielding and sound dampeners within each plate of the hull so even though the outside may get shot up, the passengers will receive little to no damage inside the ship." Phoenix explained with assurance.

"This was developed by our engineering department." Talon bragged.

"That explains why it seemed so quiet when we were inside." Kopensky noted.

"Like a plane." Gash recalled.

Jun took note of the two blood–red strokes that looked like a haphazard "X" on the side of *Lola* near the rear of the craft.

"Why the red 'X'?" Jun asked, bringing everyone's attention to the marking. "I saw it on the sides and the front of the ship when we were coming in too."

Phoenix seemed hesitant at the answer.

"You could say it's our team crest." Warlord said, jumping in.

"Like the Greek symbol 'Chi,'" Talon stated. "It represents us as Kee Warriors." He smiled with pride.

"I don't mean to correct you, but it's pronounced *kai*, not *kee*," Gash said. Phoenix, Warlord, and Talon turned to stare at Gash as if he had insulted them.

"No, it's pronounced *kee*." Talon insisted.

"I'm pretty sure it's *kai*, Talon." Gash replied, looking at Kopensky and Jun for support.

"I've heard it said both ways," Kopensky stated, attempting to remain neutral.

"Well, it's a Greek symbol, so shouldn't it be said the way the Greeks pronounced it?" Gash asked, pressing his point once again.

Jun's eyes narrowed at Gash, seemingly irritated that he felt the need to argue a point that possessed no real value to him.

"Actually the Greek pronounce the character as *kee* but with the 'K' sounding almost like an 'H'." Phoenix corrected.

"The symbol predates the Greek civilization." Warlord said, stepping forward once hearing Talon's defensive tone toward Gash.

"Where did you hear that?" Gash challenged as if doubting the authenticity of Phoenix and Warlord.

"It's a fact, Senator." Phoenix said, calmer than Warlord and Talon, having had more experience in political debate than the rest of his family. "This symbol is part of our family heritage and legacy. I assure you that the 'X' is the symbol of the Kee Warriors before Greece developed it's alphabet."

"Kee Warriors." Kopensky repeated. Phoenix gave him a hard look but said nothing. The others turned to Kopensky as Warlord continued to stare at Gash. "The Medjai were the elite military force in Egypt," Kopensky said. "Is that where your name comes from?"

Phoenix nodded. "Correct. Not just Egypt but throughout Africa."

"Your crew is patterned after the historical Medjai who protected the pharaohs and things like that?" Jun asked in surprise.

Warlord gestured at Talon, sensing that his nephew wanted

to proudly express that they were descendants of those noble warriors, but other than Kopensky, the other New Americans were not privy to their true identity or their surname.

"Yes. You could say that." Phoenix smiled slightly at Jun's knowledge of history. Gash looked at Jun and Phoenix, then noticed with a start that Warlord was staring at him, unblinking.

"That's so cool!" Jun said.

"Yes, it is!" Kopensky chuckled, sincere as always in his actions and reactions. His pure honesty was one of the many things that Phoenix admired about his friend, the politician.

Phoenix looked at Gash, who remained silent, only nodding his head in approval. Warlord and Talon continued to stare at Gash, waiting for a further challenge to their heritage, but no such challenge was forthcoming. Phoenix took Gash's silence as confirmation that there would be no further debate about *Blood Sky's* crew's totem.

"This is the primary flight deck." Phoenix said, changing the subject as he continued the tour. "Some call it a helipad because it's designed for helicopter landings. In truth, this flight deck was designed for the weight of heavier aircraft like Lola while the secondary deck above is for lighter ships and other smaller aircraft. It's also a good place to stage large cargo temporarily."

"What are they doing?" Kopensky asked, pointing at a team of men and women in gray coveralls and safety vests working on and near the helicopter.

"Those are our mechanics and engineers." Talon explained. "Whenever any of our aircraft come back to Blood Sky after a mission, they get a full diagnostic, and any repairs are done as soon as possible."

"Lola always gets priority." Phoenix added.

"Why is that?" Gash asked.

"She's the most valuable aircraft on Blood Sky." he said as he walked into the open roll-up gate, leading the others into the large hangar bay, which was bustling with people and equipment.

"Lola transports crew, supplies, and passengers from ship to shore when we're in countries or on islands that don't have a pier big enough for Blood Sky." Talon explained as he followed the others. "She's also our primary transportation for large cargo, supplies, and large parts for Blood Sky."

"And you use it to rescue people and your crew when they go on missions." Kopensky added, smiling respectfully.

"That's really useful." Gash replied before returning his attention to Phoenix.

"This is the helicopter hangar bay." Phoenix explained. "As you can see, it was originally designed for two large helicopters to be stored at the same time. Since we only have Lola, we reserve the right side for Lola's garage, parts storage, repair, and maintenance. The left side was converted into two floors. This is the lower floor, which we call 'the shop.' It's basically where all the welding and heavy metal work is done for Lola and the Enduros."

"You mentioned Enduros before on Lola." Jun said. "Those are the flying motorcycles, right?"

"Upstairs." Warlord said. Jun looked at him, wondering if he was intentionally barking an order or was simply answering her question with direction.

After hearing Warlord's deep baritone command, Gash scurried up the stairs in obedience.

Talon extended his hand, motioning for Jun to follow Gash up the metal staircase. Warlord smiled, unconcerned at Jun's challenging stare. Phoenix knew that Warlord respected a woman who was not easily intimidated. After a moment she turned to Talon, nodded politely, then followed Gash and Kopensky to the upper floor.

On the upper deck of the port side of the hangar bay, Talon

followed his father and the rest of the group to the platform directly above the shop, overlooking the helicopter area on the right. He watched everyone's initial reaction to what they saw.

Kopensky smiled at the jetbikes that were parked throughout the deck, freshly wiped down. "I recognize these," he said. "These are the mini–jets that came to save us."

Talon looked at Phoenix, who nodded and smiled, giving him approval to take over this portion of the tour. "These are Enduros." Talon said, stepping forward with pride. "We keep them up here on the second deck of the bay, which we call the garage."

Seven pilots in blue coveralls looked up from what they were doing and stared at the intruders who had invaded their personal space.

"Captain on deck!" Falcon shouted. The pilots stood and snapped to attention.

"As you were, Ravens." Phoenix smiled casually. "Talon, please do the honors."

"Senator Kopensky, Senator Gash, Miss Li, I'd like to introduce you to the Ravens, our team of pilots."

"Thank you for saving our asses last night." Kopensky said, smiling as he shook the pilots' hands.

"Nice to see you again, senators." Falcon said, wiping her hands clean before shaking theirs.

Jun looked at Falcon in surprise. Now that they weren't in fear of their lives, Falcon's beauty was evident. Her slender yet muscular physique, like a blond Olympian athlete and a Swedish runway model rolled into one, was enough to take anyone's breath away.

"You're a pilot? But you were in the building with us last night." Jun recalled.

"Commander Falcon is the Ravens' team commander. She's in charge of our pilots." Talon was quick to announce, being that he was Falcon's greatest fan. Gash looked surprised while Jun smiled broadly.

"Falcon is also one of our top field medics, so I had her join the ground team last night as precautionary detail in case on-the-spot medical treatment was needed." Phoenix said, adding to the kudos.

"It was." Gash grunted, holding his bandaged torso.

"Not to mention your skills as a fighter." Jun said. "The way you handled those men last night was remarkable."

Warlord smiled. "Yeah, my SOCIT guys aren't as politically correct with hostages as Falcon is." He smiled without a hint of forgiveness about his statement. "Falcon is good at smoothing things over during an extraction. My team can be impatient and harsh; she's better at coddling people."

Talon noticed Gash looking at Warlord with a degree of nervousness. Every time Warlord spoke, his modulation seemed to make Gash tremble.

"How long have you been a pilot, Falcon?" Kopensky asked.

"Since I was a child." she replied. "My parents had a lot of farmland back in Sweden. My father taught me to fly crop dusters as soon as I could reach the pedals and see above the console at the same time." This gave everyone a chuckle. Falcon was amazing with other people, able to make them smile even in the midst of a battle. Her slight Swedish accent simply sealed her presentation on positivity. "Then I came to New America and joined the Air Force because I wanted to be a fighter pilot."

"See how polite and friendly she is?" Warlord said. "Me and my SOCIT team would have just told you that this information is classified." He smirked as a confirmation of his previous statement.

"As you may already know, the New American Air Force has a team of specially trained airmen who run security for the Air Mobility Command." Phoenix said. "They're not pilots, but they're called Phoenix Ravens, and their primary objective in New America is counterterrorism and protecting Air Force jets, personnel, and equipment while out of the country."

"That much I know." Kopensky said, casting a sarcastic smile at Phoenix.

"When my term in the Air Force was done, I met with Phoenix, who was an old friend, and we talked about starting a team of pilots, and here I am." Falcon smiled, her hands extended.

"Since Captain Phoenix wanted all pilot call signs to be flight related, he and Falcon came up with the name 'Ravens' based on her appreciation for what the Air Force Phoenix Ravens do." Talon added. He smiled at Falcon but when he saw Warlord staring suspiciously at him, he looked away. Everyone in the family knew about his secret admiration for Falcon. Even though she was older than him and part of the team, she was the reason why he had trained to be a Raven.

"This is Raptor." Falcon said as she turned to the short, elderly man standing next to her.

Raptor or "Pops" was a Black man from South Carolina who had no patience or tolerance for people who he considered ignorant. He was shorter than Gash, and his balding gray hair simply added to his stereotypical behavior and mannerisms.

"You're the man on the radio who was leading the attack on those helicopters?" Gash asked with surprise.

Raptor stared at him with a suspicious gaze. "You look surprised. What's wrong, Politician Man? Skin too dark for ya? Hair too gray? Or am I too short?"

"Raptor!" Warlord snapped. The *Blood Sky* crew had grown accustomed to Raptor's offensive comments, but he knew better than to verbally attack guests, even though political visits were not a normal occurrence on their ship.

"And you've met Hawk and Eagle." Talon said, quickly redirecting the group to the next crew member in the semicircle of pilots. Warlord took one final glance at Raptor, but Talon saw him look up at the ceiling in an attempt to hide his amusement. Warlord always found Raptor's grumpy, smart-ass remarks entertaining, especially when they were poorly timed and grossly inappropriate.

After the tour group passed, Phoenix glared at Raptor, causing the elderly man to look down.

"You all clean up really good." Eagle said with a chiseled smile.

"It's good to see you healing up nicely." Hawk added with his deep monotone voice.

"Thank you both for everything you did for us last night." Kopensky said while shaking Eagle and Hawk's hands. "The teamwork we witnessed was unparalleled, but I'm glad it's over now." Kopensky's comment was met by a few chuckles.

"These last three to my left are Kestrel, Condor, and Vulture." Falcon said. "You didn't officially meet them before, but they were on the Enduros with Raptor last night. They're also former Air Force pilots who I recruited when I joined Blood Sky."

Gash, Kopensky, and Jun went to each of the remaining three pilots and shook their hands hardily.

"I know it may not mean much, but because of you," Gash turned to Raptor specifically and looked him in the eyes, "because of all of you, I'm alive." Gash's voice began to tremble as he fought the emotions that he had suppressed throughout the night. "And because of your heroic actions, I get to see my wife and children again. We will all be able to return home to hug our families because of you." Gash sniffled. "Thank you."

Talon couldn't tell if it was Gash's unexpectedly moving speech that got to Raptor or the fact that the elderly aviator had outlived most of his own family within the last thirty years, but his eyes started welling up with tears. Phoenix elbowed Warlord as Raptor turned away to hide his face.

"Pops? Are you crying?" Warlord asked with amusement.

"Shut up, ya damn Sasquatch! Ya know my allergies flare up 'round this time of year!" Raptor blurted. Phoenix and Warlord looked at Falcon in amusement, but she shot a stern look at her commanders. She discreetly handed Raptor a clean towel as he looked at Gash and smiled slightly while bowing his head to acknowledge the touching words.

Kopensky looked away to hide his amusement, then counted the number of jetbikes in the room.

"I noticed that you're all called pilots, but from what I saw last night, you handle these Enduros more like flying motorcycles." Kopensky stated, managing to redirect everyone's attention and rescue Raptor's pride.

"Technically, the Ravens are actually 'biker-pilots' because they're trained to fly the Enduros as well as various aircraft," Phoenix explained.

"That's a lot of training." Jun observed, impressed. Falcon bowed in agreement.

"You have a lot of Enduros, Commander. How many biker-pilots are onboard?" Kopensky asked.

"We currently have eleven Ravens, officially." Falcon said as she approached the later-model Enduros.

"And four more in training." Talon added.

"Yes," Falcon continued. "The seven of us are biker–pilots, and so are Captain Phoenix, Commander Swan, Commander Talon, and Doctor Kite." Kopensky, Gash and Jun turn to look at Talon and Phoenix, genuinely surprised.

"That's what you meant by call signs being flight related." Kopensky said in realization. "Phoenix, Swan, Kite, and Talon are all birds or bird parts."

Talon smiled as Phoenix winked his response.

"We seldom fly because we have other command responsibilities throughout the ship." Phoenix said. "But, if necessary, we're trained and qualified to fly an Enduro if necessary. Consider us second string. These are our first-string ace pilots right here."

Gash applauded the Ravens, as did Kopensky and Jun.

"I've never seen anything like these Enduros before." Jun said as she approached the older-model Enduros on the far side of the deck. "Why do these four look different from the rest?"

Talon stepped to the front of the group to address her question. "Let me tell you the history of the Enduros." he began.

"Here we go." Warlord whispered with a smirk. Talon knew his second cousin's subtle amusement was a façade to hide the pride he felt for Talon.

"These four, with the horizontal drone–like propellers away from the body of the bikes on the wings, are the original Enduros. We call them Enduro Mark Ones because they were the prototype." Talon explained.

"They came from my family farm back in Sweden." Falcon added, smiling.

"That's right," Talon continued. "When Captain Phoenix said we needed to expand our transportation vehicles for trips that Blood Sky couldn't reach, Falcon told us about the four new hoverbikes that her father had bought for agricultural maintenance."

"That explains why they look like miniature crop dusters." Gash said while walking around one of the early model hoverbikes.

The deep-blue, one–man hoverbike had brass tubing around the cylindrical framework of the propeller housings positioned at the ends of the wings. It also had an antique bicycle handlebar, a vintage motorcycle seat, intake vents on each side, and a windshield that was more for aerodynamic wind control than to protect the pilot. The exhaust pipes were on either side of the vehicle, just like classic motorcycles.

"They couldn't go more than nine or ten stories above a surface and were used for hauling grain from one side of the farm to the other in carts attached to the back. They were sturdy and fast." Talon explained.

"In the beginning they were the best." Phoenix added. "If anyone needed to make a run into a town off a coast that was too small for Lola, these were perfect. They hover over water and land, and if the incline isn't too steep, they have the power to take hills quickly. Because they use significantly less gas than Lola, they're practical for personal transportation too."

"The weapons look after–market," Kopensky noted.

"Very observant, Senator." Warlord said. "The first thing we addressed was the fact that they had no defensive equipment, so our engineering team mounted the semi–automatic guns under the front."

Kopensky nodded as he continued to stare at the Mark I Enduros.

"When we decided to use them for assault," Talon continued, "they were no longer the best equipment for the job. Because we couldn't add a lot of weight to the existing bikes, they couldn't carry a lot of ammunition, and, of course, there's no way to reload in mid-flight. However, we still use them for small cargo and supply runs and going into towns and cities."

"Smart and efficient." Gash said, glancing at Phoenix.

"Which brings us to the Enduro Mark Two." Phoenix said while walking back to the newer-model jetbikes. The tour group followed him while the pilots returned to working on their own Enduro Mark IIs.

"Where did you find these?" Gash asked.

"We didn't. Using the Mark One as a prototype, Captain

Phoenix came up with a list of what the Mark Two model needed, and then Swan designed it."

"Swan?" Jun turned to Talon in surprise. "Lola's pilot?"

Talon nodded. "Yup. She has a degree in graphic design and art, so it was easy for her to turn Captain Phoenix's ideas into three-dimensional computer renderings, and that's all it took."

"Talon is leaving out the most important part," Warlord said. "What Talon isn't telling you is that he's an aerospace engineer." Phoenix explained. "That's what he was doing in the Air Force before he joined the crew of Blood Sky. So, he was able to build the Enduros to my specifications using Swan's designs."

Gash, Kopensky, and Jun stared at Talon, their eyes wide. He often got that stare when people realized his skill level. He was shy by nature, so the sudden attention often humbled him.

"I see." Kopensky said, smiling.

"Once Swan and Captain Phoenix hashed out the upgrades and the new look, Talon drew up the 3D schematics, and built each Enduro right here in this garage." Warlord informed the group

"We put together a strong team of engineers. You can do almost anything with the right people." Talon said, meeting his father's eyes.

"We're proud of the Mark Twos. They're lighter, so they're faster and more maneuverable." Phoenix said. "They have machine gun mounts with room for automatic reload and four rockets each, which you saw in action last night." he added, pointing to each item as he mentioned them.

"Yes, we did." Kopensky nodded, impressed. Then his eyes brightened as he put the pieces together. He turned to Phoenix, smiling proudly. Phoenix winked discreetly, but Jun saw it. Kopensky now knew that Talon was the son whom Phoenix had often talked about.

"A surgical team, mechanics, engineers, aerospace technology, pilots, and a super helicopter?" Gash gazed at the people in the room in awe. "Wow! Just wow, Captain Phoenix!"

"Hey, don't forget the kickass elite commandos who risked everything to go into enemy territory and save your butts!" Warlord said, stepping up with a braggadocious tone, causing the other crew members to erupt in laughter.

Kopensky and Gash chuckled. "Yes, SOCIT!" Gash smiled. "We won't forget SOCIT, Commander Warlord."

"After what you did with those two insurgents and that wall, I will never forget *you* or you're capabilities." Jun said, putting her hand on the man-giant, her face full of admiration.

Phoenix shrugged. "What can I say? He eats his Wheaties every morning."

"And let me guess, a hell of a lot of spinach too?" Kopensky teased. Talon did not understand the correlation between spinach and strength, but he decided to ask his father about it another time.

"You know it!" Warlord smiled and winked. Kopensky shook his head in amusement before turning back to the Enduros.

"I know a couple of generals who would love to get a few of these for our Air Force." Gash said, impressed.

Everyone fell silent, tension replacing their laughter.

"They're not for sale." Talon said curtly.

"What about the design plans?" Jun asked. "You'd make so much money selling designs like this to the US military, or any other military."

Talon shook his head. "Not for sale."

"Commander Talon and our engineers are very attached to their inventions." Warlord explained.

"Inventions, plural? Are you sure you don't want to give us a peek?" Gash tried his best to look humble and cute but only came off appearing pathetic and pitiful.

"Next stop on our tour is the ship's bow." Phoenix stated, ignoring Gash's comment.

"But—"

"Please," Warlord said, his voice booming. Talon stood unmoving between the Enduros and the tour group. Warlord smiled pleasantly. "This way, senators." He directed them to follow Phoenix, ending the conversation.

"Uh, bow? That's the front, right?" Gash whispered to Jun. She smiled and nodded.

As the group walked along the deck, Gash looked at the front portion of the destroyer, staring at the blood–red "X" painted on the black plates as a badge of honor. He glanced at Warlord to confirm that the giant was still watching him, then continued walking. Jun watched as crew members greeted them cordially while passing. She occasionally looked behind her to catch people staring at them after they passed. Talon continued his role as tour guide, describing portions of the ship as they walked.

"Why is everyone staring at us?" Jun asked, picking up her pace to direct her question to Phoenix.

"We don't get a lot of visitors." Phoenix answered, smiling. "We tend to keep to ourselves most of the time."

"But I've heard so many stories about how Blood Sky rescues people in need."

"Yes, well, we do rescue people in need." Phoenix continued as they all stopped at the ship's bow.

"I'd think that helping so many people means you get a lot of visitors, especially since some of your work involves trans-porting people between islands, and countries." Jun said.

"True, but we haven't been in the business of bulk transportation in a while, and when we were, we restricted our passengers to certain sections of the ship."

Jun nodded. "I can see that."

"I heard Blood Sky was a pirate ship." Gash said while looking back at the red "X." When no one responded, Gash turned to see that everyone in the tour party was staring at him with disdain.

Jun knew Gash better than most and assumed he had connected the "X" on *Blood Sky* with the skull and crossbones that were often seen on pirate ships in stories. His obliviousness when it came to topics outside his purview was often seen as intentionally offensive. She knew that was far from the case, but she still tended to get frustrated at his assumptions and bad timing.

"Chad?" Kopensky said, his voice filled with disappointment.

"I'm sorry!" Gash said, sounding sincere. "It's just what I heard. It wasn't an accusation."

"Senator, we have rescued civilian and cargo ships from pirates for years." Warlord said. "We have seen what happens to the ships that we don't reach in time. The unnecessary violence, rape, and torture that pirates do when they don't get what they want or just because they were in the mood. Pirates do things that would keep you up at night for the rest of your life if you witnessed them firsthand, as we have. Now imagine being compared to the same animals that you've been fighting for years. It's more than an insult."

"I understand and apologize." Gash said, nodding. "I can assure you that once we get back, the world will know that you are anything but pirates."

"I doubt that." Warlord mumbled under his breath.

"Actually, we would prefer that this rescue operation remain classified." Phoenix said.

"Why? I would have thought that you'd want the positive publicity." Gash said.

"We don't want any publicity." Phoenix replied. "We just want to live our lives as merchants. If we can help a few people along the way, that's fine."

"Still the humble Boy Scout." Kopensky said.

"Do you two know each other?" Jun asked, no longer able to hold in the question as she stared at Phoenix and Kopensky.

"Let's just say we have a history." Kopensky replied. "Back when he lived in New America." Phoenix looked at Kopensky but remained silent.

"Really?" Gash sounded deeply interested. "Did you work in the military? You seem like you have a lot of experience."

"I have teamed up with military personnel and learned a lot. However, I have never been a member of the New American Military." Phoenix said, walking forward as he urged the tour to continue. Jun followed, not wanting to add space between them.

"That was a long time ago, Chad." Kopensky said. "You weren't involved in special operations back then."

"If you weren't a soldier, Phoenix, what did you do for the government?" Gash inquired, asking the obvious question.

"Classified!" Warlord warned, ending the discussion.

"Were you called Phoenix back then too?" Gash asked.

"That's classified too." Warlord replied, standing threateningly close to Gash while staring down at him, unblinking.

Phoenix turned to Talon, and the young commander understood immediately.

"Soooo, all this walking around has made me hungry." Talon, changing the subject. "Rescuing politicians can be exhausting work, and I'm sure they didn't give you the Sunday morning brunch buffet while you were guests at the luxurious Desert Terrorist Chalet." Everyone turned to look at Talon as

Phoenix stepped back, fading out of the limelight. Talon picked up the pace as they headed toward the exit.

"With all that's happened, it just dawned on me that we haven't eaten much since yesterday." Jun said, turning to Talon with a hand on her stomach.

"Well, our ship's chef is first class and can make anything you want, as long as the ingredients are in stock." Talon replied. "Sushi, barbecued ribs, steak, fish, candied yams, gumbo, chicken, Cajun seafood, curried goat, apple pie, peach cobbler, and all kinds of international foods that she picked up from our travels."

As Talon spoke, Jun noticed Kopensky and Gash inadvertently focusing their attention on Talon, a hungry look on their faces.

"Anybody ready to eat?" Warlord asked, smiling. Kopensky, Gash, and Jun raised their hands, followed hesitantly by Talon.

Phoenix looked at Talon and then the others, then led them off the bow.

8

A DAY WITH THE CREW

~

On *Blood Sky*, everything was a team effort. Those who could cook took their turn in the scheduled kitchen rotation. Those who could not cook were on the kitchen cleaning rotation. The menu for the week depended on who was scheduled to work those shifts. Everyone had their favorite meals and favorite cooks. Every now and then, Phoenix and the Medjinn siblings made cameo appearances in the kitchen, honoring everyone with their unique cuisines. Of the family of commanders, Swan and Warlord were the ones with the greatest culinary fanbase within the crew, but everyone on the ship knew to whom the kitchen really belonged.

Miss Cookie managed the kitchen staff, supplies, and all of the dining areas of the ship. She also cooked more than any other crew member. When experienced chefs like Deacon had to go on missions with SOCIT, Miss Cookie was always the alternate for him and anyone else who had a dual position on the ship, such as combat, bridge command, or flight crew.

Miss Cookie was a longtime friend of Phoenix after he

rescued her from an abusive relationship in New America. She was a robust Black woman with a three-inch afro and a broad, cheerful smile. Her laugh made others smile even if they didn't know why she was laughing. Miss Cookie was jolly and loving, becoming a surrogate mother to the crew of *Blood Sky*. It wasn't unheard of to stumble into the kitchen in the dead of night and find Miss Cookie and the captain in the kitchen, talking over a piece of sweet potato pie.

After breakfast, the guests had free run of designated sections of the ship while the crew went on with their daily duties of exercise, cleaning, training, and preparing the weapons and vehicles.

Gash retired to his assigned cabin to relax and rest his wounds. Once he was alone, the reality of his life being saved began to take its toll. He sat on the bed in his cabin staring at the wall. He had held his fear and frustration in for the better part of the day. Now that he was alone, he had the chance to be himself and not a senator from New America. Chadwick Gash grabbed the pillow with care, as if it were a human being, and began to whimper and then cry. It had been a long day, and while he was grateful to be alive, he had finally come to grips with the reality that his job had almost cost him his life.

Jun returned to the infirmary to check on Torres, who was still sedated, and to spend time with her friend. Zara was in better spirits, having spoken to the ship's psychologist. Nurse Zhang brought her a healthy breakfast and was amazed at how much and how fast the petite Afghan woman could eat. Jun was happy, Zara's healthy appetite a sign that she was feeling better.

Kopensky walked into the captain's cabin, following Phoenix. Both men were at ease now that they were no longer around the others, always aware of the formalities they had to maintain. Kopensky was surprised at the size of Phoenix's quarters, which looked more like a studio apartment with limited windows than cramped sleeping quarters on a ship. He stopped at the large digital frame mounted to the wall. Images changed every few seconds, showing moments in Phoenix's personal life. Kopensky smiled when he saw an image of younger versions of himself, Jay Malo, Charles Bailey, and Phoenix. The four men were all smiling with golf clubs in their hands and a scenic golf course in the background.

"That's how they know about me." Kopensky said, chuckling at the realization.

"I told you, your name might have come up once or twice." Phoenix said, gesturing for Kopensky to choose a cigar from his built-in humidor.

"Oh my!" the senator said, smiling boyishly. "Cubans? Where did you get these, I wonder?"

"I have no restrictions at sea, remember?" Phoenix clipped the tip of his cigar and then handed the cutter to his friend. "It was part of a payment for a job we did a few months back." Phoenix laughed as he ran the cigar under his nose, inhaling deeply with his eyes closed.

"I haven't had a cigar in almost eight years." Kopensky admitted. "It most certainly is not one of the priorities that New America imports these days."

"But it's still one of life's luxuries." Phoenix smiled as Kopensky grabbed a cigar before closing the fine cedar humidor.

"Can we smoke in here?" Kopensky asked.

"Only if you want the fire brigade running in here to hose the place down." Phoenix replied as he walked toward a large steel door at the far end of the room. He opened it, leading

Kopensky onto a luxurious balcony that jutted out from the side of the ship.

"What a view!" Kopensky stared in awe at the never–ending ocean, the plush outdoor furniture, and the ability to observe the activity on the deck a few levels below. The afternoon sky had only a few clouds, and the sound of ocean waves rolling by which added to the tranquility of the moment.

"I had the engineers build the balcony on the starboard side of the ship, so I can look at the cities whenever we make port." Phoenix explained.

Kopensky looked around at the balcony. "You had this built?"

"Yup. Designed and reinforced. I had to cut a hole into the hull. That's why my cabin is on this side of the ship."

"Amazing!" Kopensky leaned on the railing as he looked out at the ocean.

"Best seats in the house." Phoenix said. "When we have nothing to do, I have the helm turn toward the sunset, then I come out here and relax." He smiled while taking in the sweet ocean air. "Relax, Kris. The worst is over."

Kopensky looked at Phoenix with concern as Phoenix poured a glass of decades-old scotch. He knew that Kopensky usually had wine with and after a meal, but he assumed that after all they had been through, a glass or two of quality scotch would be better.

"How can you be so calm?" Kopensky asked as they each took a chair at the table. He had been holding the question in for hours.

"About what?"

"Xander, we've just been through some crazy shit! Guns shooting everywhere, your cousin plowing people through walls! You stormed in looking like fucking Captain Courageous with a team of hardcore, supersized GI Joe soldiers! An aerial rescue and a damn dogfight with jetbikes and helicopters?" His voice cracked on the last word, finally able to release his intensity and excitement. "Then we get to this," Kopensky waved his hands, gesturing broadly at *Blood Sky.* "And you're walking around giving tours like a damn cruise director! What the hell do you mean, 'about what'?"

"It gets intense out here sometimes, Kris." Phoenix said, amused at his friend's excitement.

"Intense?" Kopensky stared at Phoenix in disbelief. "Fucking *intense*? That was insane!"

"I told you that I was an extraction specialist."

Kopensky glared at Phoenix, who maintained his calm demeanor, waiting for Kopensky to get it all out of his system and relax.

"Extraction specialist? You watered that down just a bit, Xander! How can you do all that shit and still be so calm?"

Phoenix chuckled. "You're funny. We do that and worse. More than I'd like to admit. But some days it's not so bad."

"Why haven't you died of a heart attack or something? Or just died?"

Phoenix shrugged. "We're used to it, I guess. Experience reduces loss. Fewer mistakes means we live longer."

"OK." Kopensky said, the word dripping with sarcasm, typical Alexander. He rubbed his hands together and felt himself finally relax. After a few moments of silence, he turned to Phoenix, who continued to watch him like a concerned therapist.

"You okay?" Phoenix's voice was tranquil, like a radio announcer on a late-night jazz station.

"I owe you an apology." Kopensky admitted with a grimace.

"For what?" Phoenix asked. Kopensky looked down at his scotch, then glanced up at Phoenix, who was staring out at the horizon, swirling the ice in his glass.

"You're really going to make me say it, aren't you?" Kopensky shook his head before taking a sip from his glass. Unlike Phoenix, he took his scotch neat. "Thanks for saving our asses last night."

"Is that it?" Phoenix responded, using his butane lighter to toast the end of his cigar before lighting up. He took a few deep draws on his cigar, then passed the lighter to Kopensky.

"Damn it, Xander! You were right, and I was wrong."

"About?"

"You can be an arrogant ass sometimes!" Kopensky snapped before lighting his cigar in the same manner as Phoenix. "You were right about the damn tracker!"

"I was?" Phoenix asked in mock surprise.

"Yes. You always said that if I put that shit in my blood, no one would ever find it except you. I'll be damned if you weren't right again, rescuing me from a real shit situation. The first thing they did was scan us for tracking devices."

"In all fairness, you were right the last three times, Kris."

"Four." Kopensky corrected. Phoenix pondered that for a moment, then smiled and tapped his ashes in the custom black marble ashtray on the table between them. "Brazil." Kopensky added.

"Yeah, four." Phoenix smiled at the recollection. "But with that said, Senator Kopensky, you are indeed welcome."

"How did you know?"

"Common sense. You piss a lot of people off. And you've made a lot of enemies in office with your fast-tracking through the political ranks."

"Common sense, my ass! You're like a damn fortune teller."

Phoenix shrugged. "Call it a sixth sense."

Kopensky grunted, frustrated at Phoenix's casualness. He sat back for a moment, turning everything over in his head. "You think this was politically motivated?" he asked, his eyebrows furrowed in concern.

Phoenix pondered the question for a moment. "Politically motivated? No. Politically instigated? Maybe."

"What do you mean?"

"What they were spewing had merit to be the potential views of terrorists or maybe freedom fighters in their own minds, but there's a lot of things that don't make any sense."

"Like how they knew where to attack us?" Kopensky took a long draw on his cigar, squinting from the smoke as it passed his eyes. "Even if it was leaked that we were heading to Ankara, we were going to take an indirect route to avoid an ambush."

"There's that, yes. But other than their leader, those men were the backwater insurgent variety. More like pirates than terrorists. Very little to no formal combat or military training."

"Yes." Kopensky agreed, thinking back to his abductors' overall appearance and actions.

"So, where would they get the training and funding to buy and pilot assault choppers?" Phoenix asked. "Information is one thing; funding is another."

"I didn't think about that."

"You were a bit occupied."

"And where the hell did they get the fuel?" Kopensky asked.

Phoenix looked at him out of the corner of his eye as he blew smoke rings. "I thought only a few governing countries had the resources to manufacture jet fuel."

"The Middle East is one of the largest suppliers left for crude oil." Kopensky said.

"Yeah, but pirates, bandits, and terrorists usually don't have the resources to refine crude oil into jet fuel no matter how much raw oil they have."

"I'll look into it." Kopensky said, then pondered for a moment. "Chad and I agree there's a mole, someone high ranking too. I'm now certain those supplies were sent, Xander.

At first I thought that guy just took the supplies and was going to use us as ransom for more, but now that I'm thinking back on it, he always seemed to lose his control at the mention of them. I really believe he thinks we intentionally screwed his country over."

"Who was your contact in Saudi Arabia?"

"Demir Sahin, an ambassador. We've only communicated through Comtext messages and emails. We were supposed to meet for the first time this week, but, well, you know the rest. I'll have to contact him once we're back in New America and ask him if he really didn't receive the supplies. If he didn't then—"

Phoenix let out a quiet hum before taking a drag on his cigar. "Then someone intercepted it for their own use or reason. There are still a lot of pirates out at sea."

"We hired a third-party protection escort assigned to the shipment! Even if the ship the supplies were on was attacked, we would've gotten word about it."

Phoenix closed his eyes as he thought about it. "So, the supplies were taken without a word between New America and Saudi Arabia. You might have been used as a scapegoat for something much bigger."

"Why do you think that?"

"Only someone in either the government or the military could make an entire ship and crew disappear without you knowing."

"There you go with those espionage conspiracy theories."

"Think about it, Kris. If the Saudis intercepted the ship, someone in New America would have found out and said something. Instead, you think it arrived, and this guy is saying it didn't. That's deception coming from the American side."

Kopensky took a moment to ponder what Phoenix was implying, and he didn't like what came to his mind. The thought that someone in New America would prevent a shipment of supplies from reaching the Middle East, then remove all records of it getting there or being intercepted, meant it had to be someone who held a higher position in the government or the military than he originally thought.

"You could be right, but I'll have to look into it when I get back."

"I'm glad I made sure a team was in position within a hundred miles of you."

"I owe you." Kopensky took a long draw on his cigar, then sat back to enjoy the view. "Why don't you let me take this liquid tracker formula back with me, so we can issue it to all the heads of state? I'm not the most important person in politics, you know."

"You already know the answer to that, Kris."

"Come on, Xander. Things have changed since then."

Phoenix shook his head. "Not enough. You still have idiots like Ward in high military positions and racist witches like Harpy in office."

Kopensky smiled. "Harp. Karen Harp. Not Harpy." He chuckled. "And your accusations about her being a racist have never been proven."

"That's because that scared lieutenant would never document all the garbage she was saying. He just took it for years until it killed him."

"Well, let's not talk about her anymore."

"Good idea." Phoenix frowned with disgust.

It was due to Harp's decisions and actions that Phoenix and his team had been deployed on a mission with poor information to a location where they had no jurisdiction. Because of her, he and his team were disavowed and reported as killed in action to cover up the truth that they had been operating under orders from the New American government. Kopensky knew that his friend was accustomed to doing things and never getting credit for his heroism, but this was different. Phoenix never let go of the fact that he had to agree to be dead after supposedly acting on his own, never able to use his real identity again. Meanwhile, Naval Commander Ward received the credit for a rescue operation that the military had never conducted. Kopensky understood why these events still fueled Phoenix's anger at everyone involved in changing his life forever.

Phoenix took another puff on his cigar and looked out at the ocean to calm himself. "Tell me about your colleague, Gash." he said, changing the subject.

"What about him?"

"He asks a lot of questions." Phoenix said, annoyance in his tone.

"He's okay. He means well. He's just out of his element."

"How so?"

Kopensky saw the suspicion in his friend's eyes. "He's really big on family values in and out of the office. Some say he was turned down for promotion because he puts his family first over his career as a senator."

"That's not a bad thing."

"Not to you and me, but to the decision makers, it can be a problem."

"So, you don't think he could be the one who ratted you out?"

"Not at all! What's your take on him?"

"He's probably a good guy and an honest man, but damn, he can push a lot."

"He means well."

"If you say so, then I'm fine with it." Phoenix sipped his scotch, and then a mischievous smile appeared on his face. "So, who's this Jun Li woman?" he asked nonchalantly.

Kopensky hesitated before answering. "She's been with us for a few years. Gash hired her to be his assistant. I think she was recommended by Vice President O'Leary. I'm not sure if she's learning foreign policies or just working her way up the political ladder. I don't know much about her."

"A beautiful Asian woman is part of your entourage, and you don't know anything about her? I find that a little hard to believe, Kris."

"I think she's alright, but I don't know about beautiful. Are you still hanging on to that dream of yours?"

"I told you that in confidence." Phoenix said.

"I know. But a mystery woman being handed over to you by a king is a little out there. You didn't even see her face in your dream. You just know she's tall and Asian."

"She wasn't 'handed over' to me. It was more like a father figure giving his blessing."

Kopensky shrugged. "Same thing."

"Did your father–in–law 'hand over' your wife at your wedding?"

"Valid point."

"Well, that's not why I'm asking about her. That dream was just a dream. I haven't had it for years. That's all it was."

Kopensky didn't buy that for a moment. "Oh? I didn't see your whole crew, but I would bet that there are more than a fair number of Asian women on board this ship. How do you explain that, Mr. Phoenix?"

"Natural selection." Phoenix smirked, looking away.

"You're so full of shit!"

"It's true!" Phoenix said with a smile. "I brought on Nitro and her cousin, Jet, after we rescued them from a slave ship, then they recruited the others. I had nothing to do with it." Phoenix smiled mischievously, holding his hands up. "Like I said, natural selection."

"Well, there are a lot of Asian refugees in the world since most major Asian countries in the Pacific Rim were destroyed in

2029 and are still radioactive." Kopensky reasoned. "But they can always look for safe passage to Shangri-La. Why would they join Blood Sky?"

"First of all, Shangri-La is impossible to find. As a newly formed empire, it's heavily controlled. This is a freedom ship. There's a difference. Here, people make their own choices, as long as they abide by the rules of the ship."

"You travel all around the world. I'm sure you run across islands that didn't exist before."

"Yes, I have."

"Have you ever been to Shangri-La?" Kopensky watched Phoenix closely, something he did when asking Phoenix direct questions that he would otherwise avoid. Phoenix seldom lied, but he often shied away from the truth. For whatever reason, avoiding the truth was his witty way of not actually telling a lie. Phoenix allowed a few moments of silence to pass before speaking.

"I have."

"I knew it!" Kopensky exploded as he sat up straight in his chair. "What's it like?"

"It's everything they say it is. At least the part that I saw."

"What's that mean?"

"I only do trade there. My crew goes to the harbor city to drop off and pick up."

"I heard it's lit up like Manhattan City."

"It is. They have a way of illuminating the streets with neon lights more than any place I've ever seen."

"Well, you're the only person I know who has admitted to being there. Why do you think that is?"

"Trust," Phoenix said. "Trust and neutrality."

"That's cryptic."

"As long as you hold a political office in New America, I have to be cryptic when it comes to political conversations, for your protection. I wouldn't want you to ever have to lie for me, Kris."

"Fair enough," Kopensky said before sipping his scotch. He paused, his stomach tightening as he dared to pose the question that he dreaded asking his friend. "What about you?"

"What about me?"

"Would you go against your country if a neutral power decided it was no longer neutral?"

"Well, that was a 'slam on the brakes and change direction' twist in the conversation. Where's this coming from?"

"You mentioned neutrality." Kopensky said, picking his next words carefully. Phoenix was his friend, and he didn't want to offend him, but this was the best time for the conversation. "You know what I think."

"But?"

"But there has always been talk that someone with your experience may hold a grudge against New America." Kopensky said, not wanting to sound accusatory.

"And?"

"You're the only one left who made a reputation for yourself even after the . . . Harp situation."

"I see." Phoenix took a moment to draw on his cigar. "So, you're not asking because you think it's a possibility; you're asking because others are asking."

"Yes, and I know when I get back, someone's going to bring it up, and I want to be honest and say I asked you directly."

"This is why I don't like politics, but I'll answer because it's you, Kris." Phoenix sighed. "First, remember that New America is no longer *my* country. Harpy saw to that. Second, I will try to always remain neutral. I don't always agree with the policies of New America or other countries, so it's best that I stay neutral and live out my life on the open seas where I only have to abide by maritime law. And as long as no one bothers me or my people or the clients I take on, I won't get involved in national or international politics."

"Are you saying you would turn against New America if challenged?"

"No, I'm saying I don't agree with everything that New America has done, but if people don't bother me, I promise not to bother them. So, out of loyalty to you and other select people in government whom I respect, like George, I choose to stay out of politics completely."

"I know, but would you make us your enemy because of people like Karen?"

"I have no enemies anymore, Kris. You know that more than anyone. I'm retired."

"That's good."

Phoenix paused for thought before continuing. "But you do have some power–hungry people in office who may one day decide to make me and my people their enemy. I'm not looking to fight an entire country, but if that day comes, and my enemy has a country I can align with to survive . . ." Phoenix shrugged.

"The enemy of your enemy is your friend." Kopensky said with concern, then realization. "The tour today was a strategic move, not a hospitable gesture?"

"I trust you. I know you. I don't know Gash very well, and I have no idea who Jun Li is." Phoenix said. "If details about this ship happen to get out, it will be controlled and limited."

"That's why you only showed the advanced technology of your jetbikes." Kopensky said.

"Yes. Only the offensive technology. Specifically, the vehicles that we used to rescue you. Besides, I'm sure the Navy pilots already gave their commander an earful of what they saw that our Enduros can do in aerial combat."

"I'm sure they did."

"The rest of our tech advancements remain classified to

specific crew members only. I must make sure that my people and our technology don't become a tool in some sort of arms race that leads to another world war. I don't want that blood on my hands, Kris."

"I would never let that happen, Xander."

"You're not high enough on the political food chain to make a difference yet, Mr. Senator."

"Yet?" Kopensky caught that last portion of Phoenix's statement. "But you're saying one day I will be?"

"I'm sure you will. I've seen it."

"Like you saw me becoming a senator?"

"Exactly."

"Is that another official Nostradamus prediction, or are you just throwing out compliments?"

Rather than reply, Phoenix continued to stare out at the ocean, a focused expression on his face. Finally, he turned to his friend, who had a puzzled look on his face. "When that day comes, I will sigh in relief, my friend. Might even sell you some tech if you ask me nicely and buy me a fancy steak dinner." Phoenix looked out at the horizon again. "But until you're in a position to make a difference, I will continue living for today."

Kopensky took a long drag on his cigar, knowing that his friend and ally spoke some form of truth. Over the years he had seen Phoenix make many bizarre yet accurate predictions. He often explained it away as a result of wisdom and experience gained from watching how the streams of life flowed. Many people saw Phoenix as a strategic leader who could sense danger and foretell possible outcomes. What worried Kopensky was that Phoenix might be right, again, about the impending threat.

9

HISTORY LESSON

~

K ite sat in her office, working on her tablet, the holographic keyboard projected onto the stand. She rubbed her eyes in exhaustion, looking away from the screen. She noticed movement off to one side. She leaned back, looking out of her open door to see Jun Li standing over Zara, who was sleeping, unaware that Kite was watching from her office.

"She was restless, so I gave her a sedative to help her sleep through the night." Nurse Zhang said. Her voice was so calm and peaceful that it seemed to whisper kindness and care. It was one of the many reasons that Kite had hired her for the head nurse position. Zhang had superior skills, but her ability to remain tranquil in chaotic situations set her above the rest.

"Thank you." Jun replied. Jun sighed deeply, then turned to walk out of the infirmary. Zhang stared at Jun with sadness on her face before returning to her workstation in the corner of the room.

Kite watched Jun leave the infirmary, wondering if the woman was concerned about losing her friend or something else entirely. It wasn't unusual for someone in Jun's position to feel alone and isolated so soon after her rescue. She didn't have access to a phone, so she couldn't talk to her friends and family to update them. The only person she could relate to at that time was unconscious. Kite turned off her desk lamp and walked out of her office.

Swan sat in front of her monitor, laughing while editing footage. Half of her personal quarters looked like a cross between a home theater and a security command center. Monitors of various sizes were mounted to the wall in front of a massive desktop computer and first-rate sound system. That was where she currently sat in the dark, entertaining herself with family and crew moments that she had spliced together from old video files.

The other half of her room was a bizarre combination of delicate trinkets, high-tech gadgets, and comic book illustrations. It was her own little private domain where she was free to be completely herself with no orders to give or people to manage. One section of her wall displayed her original artwork. Muscular griffins, peaceful animals, her family in different suits of futuristic armor fighting a trio of scarred men, an armored minotaur, and a giant flying above them all. Above were sketches of *Blood Sky*, leading a fleet of flying ships in the clouds. Her bed was surrounded by art and creative designs in various stages of completion. Swan was a talented artist and was her father's personal human encyclopedia. She got the art gene from her father but far exceeded his own sketches and drawings.

She reached over to take a bite of her freshly made sandwich when she noticed movement on one of the surveillance monitors. She stopped laughing and watched Jun walk out onto the aft deck into the cool night air. The woman rested a hand on her slung arm and leaned against the ship's rail.

Using the joystick, Swan zoomed in on Jun's bleak expression as she looked down at the rushing water below.

Jun stared out at the clear night sky and the crescent moon, allowing the crashing breakers below to lull her into a false sense of escape. She closed her eyes, only to open them moments later when she felt the presence of another person.

"Hi." someone said, approaching Jun from behind. She didn't turn at first, but after realizing her lack of response would be considered rude, she turned to see that the person approaching was the onboard physician, Kite.

"Doctor? Do you always work so late?" Jun asked as Kite approached the rail and stood next to Jun, looking out at the ocean.

"Sometimes." Kite replied, then turned to face Jun. "How are you doing? How's the shoulder?" Kite watched as Jun shifted her left arm in the sling slightly and moved her fingers to demonstrate free range of motion.

"Are you asking professionally?"

"Checking in on someone who's been through a traumatic event shouldn't be classified as personal or professional."

Jun smirked. "That's fair. The shoulder is still sore. The painkillers you gave me are helping." She paused, considering the original question. "I will . . . I will be alright. I just . . ." Her voice trailed off as she tried to figure out how much she should tell this stranger. "This might be the last time I'll see New America." Jun paused to choose her words. "You see, I was only supposed to be here to learn American politics. Now that this has happened, my father will want me to come home."

Kite nodded. "My father would do the same thing. He feels that no one can protect me better than him." Kite smiled taking note that while Jun's Chinese accent was not as heavy as her head nurse Qin Zhang, there was a smooth combination of American speech patterns mixed subtly in with the proper Chinese dialect.

"My father is the same." Jun said. "But after this it's going to be difficult to argue with him."

"You don't want to go home?" Kite asked, realizing she already knew the answer.

"I was born and raised in New America. My father moved us after the Blitz War when I was still young, about six or seven. Working in New America felt like coming back to my childhood, even if it's different from what I remember." Jun hesitated for a moment. "Once I go back home, it'll be hard for me to leave again. Despite what happened last night, my entire life has always been an adventure in one way or another." She sighed. "I just don't want to see it all end."

"I hope you don't mind my asking, but what do you do for the senators?"

Jun studied Kite, wondering if she could trust her. "My father is wealthy and well-connected. He wanted me to learn about New American politics. He spoke to his contacts in the government and got me this job for experience."

"I don't understand. How would that put you in such a high-profile position?"

"After I had a few years of experience, my father pulled strings to get me to be Senator Gash's assistant."

"Oh. So you could shadow a senator before you decided if you wanted to go into politics yourself?"

"Something like that. Only I don't have much of a choice. My father wants me to go into politics."

"That must be hard." Kite said. "What do you want to do?"

"I want to help my father and the family business, just not in the way he wants me to." She paused, deciding the conversation was moving in a direction she was not prepared to discuss. "Do you mind if I ask you a question?"

"Sure, go ahead." Kite looked pleasantly surprised.

"Phoenix."

"What about him?"

"What's he like?"

"Do you mean as a man or as our captain?"

"Was he one of the special commanders who did covert assignments after the Blitz War? Why was he reported dead?"

"How do you know about that? He doesn't talk to anyone on the ship about what he did before Blood Sky, not even me."

Jun smiled. "There weren't a lot of Black men commanding covert operations with a real–life Black giant as his right hand."

Kite realized the connection but questioned the access to the classified information. A senator's aide wouldn't have that level of clearance.

Jun read the concern on Kite's face and decided to answer her unasked question. "Like I said, my father has connections."

"He must. You know more than most of the crew of Blood Sky."

"Can you talk about what you do know?"

"Why do you want to know?" Now it was Kite's turn to wonder if she could trust her conversation partner.

"I don't know." Jun said, looking away embarrassment. "I've heard rumors about Blood Sky, but everything was always so vague and contradicting. I thought he was a real–life Robin Hood who lived the life of a swashbuckling 'good' pirate, sailing the seven seas, saving women, and punishing evil men. And what a cool name, 'Blood Sky.'" Jun smiled, hearing the sound of a heroic orchestra in her mind. Kite looked around, almost as if she heard it too.

"Surprising," Kite said, smiling. "You don't look like the romantic adventure type."

"What type do I look like?"

"Smarter than you want people to know." Kite looked at Jun, assessing her appearance. "With the type of work you do, you would have to be professional too, or you couldn't pull it off."

"Pull what off?"

"That you're a tough rich kid pretending to be a politician."

"Pretending?" Jun blurted, offended.

"Don't take it the wrong way, but aren't you pretending? Really? Most politicians are liars and con artists, but you seem like a person who says what's on her mind and doesn't take any crap."

Jun finally lowered her guard and smiled at the compliment. "You're right about that."

"I wouldn't want to be you." Kite admitted. "Your father wants you to be a politician, but you want a different life. Now that you're caught up in this mess with the abduction, he'll probably never let you do what you want."

"That's my fear." Jun frowned. Kite remained silent for several moments as both women looked out at the ocean.

"I have an idea." Kite said.

"Yes?" Jun turned to Kite with hope and a bit of desperation, wondering how this young curly haired doctor had found a solution that she herself could not fathom.

"Tomorrow we make port in York Jersey Harbor."

"Yes?"

"Swan and I were going shopping when we make port. How about you come with us? Our treat." Kite's broad smile was infectious.

As Jun stared at the young physician, she noticed the resemblance between Kite and Swan. Having no idea that they were fraternal twins, Jun took at Kite's light brown large curls in her hair, kind eyes, and broad smile. It was obvious when she thought about it. Kite had a fairer complexion and was slightly taller, but their physical appearance was nearly identical, except for Swan's jet-black curls and darker skin. Jun realized that in a black-and-white photo, the two would look identical.

"Shopping?" Jun asked, smiling.

"It's kind of a ritual with me and Swan. We treat ourselves to a few things whenever we get to a safe port."

Jun pondered the thought of shopping in Manhattan City one last time before the possibility of having to leave New America for good. She smirked. "I guess I could buy more shoes. My collection is a little sparse."

"Collection?" Kite smiled. "How big of a collection are we talking about?"

"Well, I might have a small closet dedicated to it." Jun admitted, blushing.

"Is it full?" Swan asked as she approached the two women.

Kite turned to her sister. "Were you eavesdropping?"

Swan ignored Kit's question, her gaze fixed on Jun. "You have an entire closet full of shoes?"

"Not completely full," Jun said. "Just a few shelves."

Swan folded her arms. "Just a few huh?"

"We'll be the judge of that," Kite said. "You'll have to invite us over sometime."

Jun smiled hesitantly. "One day, yes."

10

RECOVERING DEBRIEF

~

D emir Sahin sat in a luxury suite that had been transformed into a room for medical care, complete with a hospital bed and monitoring equipment. He was at ease when he woke up, realizing he was in his private compound, which resembled a desert fortress more than a house. The spacious recovery room was reserved for tending to his personal injuries. The soft aroma of attar oil from a fragrant flower he knew to have relaxing healing powers filled the room. One of his arms had been dressed, as had his abdomen. He was certain his trusted general and oldest friend, Abdul Jalil, had been responsible for ensuring his care while he was sedated.

Sahin sat in silence, contemplating his injuries. Any of his followers who survived the attack and were worthy of his hospitality would have been placed somewhere within the compound. Sahin took a deep breath and cringed at the pain in his chest. The fact that he could breathe so easily meant his fake nose was gone, as was all the makeup and plastic skin he wore to hide his true features.

Upon seeing that Sahin was awake, the nurse stood up from her seat in the corner of the room. Her head and body were covered in white cloth, except for her eyes. She said nothing as she approached, bowing in reverence to Sahin before pouring a hot cup of tea for him from a classic Arabian tea pot.

Taking a sip, Sahin closed his eyes and meditated on recent events. Like most competitive individuals, he did not like losing, but he understood the value of learning from failure.

His plan had been flawless, or so he had thought. The New American military had no method of discovering the location of the two senators in time, and none of the hostages had tracking devices on their person. A traitor was not possible. His men were too loyal. Something was missing, some information of which he was not aware.

His men reported that the helicopter the senators had escaped in was joined and protected by flying motorcycles before New America's military helicopters arrived. They said that the flying motorcycles were faster and more maneuverable than anything they had seen. Were the motorcycles some sort of New American prototype? No, he was certain that he would have known about them if they were American. But that would only be true if his contacts in New America knew about them. Even if the motorcycles were not from New America, that would not explain how they had learned about the senators' whereabouts almost immediately.

His brow furrowed. What was he missing?

A knock at his door tore him from his barrage of internal questions, causing him to sigh deeply. "Come in." His mental investigation would have to wait.

Abdul Jalil, Sahin's second in command, stepped through the doorway, bowing his head in respect as he entered. "My Sheik, how are you feeling?"

"I'll live, Abdul." Sahin replied, signaling for the nurse to leave them. She bowed to Sahin before exiting the room. Jalil stood in silence, waiting for the door to close completely before returning his full attention to Sahin.

"What of the senators? Were any killed during the escape?" Sahin asked.

"Nothing public has been announced regarding any deaths. One American spokesperson held a brief press conference to say that everyone was rescued and in protective custody while being debriefed. We are unsure if the American government is silent because their injuries were too severe or for other reasons. I am hopeful that you were successful in causing enough injury to bring about a mortal and fatal end, my Sheik." Jalil straightened his back and gave Sahin a small but confident smile.

Sahin nodded. He did not think that was the case, but Abdul was always more optimistic than him. Even when they were children, running around their village, Sahin would be more cautious and analyze a situation while Abdul would dive right in. The two were separated as teenagers when Sahin's well-off family sent him to be educated in America and London. Jalil followed his father and joined the military. The two friends reunited more than a decade after 2029 when they learned that their home village had been destroyed by an American attack. Having lost their village, their history, and their families, when the two found each other, they vowed to stay together. Not long after that, Sahin used his political power to gain access to confidential information, and using his family's wealth, the Patriot Knight was born as the masked avenger who fought for the justice of all Middle Easterners.

"How did things go with Marco?" Sahin asked, watching Jalil closely. The answer was extremely important to him.

"Your new doppelgänger performed well, as you expected." Jalil smiled.

"Excellent." Sahin smiled back, though his face was pained.

"He waited for the senators at the embassy and was seen by many reporters expressing his—your—regret that the senators were brutally kidnapped before we left and headed for Cairo a day ahead of schedule. He attended the conference in Cairo and made all public appearances. I was with him at every moment and made sure that the press took photos and video recordings of him with the other delegates. He even went as far as to speak briefly to the press, expressing concern for the abduction that was going on, as directed."

"Wonderful! People always see you at my side. I know you wanted to be with me, but it was more important that you kept up appearances."

"But you could have been killed, Demir." Abdul said, his eyes filled with concern for his best friend.

"But I was not. That's what is important."

"Yes, Demir."

"Where is Marco now?"

"Downstairs, in his quarters, out of sight from everyone, as instructed. He and I will leave for Saudi tonight and make sure the world sees that you have not changed your public appearances, which you have scheduled."

"But he is not speaking often, correct?"

"Briefly, as per your command, and only when asked a direct question. As you instructed, he tells the people that he is coming down with a cold, coughs, and the questions stop, the press keeps away." Jalil smiled.

Sahin nodded in satisfaction. "As an actor, he was worth the cost."

"I agree. Now no one can claim your involvement in the American abduction."

Sahin took a sip of his tea. As Sheik Demir Sahin, he was a

pacifist ambassador who wanted nothing but peace and prosperity not just for Saudi Arabia but for all Middle Eastern countries that had been mistreated by the Western world. As the masked and mysterious Patriot Knight, he was a vengeful vigilante who did whatever was necessary to make sure the Middle East was fed and protected from those who preyed on their weakened state. The idea was not entirely his own, inspired in part by an American comic book.

A soft knock came moments before the door opened. A young boy with a small bag strapped across his chest entered the room and bowed. "My Sheik, I have a message for you."

The young messenger reached into his bag. Jalil subtly, but quickly, moved to rest his hand on his pistol, previously concealed under his jacket. The boy froze at the sight of the gun. Sahin's nod was the only signal that Jalil needed to lower his guard, but he still did not remove his hand from the weapon.

"It's alright, Abdul. Yusuf is one of my personal messengers. He's been abroad for years. That's why you don't know him."

"My Sheik?" Jalil asked with caution.

"Yusuf is a third-generation messenger." Sahin said. Jalil relaxed his hand but continued to watch the boy for any sudden moves. "Yusuf?"

"Yes, my Sheik. This arrived for you over the Comtext on your private channel." Yusuf removed a folded piece of paper with an emerald colored silk bow wrapped around it and handed it to Sahin. Yusuf turned to leave the room, but Sahin's voice stopped him.

"Wait! Come here, Yusuf." He beckoned to the boy with his good arm. Yusuf walked back toward Sahin, his head bowed. Sahin reached for his wallet on the nightstand and removed a $100 bill printed in New America. With a kind smile, he handed it to the dumbstruck boy.

"My Sheik! I cannot accept this! It is too much!" the boy said, shaking his head. Sahin gave him a reassuring nod and put the money in his hand.

"You can, and you will, Yusuf. You and your family have done well for me and deserve a reward. Take it to your father with my appreciation."

Yusuf looked at the money in disbelief, then looked up at Sahin with a tearful smile. "But you already give our family so much, my Sheik."

"This is a simple demonstration of my appreciation, Yusuf."

"Thank you, my Sheik!" The boy bowed deeply before racing out of the room.

Sahin smiled as he watched Yusuf leave, closing the door behind him. Turning the folded note over in his lap, his smile faded as he unfolded paper and read the coded message.

Jalil's posture had relaxed once Yusuf left the room, but when he saw the expression on Sahin's face, he stiffened once more. "What does it say?"

Sahin frowned as he concentrated on the paper. "It would appear that not only did the senators and their underlings survive, they are on a merchant ship called Blood Sky. Apparently, those jet–powered motorcycles that aided in the rescue belonged to Blood Sky's combat team."

Jalil's face contorted slightly. "How can that be? What kind of merchant ship has such technology if New America does not?"

"It would seem that New America's military is just as baffled as you are."

"You have spies in New America?"

"Of course. One of my spies holds a high seat in New America's government and has secretly volunteered to help our cause."

"This is how you knew the details of the senators' travel plans?" Jalil asked.

"Yes. Travel plans, military accompaniment, and everything else we needed to complete the task."

"Everything except Blood Sky."

"It would seem that my spy has failed to gain intelligence on this vessel." Sahin admitted with disappointment.

"You don't seem surprised."

"I have heard stories about this Blood Sky ship and its crew. The Pirate King himself told me that this Blood Sky ship has a reputation for attacking roaming pirate ships. They have never before involved themselves with political matters, at least not to my knowledge."

"Then why did they interfere now?" Jalil asked.

"The details have yet to come in, but it seems that Blood Sky's captain has some sort of connection with the New American government." Sahin said as he held the letter over the candle closest to him on his nightstand. The paper caught fire, and Sahin waited until the flames were almost touching his fingers before he dropped the burning message on an empty plate near his teacup.

"What is next?" Jalil asked, ready to serve.

"Find all you can about Blood Sky and the identity of its captain." Sahin said. He smiled. It had been a while since he had had a formidable opponent.

"And the senators?"

"Let them have this one, Abdul. Allow New America to gloat and strut their peacock feathers at the victory."

"But you said Blood Sky is not a ship from New America."

"No, but New America will take credit for the win, I assure you. They have no choice." Sahin stopped and pondered. "This Blood Sky may not be from New America, but there is a connection."

"Yes, Demir."

"Before we move against Blood Sky, we must investigate. As I always say, if you want to assure victory, know your opponent."

"Yes, Demir."

"We will investigate while I recover and heal. The next time we encounter this Blood Sky and its crew, we will be prepared with the greatest ammunition of all: knowledge."

"Yes, my Sheik." Jalil bowed and smiled.

11

MEMORIES

~

A s the morning sun rose over the horizon the following day, sadness was in the air as Phoenix watched the three helicopters loom closer to *Blood Sky* from the west. Behind the aircraft in the distance was Manhattan City Harbor, their destination. Phoenix already knew that *Blood Sky* would not be granted the honor of bringing the two senators to port. He confirmed with Kopensky that the approaching helicopters were just another opportunity for politicians to take the credit for Phoenix's accomplishments. The rescue would be awarded to the New American Military, as far as the world was concerned. It was good press. Although he had grown accustomed to it, it still left a bitter taste in Phoenix's mouth. He didn't really care who took credit for the mission. He liked staying in the shadows along with all the unsung heroes around the world. He had taken on the mission because his friend was in trouble, and Phoenix knew he had the resources to help. What he found distasteful was how often people placed their lives on the line without hesitation while the politicians made public announcements as if they were the ones who were in the trenches risking life and limb. Paramedics, firemen, police, military, government agents, it was always the same. For every heroic action, some politician almost always took public credit for the decision while the faceless heroes got a private handshake for their remarkable efforts. Such actions made him avoid and disdain politics.

Hawk and Eagle approached Phoenix from below deck as he stood at the bow watching the helicopters. Even though the approaching aircraft were still at some distance, he knew that one was a transport chopper, and the two flanking crafts were gunships. The formation brought back bittersweet memories. His mind flashed back to a past life when he was a civilian commander of a small New American covert team charged with rescuing high-value targets similar to Kopensky and Gash from dangerous locations that the military could not get to, at least not officially. That was a different time. A time when the task of extraction was not always easy. A time before he was Captain Phoenix. Back then he was still using his birth name, Alexander Medjinn, call sign: Thor.

Thor held his rifle in the ready position as he sat firm in the opening of the transport Chinook helicopter in an open field. Blood and dirt stained his black tactical clothing, and one of his lapels was missing. He couldn't remember when he had lost it. His body was exhausted, his muscles burning from battles earlier in the week, but his eyes remained sharp, awake, and focused.

He adjusted his harness and turned to Jesse Smythe, a short yet brawny man who was manning the big gun mounted to the helicopter's floor. Smythe looked fresh for the fight. His alertness would be needed in this last portion of the mission. Thor turned from Jesse to Javier "Proctor" Padilla, who had just finished strapping in the uncon-

scious passenger whom Thor had brought onboard the helicopter and was now checking her vitals.

"Where's everyone else?" Petros asked as he exited the helicopter's cockpit. Thomas Petros was Thor's Greek civilian pilot. He was efficient and intelligent but occasionally sarcastic in comfortable surroundings.

"Right behind me," Thor replied, continuing to stare at the tree line. "Start the engines. We'll need to get out of here fast!"

"Here they come now!" Proctor announced as he stepped to Thor's opposite side, pointing at what resembled fireworks over one hundred meters in the distance.

It was all like a silent dream as Thor issued orders over his radio headset, directing the pilots of the two gunship helicopters that were out of sight to move into striking position.

On the ground, Aaron "War Chief" Medjinn easily carried the wounded unconscious body slung over his shoulders while holding his automatic rifle in position in his free hand. He felt the pain from the bullet wound in his side, but he could not allow it to distract him. After sprinting for a few moments, War Chief turned to shoot the enemy who was exiting the tree line, without thought for his own safety. Then he resumed his sprint toward the Chinook, which was activating its engines for lift off.

Lawrence "Law" Mackenzie, Sean "Savage" McAllister, and Andrew "Sandbags" Simms ran out from the dense forest as something exploded behind them. They did not slow their pace or hesitate. There was no time. They were still under heavy fire.

The three men ran in a diagonal pattern toward War Chief and the Chinook. Sandbags ran through the high grass at full speed while Law turned and dropped to one knee to fire on their pursuers.

As War Chief got close, he saw Smythe open fire with his heavy mounted machine gun at the vehicle that was approaching from the far side of the jungle. Thor killed several enemy soldiers who charged the tail end of the Chinook. When he ran out of ammunition, Proctor *stepped forward to continue the barrage of bullets while Thor reloaded.*

One by one the rest of his team boarded the helicopter while those already inside laid down suppressing fire, keeping their enemy low and disoriented.

"Everybody's in!" Thor roared once Law leapt into the helicopter. "Go, go, go!"

Without another word Petros and Smythe piloted the Chinook into the air while two unmarked American gunships flew in low battle formation, shooting rockets at the continuous onslaught of enemy soldiers who rushed out of the jungle. Then the gunships turned and flanked the Chinook in standard escort position as the three choppers made their way to safer airspace.

While Proctor gave medical support to the two wounded passengers buckled into seats, the rest of Thor's team sat back, feeling at ease now that they were out of range of enemy fire and heading toward the safety of the ocean. They were covered with dirt, sweat, and blood. They had been in the jungle for a week waiting for the right opportunity. They were tired, starving, and wounded, but most of all, they were all safe, and there would never be a record of their having been there.

"American military squadron requesting permission to land." Hawk said, cupping the small earpiece to muffle out the background noise of the ocean and engines. "What do you want me to tell them?"

Hawk's voice broke Phoenix out of his haze of memories, but he continued watching the approaching helicopters.

"Permission granted." he replied with a troubled sigh.

Phoenix and his escorts walked onto the primary flight deck at the rear of the ship. He turned to see Gash, Kopensky, and Torres entering onto the deck from within the ship behind him. As he approached the three men, Jun and Zara were saying goodbye to each other and to the male members of their original group. Jun had decided to remain on *Blood Sky* until the ship made port.

"Do you think she'll be okay?" Kopensky asked, nodding toward Zara.

"Oh." Phoenix said, considering the best way to respond. "Our therapist said that she'll cry it out in a few days if she hasn't already. Sometimes the shock takes a while to register, and everyone handles these type of traumas differently. Once she's in a familiar environment, like her home, it'll all come out. That's when she'll need professional help to get through this. Give her some time. She'll probably want to transfer to a position where she doesn't have to travel."

The first Black Hawk helicopter made wide circles around *Blood Sky* while the second identical gunship stayed close by, its arsenal facing the ship's deck. Despite all that Phoenix had done for New America, it seemed that he still was not to be trusted.

"Old memories?" Kopensky ask, noticing Phoenix staring at the gunships hovering around his ship.

"I haven't seen this formation since I left." Phoenix admitted. Eagle and Hawk flanked him, always remaining in his peripheral view. "The Black Hawks weren't as heavily armed." Phoenix stared at the excessive number of guns and missile launchers on each gunship.

"I can't imagine what it's like being on the other side of one." Kopensky replied, sensing his friend's turmoil.

"No, you can't."

"What's it like for you?"

"Like I need new memories to replace the old ones."

Phoenix admitted, turning to face Kopensky as Gash approached them. Torres followed, pushed in a wheelchair by Nurse Zhang.

"If I know you, you'll find a way." Kopensky said. "Memories born from your dreams of a better tomorrow."

"A better tomorrow?" Gash asked with a mischievous smile. "I hope I'm part of that dream."

"You never know, Senator." Phoenix smiled. "Maybe you will be."

"Captain Phoenix, thank you for everything. The hospitality, the food, the accommodations, and especially for rescuing us." Gash smiled as he extended his hand. Phoenix looked down at it, pausing for a moment before shaking it.

He had become bitter against politicians of New America and maybe politicians in general. Now this one had extended a hand of appreciation for the second time. It was a common gesture for a job well done but an uncommon act from a senator of the United States of New America. Maybe things were different now. Maybe now was a time for change, and Kopensky was right. Maybe, just maybe, the old memories were going to fade, making room for new ones after all.

Phoenix smiled sincerely. "You're welcome, Chad."

"If there's anything you need in New America, you know you have a friend in the senate." Gash glanced at Kopensky and nodded. "Another friend."

"I appreciate that."

Gash turned to board the Chinook as the soldiers who had exited the chopper stood flanking the craft's entrance with rifles at rest position. Nurse Zhang wheeled her patient closer to Phoenix. Torres extended his hand as well.

"Thank you, Captain Phoenix." Torres said with humility.

"You're welcome, Neil. How do you feel?" Phoenix asked, looking down at Torres with concern.

"I'll live, thanks to you. The doctor said I should be able to walk in a couple of days. I'm going to be okay."

"That was a brave thing you did back there, Neil. There aren't too many men who would take that kind of abuse to protect other people." Phoenix said while continuing to hold Torres's hand.

Torres shook his head. "You and your crew are the heroes."

"To the world that watched you a few days ago, you're a hero. They never saw us. They saw you standing up to violent abductors while you were injured. The higher-ups will make a blanket statement that it was a well-planned military operation, then close the books as classified. So, you can tell people whatever you want; no one can dispute it." Phoenix smiled at Torres. Having a son in his mid twenties, Phoenix knew the value of encouragement at that age. Knowing that Torres probably felt defeated from his actions during the torture on the Global Comtext, this young man needed to see the positive side of the events of the past now that the worst of his pain was over. Torres was a young hero who had taken abuse and torture and lived to talk about it. This little encouragement would open the door for a future of confidence.

"I didn't think of it like that." Torres said, his face turning thoughtful.

Phoenix stood up straight and winked. "Good luck with your new fan club, Mr. Torres."

Torres frowned in wonder before the realization washed over him. He grinned as he directed Nurse Zhang to wheel him toward the helicopter. Phoenix stood by as the soldiers assisted Torres into a standing position before helping him climb into the helicopter.

Zara walked to the helicopter but stopped before getting inside. She turned around and mouthed a whispered thank-you to Phoenix before slowly getting inside the helicopter. Phoenix nodded as Zara, Gash, and Torres fastened themselves into their seats before turning to face Kopensky, who was still standing outside the helicopter.

"As long as there are people like you around, there will always be hope." Kopensky said, placing a supportive hand on Phoenix's shoulder. Kopensky knew that his friend remained heavily burdened by the memories of the distant past and felt the need to give encouragement as well.

"As long as there are people like you and George in government, New America has a chance to be more humane again." Phoenix replied, shaking Kopensky's hand. Kopensky looked past Phoenix to observe Jun, who had managed to make her way up to the deck on top of the helicopter hangar bay.

"And what about her?" Kopensky asked dryly.

"She'll be okay. Doctor Kite has some subtle therapy in mind to get her head back on track." Phoenix assured him, not turning to look at Jun. "I promise we'll take good care of her. She'll be at the briefing tomorrow, Kris."

"I didn't mean like that. How do you think Jun will be long term?"

"Hard to say." Phoenix turned to look at Jun, only to find that she was staring at him as she pulled her blowing brown hair from her face. "She's tough, but she's still not used to this. She'll break down, but she'll probably do it when it's convenient for her, in private."

"You got all that with one look?"

"I was a professional profiler, remember?" He turned back to Kopensky, who was smiling. "But you know that, wise ass."

Kopensky grinned. "Will you be in the city for a while?"

"A few days. Long enough to get supplies and give my crew a round of shore leave."

"Send me the bill for the supplies."

"You don't have to tell me twice." Phoenix chuckled.

"Hopefully, I'll see you before you cast off."

"Hopefully." Phoenix said with a slight bow toward Kopensky. They shook hands again, then Kopensky turned to enter the Chinook.

Once Kopensky was inside the chopper, something unexpected happened. The American soldiers in and around the helicopter stepped out of the craft and snapped to attention, raising a civilian salute.

Hawk and Eagle were as surprised as Phoenix. After a few moments, Phoenix responded to the show of respect by returning the salute.

No words were spoken, and none were needed. Phoenix was not military, so the gesture was not mandatory, but it showed there were still soldiers that held a high level of respect for the merchant captain, especially for rescuing the New American citizens. It was something to be proud of, something these enlisted men chose not to disregard.

With that done, the soldiers of New America boarded the Chinook before it spooled up its engines and lifted off *Blood Sky's* flight deck. As Phoenix exited the flight deck with Hawk and Eagle walking close behind him, the three helicopters maneuvered back into formation before flying toward the distant shore of Manhattan Harbor on York Jersey Island.

Later that morning, Kite and Swan stood with Jun at the bow of the ship as *Blood Sky* approached the main international harbor of York Jersey Island. For Jun it was like a breath of fresh air just to see a familiar, non–hostile shoreline. From a distance, Phoenix stared at the distant Capitol building of New America with mixed feelings of loss and nostalgia. So much had changed since America had become New America.

Targeted by the Vapor Incursion and attacked again during the Blitz War by a nuclear missile, Washington, DC, and part of Virginia were now a radioactive wasteland, too toxic to inhabit. It was for this reason that the nation's capital had been permanently relocated to One World Trade Center, ground zero for the first "successful" terrorist strike on Old America, so-called because the building was attacked years prior to September 11, 2001, with bombs in the lower-level garage that were thought to be a failed attempt at bringing down what was then called the Twin Towers. Phoenix lost family in that attack, so it had always been a sensitive subject for him.

Phoenix always thought it was interesting to establish the Capitol building at the same address as a former terrorist attack, but he also understood that doing so brought hope to older Americans and New Yorkers. The building was also heavily fortified, so it could never become the target of a successful attack again. In fact, the One World Trade Center building had become one of the most fortified buildings on York Jersey Island.

12

YORK JERSEY LIFE

~

J un, Kite, and Swan stood on the pier watching as many of the crew members secured the ship. It was obvious that trade agreements had been arranged prior to their arrival in Manhattan City. The *Blood Sky* crew was already wheeling crates on handcarts and forklifts to the loading gangplank at the ship's rear deck. Deck Chief Marcus Medina, who oversaw the shipping and receiving of all cargo, stood at the cargo bay entrance, making notes on his digital tablet.

Jun had barely stepped onto the pier with her companions when a pearl-white and blood-red high-class British stretch limousine drove toward them. Kite was hesitant as the vehicle slowed to a stop near them. Jun found Kite's actions interesting. Kite didn't respond with fright but with combative readiness, adjusting her stance in a subtle manner to defend herself if the situation called for it. Jun didn't expect that from a physician, but she appreciated it.

"It's okay, Kite," she said, "that's one of my father's cars."

"Oh, fancy!" Kite smiled, her body relaxing slightly. "So, we're going shopping in style!"

"Is there any other way?" Jun teased as they moved toward the limousine. Kim was her Korean driver, assigned specifically to this limousine. She didn't like his constant scowling expression, but she knew it served its purpose of intimidation. When Kim stepped out of the driver's seat to walk around the car and open the rear door for the women, he bowed respectfully to Jun. Like the rest of the world, he had heard the reports and had probably seen the Comtext. She detected a hint of relief in his eyes that she was safe, although injured, still wearing the sling. His expression of relief made her smile.

"Hold on!" Warlord said, approaching the group. As the women turned to address him, Kim stepped toward Warlord, giving him a challenging stare. Warlord took a moment to size up the driver. Although Warlord admired Kim's bravery, he did not appear concerned or threatened.

"Is everything okay, Warlord?" Swan asked.

"You know the captain's protocols when off ship." Warlord said in a slightly scolding tone. Jun saw Swan smile mischievously at Warlord, as if she had been caught with her hand in the preverbal cookie jar.

"I don't understand." Jun turned to Kite while Swan attempted to bargain with Warlord. "What protocol?"

"Protective escort." Warlord replied.

"This is supposed to be a girl's day out, just us. We would rather not ruin the experience by having muscle–bound men walking around us all day." Jun protested.

Warlord looked at Kim, who was dressed in a snugly fitting business suit as he stood sentry at the limousine's open rear door, then back at her.

"He's different," Jun explained. "He's staying with the car."

"Even more reason to have protection when you're in the stores, just in case."

"Once we stepped onto that dock, you were off the clock, Commander. Your mission is over. We are back on friendly ground and no longer in need of your protection, good sir." Jun said. "And I would prefer not to be surrounded by men watching my every move." It was her last chance to be out in the world without a heavy security detail, and she wanted to savor it. After seeing the personnel on *Blood Sky* and what they were capable of, she didn't want to draw attention to herself all day, as she imagined hulking men in mercenary attire and tactical rifles in their ready positions.

"Who said anything about men?" Warlord asked, raising one hand to gesture behind him.

Jun looked past Warlord's massive frame and saw three athletic women walking down the gangplank. She was puzzled at the sight of them.

"Jun, this is Nitro, Snow, and Dizzy."

"I don't understand." Jun said, turning to Kite.

Kite gestured to the petite Vietnamese woman with a gymnast's physique standing in the center of the trio. "Nitro is in charge of Blood Sky's special missions team." she explained. "They're our infiltrators."

"But me and my cousin, Jet, like to call us 'The Blood Sky Ninjas.'" Nitro added with a broad smile. Jun smiled back at Nitro's positive energy. She looked like she had caffeine pulsing through her veins.

"They go in undercover and gather information when the captain wants discreet intelligence before the violence starts up." Swan explained. "They're trained for recon, surveillance, and elimination."

"So, why are they here?" Jun asked.

Before Nitro could respond, Warlord stepped in. "Because

we also use them for protection details when blending in is preferred."

"Snow and Dizzy are female members of our protection team." Kite said, continuing the introductions.

Snow was a tall, voluptuous blonde who looked like a female superhero out of a comic book in her alter-ego's clothing. Jun wondered if she did bodybuilding exercises with the members of SOCIT. Dizzy was a Black woman who looked like a model who did bare-knuckle boxing on weekends. Jun glanced at the woman's hands. They were covered in scars and appeared to have suffered more than a few broken bones. She wondered if her nickname had anything to do with her right hook.

"You look like badass women soldiers." Jun observed.

"We don't have any actual military experience." Dizzy said. "We consider ourselves warriors, not soldiers."

"Woman warriors." Jun added.

Snow smiled. "We do a lot of high-profile protection."

"Commandos, combat pilots, assassins, and badass femme fatales?" Jun chuckled, surprisingly please as she looked at the three of them, then at Warlord. "All on one ship. I like that. Makes you wonder what kind of a merchant ship this is." Nitro, Snow, and Dizzy smiled at Jun in appreciation.

"One that's prepared for any problem at any port." Swan said.

"Are you girls going to just hang around, or are you going shopping too?" Jun asked, changing the subject.

As if on cue, Nitro, Snow, and Dizzy all raised their sky-blue, pen-sized credit rods.

"Dizzy is from Manhattan City; she's going to be our guide today." Kite announced.

Dizzy flipped the long black hair that flowed down her back. "I'll take you to the best places to shop in Manhattan City. The stores, the restaurants, the shoes . . ." The dreamy emphasis that Dizzy put on the word "shoes" made Jun smile.

"All right then!" Jun said before turning to step into the limousine.

"Today is about us!" Dizzy said, flashing a glamorous smile that caught Jun by surprise.

"One more thing." Warlord said amidst the cheering women. Jun turned back with a deep sigh. "What is it?"

Warlord handed Swan a black credit rod. Black credit rods had no limit and came with a level of status that Jun was all too familiar with.

"For your inconveniences, Captain Phoenix would like each of you to enjoy your day in the stores as his treat." Warlord said. The women exploded in cheers.

"Wait a minute!" Jun said, silencing the others. "What inconveniences are you talking about?"

Warlord smiled. "A little inconspicuous additional protection, an added precaution."

"No need, commander." Jun said, her patience dwindling as another vehicle driving up the pier caught her attention. She let out another deep sigh. "My father sent added protection." She directed Warlord's attention to the black military Hummer that had pulled up behind the limousine. Warlord looked at the shiny black vehicle as four Asian men stepped out of it. Then he glanced at Kim, who was still standing by the limousine's open rear door. They were all wearing identical black suits and button-down shirts with no ties.

"Impressive," he said, turning back to Jun. "But like your father, Miss Li, Captain Phoenix would feel more comfortable if he sent his team to tag along as well, just in case." Warlord gestured behind them.

Suddenly, revving engines could be heard from *Blood Sky's* stern. Two Enduro Mark I's lifted off the ship's aft section and then flew over and landed near Swan and Kite. The biker–pilots turned off their engines.

"This is Condor and Vulture. You met them before on your tour." Warlord said. Both biker-pilots nodded politely at Jun. "They'll be discreetly following your convoy."

"Why?" Jun asked.

"Ship protocol. Any time a commanding officer goes ashore, they are to be accompanied by a protection escort and a contingency." Swan recited dryly.

"They are the contingency." Warlord added, smiling.

Jun turned to Kite and Swan with realization. "Of course! Falcon said it when we were touring the ship. You're both commanders."

Kite and Swan appeared embarrassed to admit the truth. Jun wondered if they had been enjoying being treated like one of the girls for a change.

"Let me formally introduce you." Warlord said. "This is Senior Pilot Swan, Commander, Engineering Division." Warlord motioned to Kite, "And this is Doctor Kite, Commander, Medical Division."

"You're both so young to be commanders," Jun commented. "It's very impressive."

"The hoverbikes are a precaution since the commanders are not traveling with one of our own vehicles, ma'am." Condor stated in military manner while staring at Jun.

"In case of an emergency or an assault on a commander, we are ordered to relinquish our Enduros to both commanders, so they can escape, ma'am." Vulture added.

"And you say this is inconspicuous?" Jun asked, eyeing Warlord.

"It won't be a problem." Kite assured her. "They'll be behind us the whole time and staying with the others. They have their orders."

"It'll be fine." Swan said, then turned to Vulture and Condor, who were still seated on the Enduros. "Soft shadow today." The two biker-pilots nodded in agreement, then put on their helmets and saluted Swan and Kite, who returned the gesture.

Looking at the hoverbikes, Jun accepted the fact that at least they had brought a version that would blend in with traffic more than the jetbikes that were used to defend them in the sky. Jun realized that, like her, Swan and Kite were also hoping for a normal girl's day out.

Jun looked back at Phoenix, who was watching from the observation deck like a ruler from his palace balcony. "Let's go!" she said after a brief shrug.

Jun's face showed no expression, but Kite saw the wheels turning behind Jun's eyes. It became clear at that moment that she was correct in assuming that Jun had been pretending. This was not the expression of a career senator's assistant. This woman was clearly comfortable being in some form of leadership. However, Kite wondered what the reason for Jun's charade was and who she really was below the surface.

Jun smiled at the other women. Kite and Swan looked at each other, both of them relieved that they were not going to be in charge for the day, leaving them free to be themselves or, in this case, Jun's guests. They followed Jun into the customized extended limousine, their casually dressed female protection team right behind them.

Warlord watched as the limousine followed the Hummer, the two hoverbikes following a short distance behind them. Once they were out of sight, Warlord turned to see that Phoenix was still standing on the observation deck, now staring down at him. Phoenix was not smiling, but he was not angry. As first cousin to the ship's captain, Warlord had learned which blank look was associated with which emotion. He recognized a look of fatherly concern. Phoenix was never comfortable with letting his daughters out on the town. He seldom informed people that they were his children, but they were adults now. Not just adults but experienced women in their late twenties with their own thoughts, dreams, and aspirations.

Warlord went up to the observation deck and gave his cousin's shoulder a reassuring squeeze.

13

NEW TOYS

~

Talon stared at a whiteboard, tapping a marker on his chin in a fast-paced beat while two of his team members stood behind him. All of them were fixated on a series of drawings and calculations on the whiteboard. *Blood Sky's* research department was a large storage room that had been converted into an advanced laboratory facility for scientists and engineers to create and develop new ideas. Laptops, digital tablets, engine parts, and vials of a gray liquid were littered across the various boxes and desks in the room while small screws and scraps of plastic littered the floor. Techno-rap music blared through the room's speakers but didn't seem to disturb the three researchers.

"If it's too thick to come out the can like a spray, why not extend the nozzle?" Yahia suggested. "Something like those bug spray cans with the narrow attachment." Yahia was a tall, fair complexioned Algerian man who was a few years older than Talon. His curly afro always hid the pen tucked behind his ear.

"That'd work for cracks and holes but not for something

big." Talon mused, drawing a can with a long line attached to the top. He scribbled a note under the line.

"Depending on what we're talking about." Morty said. "This would only work for surface-level damage. If an Enduro's engine gets hit, no amount of this stuff is gonna fix it." Morty was the shortest in the room but one of the brightest. While Morty never believed it, Talon always said that Morty was smarter than him.

Talon frowned, staring at the whiteboard. "Yeah. Let's do some conductivity tests. Maybe we can use it to create a conductive surface . . ." He paused when he saw Phoenix and Warlord enter the lab and spun on his heel toward them. "Captain on deck!" He saluted with the marker in his hand before dropping it to the floor. Yahia and Morty also turned and snapped to attention. All three researchers were wearing jeans and T-shirts stained with everything from food to chemical solvents.

Phoenix smiled. "We're off duty. Just wanted to check in and see what you and your team have been up to."

Talon dropped the salute, then hurried over to a laptop and turned off the music. "Just working on the distribution system for our next project." he said, gesturing to the engine on the table. Upon closer inspection, Phoenix saw a series of gray dots along the fuselage, next to bullet holes. "The product works, but we want to make the distribution more streamline before we present a finished product to you."

Yahia grabbed a small cup and showed the gray contents to Phoenix and Warlord. "We're still working on a name for it, but it's a metal-like plaster for fixing holes."

Phoenix raised his eyebrows, impressed.

"It-t-t-t's . . .we're st-t-till t-t-testing it, sir." Morty stuttered, unnerved by the two large men. While Talon was taller than Phoenix, the captain of *Blood Sky* was more intimidatingly stoic and much more unreadable than his son, which made Morty feel minuscule, especially when added to the fact that the commander was a real-life giant, and the captain was built like a linebacker.

Talon nodded slowly. "Once finished, it should make emergency repairs and rescue efforts easier."

"Sounds good." Phoenix replied. "Keep me updated."

"Yes, sir!" the three researchers said at once.

Talon looked down at his watch and then glanced over at Morty and Yahia. "Let's break for lunch. You guys in the mood for pizza?"

Yahia laughed. "Sure. Will the captain be joining us?" He looked over at Phoenix.

"Not today." Phoenix said. "Would you mind giving us a minute?"

"Y-y-yes sir!" Morty replied, grabbing some of his belongings and going out the door, avoiding Warlord's gaze.

Yahia bowed his head to the two of them before following Morty.

Once the two were gone, and the door was closed, Talon visibly relaxed with a quiet sigh. Warlord chuckled. "Still getting used to being in charge?"

Talon rubbed the back of his neck. "It's a lot different from school projects, Uncle Aaron. My time in the Air Force helped, though."

Talon and his sisters were only allowed to use family titles when alone with each other and the ship's commanders. Phoenix had insisted on it to reduce the expectation of nepotism among the crew. Those who knew Captain Phoenix well were aware that he expected a higher level of professionalism from his family than he did from the rest of the crew, but to help maintain ship morale, the family connections were not discussed. The strict use of call signs in public was a great help.

"And now you get to build everything you've been theorizing in college, son." Phoenix said, smiling.

With the massive loss of resources, most education became theory-based rather than hands-on. While this was more of an annoyance for engineering majors, Talon had heard about music majors who had to share one instrument among an entire group. In the Air Force, he was allowed more hands-on opportunities, but the challenging projects were reserved for veteran commanding officers, as materials for research and development were scarce.

"Yes. Speaking of . . ." Talon opened a small container and revealed a pair of futuristic-looking metal-framed goggles. After removing the elastic strap that would secure the goggles to an individual's head, he turned to his audience.

"Are they for the shooting range?" Warlord asked. "Or for skiing?"

"I'm assuming this does more than what we can buy in the store, right?" Phoenix said with controlled patience.

"This may look like an ordinary pair of eyewear," Talon said, "but these have interchangeable plasma-filled electromagnetic lenses that allow you to see at different variations of vision." Talon handed them to Phoenix. They were charcoal gray with a sleek design, a sturdy frame, and a small elliptical button on each side.

"Explain electromagnetic lenses." Phoenix said, looking up at Talon.

"Simply put, they detect energy waves."

Warlord raised an eyebrow.

"Heavier than I expected." Phoenix noted, feeling the goggles' weight in his palm

"They're armor-plated. The frame and lenses are bullet resistant."

"Why?"

Talon shrugged. "In case someone gets a lucky shot."

"You're saying it's okay to get shot in the mouth as long as I can see?" Warlord teased.

Talon chuckled. "No. Once we perfect them, we'll add the same lenses to the face masks we're working on for the Raven helmets. Eventually, they'll come in a version where they'll look like everyday glasses for anyone who needs them but doesn't want to bring attention to themselves. The upgrades will look like designer sunglasses."

Warlord nodded and winked. Phoenix nodded his approval as he turned the goggles over in his hands, examining them from every angle.

"So, what were you saying about the vision variations?" Phoenix asked.

"Specifically, the goggles can detect various energy waves— microwaves, infrared, ultraviolet, X-ray, and radio waves." Phoenix and Warlord looked at each other mildly impressed. "The radio wave detection allows it to double as a two-way communicator and can link to other wireless communication devices, like phones, once programmed."

"I'm liking it so far." Warlord said.

"How does it work?" Phoenix inquired.

"Well, for starters, you're in normal mode where you use them as regular ultraviolet-reducing sunglasses. You can go blue or clear. I picked blue because I knew you'd like that." Talon said, staring at Phoenix.

Phoenix grinned and nodded. "Good choice."

"Then if you press this button here," Talon pointed to the thin button on the right side of the goggles, "it cycles to the next option from normal mode to microwave detection." Talon pressed the button, and the lens changed from blue to orange. Phoenix and Warlord stared at the lens in awe.

"Microwaves are used for communication, but this particular visual detection mode is for radar frequency of the microwave energy source. Radar uses minor microwave radiation to identify range, speed, and other characteristics of remote objects. With this feature they can see and calculate range to targets and other objects in the area."

"Cool!" Warlord smiled proudly at Talon.

"Press it again, and it changes to infrared mode, so you can detect any thermal radiation in the vicinity."

Phoenix put the goggles on and looked around the room, confirming the difference in heat between his family members and various objects.

"Yeah, they work!" Phoenix smiled as he removed the goggles. He turned to pass the goggles to Warlord, but Talon intercepted them.

"Another press, and it becomes an NVD." Talon said while pressing the button again, activating the night-vision mode. This time the lens turned emerald green. "This phase is the standard night-vision mode, allowing images to be visible with low levels of light, approaching total darkness. A moonless night would provide enough light for this to show everything in the area, but these change the intensity based on the level of light in the room."

"Which means?" Phoenix asked.

"Sudden light won't blind the wearer. Not even a flash–bang."

"So, you combined our standard vision wear into a pair of multipurpose goggles?" Phoenix asked.

"Yes, sir."

"And you gave them style, nephew." Warlord noted as he reached for the goggles. Talon pulled them away again, eliciting a glare from Warlord.

"There's more." Talon said, smiling. "Next, we have the ultraviolet mode." He pressed the button again, and the lens turned to a light purple. "In this mode, the user is able to detect harmless to severe ultraviolet radiation or energy waves in the immediate area. This is also useful for detecting solar energy in a power source or device. Sometimes, knowing how a vehicle or a ship is powered can give you an idea of how to disable it." Talon pressed the button again.

"Anything else?" Warlord asked, frustrated at not being able to handle the goggles.

"The last press of the button takes you to X-ray mode. As you can see, the lens changed to a dark gray that matched the frames perfectly. Of course, in X-ray mode you can see through objects, but when you press the left button, it acts as a dimmer to increase or decrease the level of intensity, so you can go from just looking for weapons under someone's clothes to visually removing their clothes completely."

"Hey, now!" Warlord said, grinning at the possibilities.

"All the way to the highest intensity to see to the skeleton and allowing you to see through walls or containers if you're looking for bombs or traps." Talon continued. "This is also good for seeing metal objects in someone's body or behind walls."

"Nice." Phoenix said, nodding. "Perfect for those suicide bomber body implants."

"The left button only functions for the optical versions in X-ray mode. At all other times it manages your communication."

"Wow, son!" Phoenix said. He examined the goggles again, then looked up at Talon and smiled. Pride filled Talon's chest. He always enjoyed impressing his father.

"Kayla and her medical team can use these for surgery," Phoenix realized.

"Surgery, check-ups, anything." Talon agreed. "Imagine being able to find the position of a bullet while in the field doing surgery. Kayla and I already talked about the medical implications, so we'll be making them for the medical team here and on Thunder Island."

"This is genius." Phoenix said. "What do you call them?"

"Special Purpose Eyewear, model X. 'SPEX' for short."

"Does the 'X' stand for X-ray?" Warlord asked.

"Probably the roman numeral for ten." Phoenix said. "Assuming it's the tenth prototype?"

"Does that mean the first nine didn't work, or you just wanted to use 'X' because it worked with your acronym?" Warlord teased.

"You're both wrong. The 'X' is for the letter Chi, which represents our ancestors." The look of pride that overwhelmed Phoenix at that moment almost brought a smile to Warlord's face. Almost.

"Somebody just earned a promotion! Way to kiss up to your old man, Axel." Warlord teased.

"You did good, son." Phoenix said, placing a loving hand on Talon's shoulder.

"I almost forgot." Talon said. "After our last mission, I added special optics that work in all modes, including regular mode. Now each of these will be able to detect liquid trackers."

"How's that?"

"Anyone that has been injected with our tracking enzyme, like Senator Kopensky, will have an aura emitting from their body, so you can find such people in a crowd without using our standard tracking devices. We'll still need the scanners to find them in a place with obstructions, like buildings, but if there's a clear line of sight, they'll look different from anyone else. It's short range for now, only about two hundred feet."

"They don't work around walls?" Warlord asked.

"They haven't been field tested yet, but so far they don't work very well around the ship, but that could be because Blood Sky's hull is made from dense metals, which wouldn't be the case in older corporate and industrial buildings. The newer buildings that are built with limestone and synthetic materials would be more transparent. So, yes and no for this model, depending on the structure."

"How soon can you have enough of these made for each member of the medical team, SOCIT, and the Ravens?" Phoenix asked, finally passing the goggles to Warlord.

"The mold is done, so give us about a week to put three dozen together and an additional day for testing." Talon said.

"Get on it," Phoenix ordered. "Now, what about the side project we talked about? Any updates on that? It's been months."

"Yes, sir." Talon replied, turning to the lab table and picking up a flask of jet–black liquid with dark-blue granite-like crystals throughout.

"What is that, tar?" Warlord asked.

"We're calling it 'Nibirium.'" Talon replied. Phoenix raised his eyebrows but said nothing.

"Is that an element on the periodic table?" Warlord asked.

Talon smiled. "Not yet."

"Remember those huge boulders we found under the base in a crater a couple of years back?" Phoenix asked, turning to Warlord.

The big man nodded. "Yeah. That's where this came from?"

"I broke off a chunk of it, and Axel has been working on it as a little side project."

"I thought Professor Dowe was working on it as a power source."

"He still is," Phoenix confirmed. "This is just to see what Axel can come up with."

"And this is the best you could come up with? Alien meteor

mud?" Warlord frowned, holding the flask closer to his face for a better look.

"It's a new type of matter, different from anything on Earth." Talon explained. "Once we broke it down, we named it."

"Nibirium," Phoenix said, "from the planet Nibiru?"

"That's what Professor Dowe thinks it is."

"You get alien rock and then what? You soften it up and turn it into alien diarrhea?" Warlord handed the flask back to Talon. "What if it's fossilized alien dinosaur poop?"

"No, Uncle Aaron, it has multiple uses."

"So does cow shit." Warlord pointed out. "You can burn it to keep flies away, fertilize your lawn with it, or mix it with mud and clay to make bricks." Phoenix chuckled at his cousin's obtuseness. "Stinky house that will smell like a never-ending fart, but if that's what you're into . . ." Warlord shrugged.

"This is different." Talon insisted. "Right now, it looks like tar because it won't harden if we keep it at a certain temperature. In its liquid form, it turns a blackish-blue color and is easy to use as a spray. Once it dries it acts like a thin sheet of armor that is almost impregnable. It's also undetectable." This last part captured Warlord's attention.

"It's invisible shit?" Warlord asked.

"Not quite, Aaron." Phoenix said. "It's just a theory, but because it's an unrecognizable element on Earth, none of our scans could detect any ore or metal present, so I thought it would render anything coated with it invisible. So, I gave it to Axel to confirm."

"It's not a theory anymore." Talon said, handing Warlord a pistol from the lab's small armory.

"You got it to work?" Phoenix asked, giving him a hopeful look.

"Yes, sir. We found that by smelting it down a different way

—I won't bore you with the details—we were able to liquefy it, then apply a light coat of it to this gun."

"But I can see it." Warlord frowned, implying that the invention was a failure. Talon handed Warlord a metal-detecting wand commonly used at airports and government buildings. When Talon waved it over the pistol, nothing happened.

"Is it broken?" Warlord asked.

Talon waved the metal detector over Warlord's personal sidearm in his hip holster. The wand flashed red and made an irritating sound.

"I guess not." Talon said, putting the wand down. "Most commercial metal detectors were developed to identify and react to weapons-grade metals, but Nibirium is not a metal from Earth. So, even if you see a gun, no metal detector will be able to identify it. What this means is that we can enter anywhere with our guns, explosives, or anything else concealed, and our enemy's sensors won't pick it up."

"Interesting. It's like a ghost gun." Warlord realized, his interest piqued. He always teased Talon about his inventions, but whenever he saw one that had military significance, he stopped his teasing and focused on the possibilities.

"And we can apply Nibirium in its liquid form to any solid surface?" Phoenix asked.

"I don't see why not." Talon replied. "We have enough of the meteor at the base to either make metal sheets or liquefy it to spray over any surface, like a coat of paint. The result is the same, undetectable by any conventional device." Talon looked at his father. "What did you have in mind?"

"All of our weapons?" Warlord asked, smiling.

"A bit more practical for starters." Phoenix said while thinking of the possibilities.

"Like?" Talon asked.

"SOCIT body armor," Phoenix replied.

Warlord's face glowed with a huge smile as the possibilities washed over him. "I love it! We would be totally stealth!"

"Not totally, Uncle Aaron. Remember, sensors won't pick you up, but you can still be seen."

"That works for me!" Warlord replied, then paused when he saw the look on Talon's face, his eyes still glued to his father. "What?"

"You said 'for starters,' Dad, what did you mean?"

"How much more of this goo can you make?"

"Now that we can synthesize the process, we only need a small portion of the ore to replicate and expand, so I guess the amount is practically endless. What did you have in mind?"

"The other teams?" Warlord guessed.

"Bigger." Phoenix said, looking at Warlord.

"Oh, the Enduro Mark Twos, weapons, and uniforms?" Warlord blurted.

Phoenix smiled. "Bigger."

Realizing what his father was thinking, Talon picked up the flask and looked at it, his mind churning. "That would take a lot of Nibirium, more than I have here on the ship." His mind raced as he calculated what he would need to make his father's idea a reality.

"What would?" Warlord asked.

"How long?" Phoenix asked, his eyes fixed on his son.

"We would need a bigger smelting plant. Too big to fit on Blood Sky. Even with that it would still take months. The process is slow."

"Get started on crunching the numbers. Have Dowe start building a second smelting plant at the base. We'll bring him everything he needs on our next trip there."

"I thought Professor Dowe's team was tied up getting everything ready for phase two." Warlord reminded him.

"He is." Phoenix paused to think for a moment. "We're going to make this part of phase two."

With that he strode out of the room with newfound determination, no doubt to record his thoughts.

"Cuz, you're going to make a ghost ship?" Warlord shouted after him. When Phoenix didn't reply, Warlord turned back to Talon and let out a frustrated sigh.

14

DOWN TIME

Phoenix leaned against the rail, taking a moment to appreciate the world around him. He always took time to be with the team for the sake of moral, but he preferred solitude and meditation. He took another deep breath, inhaling the various food aromas coming from the restaurants on the harbor. The harbor was quiet. The dock workers had left for the evening, and no new ships were coming in until the following morning. The only people wandering the docks were security guards and harbor residents out for an evening stroll or walking their pets.

Phoenix looked up at *Blood Sky* as he stood at the stern of the ship. She sat on the water like a majestic ebony beast. Strangers stopped to admire *Blood Sky*, an old warship brought back to life by modern technology. To any passersby, the ship probably looked like a slickly painted museum relic that had pulled into the harbor for a vintage boat show. The thought caused Phoenix to smile. For those who encountered *Blood Sky* in the open seas, it was a merchant ship commanded by a crew of mercenaries for hire, but for a faithful crew, *Blood Sky* was "home."

It was a clear night, offering an amazing view from Manhattan City Harbor. The neon building lights of the downtown area were a sight to see. During the city's restoration, neon lights were incorporated into buildings so that at night, passing aircraft that lacked the proper technical equipment wouldn't accidentally crash into them. Eventually, even advertisements were given a visual change with the addition of projections and holograms. From a distance, the flashing and dancing of colored lights and images formed an artistic backdrop.

Throughout the port, the sound of waves crashing mixed perfectly with the melody of a lone saxophone player playing jazz on *Blood Sky's* bow. Titus "Ace" Jackson, *Blood Sky's* Enduro specialist mechanic, was practicing, as he did almost every night they were in a neutral port. The saxophone music set the mood for a tranquil atmosphere.

Titus stood on the bow deck playing his saxophone with heart and soul. His soothing jazz melodies brought comfort to the skeleton crew that had remained behind to protect and maintain *Blood Sky*. Anyone who was off duty had the option to pull out a chair and sit comfortably on the bow deck, listening to Titus play, or to the sounds of recorded jazz and classical music when Titus wasn't in the mood. On nights such as this, *Blood Sky* was more like a cruise ship than a merchant vessel, filled with music, laughter, and conversation.

Because of how some of the combat equipment and vehicles were positioned on the ship's upper and lower rear decks, an unofficial VIP section for the higher-ranking crew members had been created. From there the lights of downtown were clearly visible, as was the open sea and the clear, cloudless sky.

Phoenix walked up to the portable card table where Warlord, Sandman, Hawk, and Eagle sat playing poker, each with a drink in one hand and a cigar in the other. Since all pilots had the night off, Falcon and Pops used their Enduro Mark IIs as seats. The jetbikes were more than advanced machinery; they were the Ravens' personal pets during quiet times and attack dogs during missions. Every now and then, Falcon's laughter filled the air in response to Pop's charming and often hilarious, lady-killer antics. Hacker and Talon had *Lola's* cabin set up as their very own entertainment center, where they challenged each other to various video games. Swan would often join them when she was onboard.

Phoenix pulled up an extra folding chair, sitting backward so his arms could rest on the back of the chair. He kept his cigar in his mouth and placed his glass of scotch, with a twist of orange peel, on the table in front of him. He alternated between watching the poker game and looking at the city lights beyond the ship.

He smiled to himself as Athena, his second in command, approached them with a bottle of beer in hand. She was an attractive Cuban-born woman from Spanish Harlem in Manhattan uptown who was athletic with long curly hair and a copper-colored complexion. She had been friends with Phoenix for so long that she felt like his little sister. The two had been fiercely loyal to each other long before she lost her left eye. Phoenix always teased her that while she had lost her left eye on their last government mission together, she had gained a great husband, to which she would reply, "Sometimes he makes me miss the eye." Phoenix had developed many family-like ties to the members of his crew, but Athena was one of the few whom he trusted with his ship when he was on missions or on shore leave.

"Who let you out of your hole, Athena?" Sandman teased.

"Captain was nice enough to give me some down time to hang out with you drunken bums."

"Says the girl holding a bottle of beer like a dude." Eagle said, smirking.

"And how am I supposed to hold my beer, 'dude'?" Athena asked, returning Eagle's grin. "Why don't you give us a little demonstration?"

"Fine, fine." Eagle waved her off as he lurched to his feet, "*This* is how a woman holds her beer." Eagle lifted his beer, extended his pinky, pursed his lips, and then swayed his hips as he took a sip, to the laughter and cheers of Athena and the officers.

"I don't know how you, Proctor, and Apache drink that piss water." Warlord snapped looking at her bottle of amber liquid as if it had a bad odor. "If you're going to drink beer, drink a man's beer! Dark and strong." With those words said, he raised his bottle of stout beer.

"In case you forget, I'm not a man, Warlord." Athena said before tipping her bottle back.

"I didn't forget. Especially when you come out here in your jeans with your hair down. You plan on slipping out to meet your Sancho?" Warlord asked.

"Does hubby know?" Sandman teased, grinning as he looked at his cards.

Athena snorted. "I don't have side action like Warlord does."

"Correction. For me to have a Sancha, I have to be in a relationship. You can't cheat on someone who's not there." Warlord raised his beer before taking a swig.

Sandman chuckled. "Yeah, you are the Sancho."

Warlord laughed and raised his beer. "Damn straight!"

Phoenix and the crew always respected Athena and her marriage, even though her husband lived at their land base thousands of miles away, but they loved to tease her about it, and she always rolled with it. That was one of the traits that Phoenix enjoyed about her. She was a tough commander and a great teacher, but she could become one of the guys without hesitation, and she was very proud of her Cuban heritage.

"You know, I was just thinking, there's a certain satisfaction that comes from doing this job." Athena said, pulling up a seat. "Especially when we have zero casualties."

"I never used to feel anything afterward, but since I started hanging out with this guy, things changed." Warlord smiled, gesturing to Phoenix.

"But you guys are cousins." Sandman pointed out. "You two haven't been doing this all the time?"

"We didn't grow up together, and not every cousin is someone you want to be close too." Phoenix said, chuckling.

"Hell, I know about that!" Sandman replied.

Warlord nodded. "Every family has one."

"Or two." Phoenix added with a smirk before taking another sip of his scotch. Warlord chuckled, knowing to which family members Phoenix was referring.

"Our fathers were very close. They were the youngest of nine kids, all from Jamaica." Warlord explained with his slightly detectable Jamaican accent. "We lived in Chicago, and Phoenix's family lived in New Jersey. As kids we never saw each other. My father would always fly to see his little brother while we stayed at home with our mother in Chicago."

"So, I got to know Uncle Ossie growing up but never met his kids until we were older." Phoenix added to the history lesson.

"You haven't been doing these missions together all your life?" Sandman asked.

"Déjà vu?" Eagle whispered, having heard Sandman ask this question for the second time. Athena tapped her half-empty bottle with Eagle's because they both knew all too well that Sandman had a tendency to repeat himself when he was getting drunk. Phoenix smiled while sipping his drink.

"Not at all." Warlord explained amused at the thought. "Like you, I put in my time in the military. It was all the adventure they promised, and I was good at it. But over the years, it got old. When I finished my last tour, I went into the protection business for a short time, working for celebrities."

"How did you end up here?"

"This guy wanted me for that first spec ops deal, and he knew I still held my classification from before, so I did it to back up my family." Warlord smiled, gesturing to Phoenix.

"We did whatever was needed." Phoenix said. "When I needed him, he came."

Eagle smirked. "Me and Hawk got called in when there was rescue stuff."

"Yeah, Eagle and Hawk were my local go-to guys when I moved to California." Phoenix said, raising his glass in appreciation to his oldest friends in the crew.

"But I thought one of you was a cop and the other was . . ."

"A racketeer from what the courts called it." Eagle said, interrupting Sandman and causing Hawk to clear his throat.

"That's how I met Eagle." Hawk explained.

"Yeah, the rescue mission that never happened." Eagle added with a puff of cigar smoke.

"How's that?" Sandman asked, eager to hear more.

"I had done some . . . undercover work in my prior life." Phoenix said. "During those assignments I worked with Eagle and Hawk separately. Eagle was a freelancer for a criminal organization, dealing with collections and racketeering, and Hawk worked with me on a few criminal cases. I trusted both of them, but they had never met."

"Until Phoenix's niece was kidnapped." Hawk added.

Phoenix nodded. "Yes. While I was living in California, my wife's niece went missing for a few days, and she managed to send an email to her mother, saying that the boyfriend she met online was holding her hostage in his house and wouldn't let her leave."

"Wow, and that was your first rescue op?" Sandman asked.

"Together, yes." Phoenix replied. "I had done them before, but they were assignments from the government or private clients who were paying me for protection. This was my first personal rescue."

"No money?" Sandman realized.

"No money. Aaron was too far away for him to get there in time, so I called the only two people in California who I trusted to do the job for no pay. They agreed without hesitation." Phoenix nodded toward Eagle and Hawk.

"Good guys." Sandman acknowledged.

"They were friends of mine who met that night for the first time. My wife at the time was shocked when these two guys who had come to the house as my friends were prepared to do whatever it took to get her niece back, just because I asked them. The fact that we each had a modest arsenal surprised her even more."

Everyone at the table laughed.

"She didn't know?" Athena asked, chuckling.

"She knew I did protection work, but she didn't know that these two were so intense until that night."

"Nice!" Sandman said.

"We were all ready to go. We were going to go across the border into Vegas, snatch my niece, and take her home, but we were prepared for resistance from lover boy or any of his friends."

"We were hoping for it." Hawk said, his cigar hanging out the side of his mouth as he stared at his cards.

"So, you all went over there and fucked him up?" Sandman asked, leaning forward eagerly.

"No, dude!" Eagle replied with disappointment. "That moth-erfucker let her go before we even made it out of Cali."

"My wife at the time, called us and said that her niece had been released and had called her from her mother's house." Phoenix said.

"Why?" Sandman asked.

"We never found out what changed his mind," Hawk replied with a shrug. "We didn't really care."

"And that was it?" Sandman sounded disappointed.

"Me and Xander still wanted to fuck him up for kidnapping a teenager, but this half-Jamaican, half-predator cop said we couldn't." Eagle said, gesturing at Hawk. "He said it wouldn't be justified because the guy was no longer holding her, so the threat was gone."

"Hawk keeps us doing the right thing." Phoenix explained.

"You're half Jamaican, Hawk?"

"No, he just says that because of the dreadlocks. Just like the crack about 'predator'." Hawk replied.

"Come on, dude! You know you look like the alien predator from the movie when he came to Earth to hunt people." Warlord, Athena, and Sandman got a good laugh looking at Hawk's dreadlocks, which went past his shoulders.

"That was back before Hawk started graying." Athena said, smiling.

"Yeah, now he looks like the predator chief from the sequel with gray dreads. All buff with weapons from all different times in history!" Eagle said, laughing.

"I remember that! Shit, Hawk, you do look like the elder predator!" Sandman said with sudden realization. Everyone laughed, including Hawk.

Athena's expression turned serious as she pressed her hand to her ear. She usually didn't do this under normal circum-stances, but with the noise of laughter around her she wanted to be sure she monitored the transmission accurately. After a moment, she turned to look at Phoenix. "You have a visitor." she said calmly. The others looked up as Warlord's on-duty SOCIT members approached the flight deck, escorting a stranger. Phoenix sipped his drink. Warlord always sat facing the entrance to the aft deck for this reason. Woody left the stranger in Lobo's custody and approached Phoenix. Warlord signaled to the other card players. Athena was already standing beside Phoenix. Sandman, Eagle, and Hawk stood up and moved to flank their captain and Warlord, who had remained seated on his right, all of them staring at the newcomer in an intimidating manner.

As the newcomer stepped forward, it was apparent that he had no idea who the ship's captain was, until he saw that several intimidating people had gathered around one man who was seated while smoking his stogy, a glass of whisky in hand. Lobo, who was dwarfed in size and muscle mass by Warlord, raised his giant paw of a hand, stopping the stranger's advance while Woody continued toward Phoenix.

"Captain." Woody snapped to attention.

"Woody." Phoenix gazed past Woody at the stranger in the business suit.

"Sir, Commander Proctor approved us to escort this government messenger directly to you, sir." Woody explained before stepping aside.

Phoenix nodded, signaling Lobo to bring the messenger closer. The messenger walked cautiously, realizing that everyone on the flight deck was watching him. Talon and Hacker were standing at *Lola's* rear gate, staring as well.

"Captain Phoenix, sir?" The young messenger began with a trembling voice. Phoenix nodded slightly, confirming he had the right person.

"Captain Phoenix, sir, the Senate Armed Services

Committee requests your attendance at a nine o'clock meeting tomorrow morning so that our government can congratulate you personally for your heroic acts in rescuing Senator Gash and Senator Kopensky."

Phoenix noted the messenger's nervous stance before he looked away, pondering the ramifications behind a semi-public need for congratulations.

"The Senate Committee wants to congratulate me publicly?" he asked, not bothering to hide his suspicion.

"The meeting will only have high officials present and a few invited guests. No press will be allowed, as the senators will be discussing details of the rescue operation, which has been deemed classified as part of national security, sir."

Phoenix thought for a moment, staring blankly at the messenger before turning to glance at Warlord, then returning his gaze to the messenger. "Please tell the Senate Committee that I will be there with my usual escort team."

"We have made arrangements to provide you with a police escort between the harbor and the Capitol building to assure your safety, sir." the messenger replied.

Phoenix shrugged. "Not necessary, but that's fine."

"Thank you, sir." The messenger bowed slightly. "Goodnight, Captain Phoenix."

After a nod from Phoenix, the messenger turned to follow Lobo and Woody as they escorted him toward the exit.

Phoenix turned to Warlord and Athena who were standing by for instructions or comments.

"Do you want me to go with you tomorrow?" Athena offered, seeing the suspicion in his expression.

"No. It's better if you standby here, just in case." Phoenix replied, appreciating that his friend always offered to go into potentially awkward situations with him.

"What about the rest of us?" Warlord asked.

"Yes." Phoenix replied, then paused to think as a bad feeling of distrust for what they were going to walk into came over him. He didn't want to worry the crew or his commanders and friends, so he did not voice his concerns. "This should be interesting." he said before tossing back the remainder of his scotch and staring out at the skyline.

15

COMMAND ENTOURAGE

～

T he following morning, Phoenix, Warlord, Swan, Kite, and Talon walked down the gangplank and onto the dock. *Blood Sky's* crew had no official uniforms and were seldom asked to attend formal events. The common family theme was black and gold, but each family member accented their business attire with their own favorite color.

Phoenix wore his classic deep-blue three-piece suit with a black shirt, black fedora hat, and a gold tie. Talon dressed like his father, donning a black three-piece suit but with a traditional white shirt and red-and-gold silk tie. In typical twin fashion, Swan and Kite wore matching black blazers with knee-length pencil skirts. Each woman also wore a silk scarf with matching stilettos. Swan's was dusty rose, and Kite's was a deep royal purple. Warlord suffered through wearing black formal pants and a vest with a black button-down shirt, custom designed and tailored for him by Snow. Phoenix requested that he wear a tie and suit jacket like the rest of the men, but Warlord had his limits, and a necktie and a restricting jacket were beyond them.

"You ready?" Warlord asked as he approached Phoenix, tugging at the bottom of his vest. Their faces were stern, distrustful of such invitations. Phoenix looked at Warlord, then at Talon.

"Everything set?" Phoenix asked.

"Yes, sir," Talon replied with confidence. "We can gear up on the way."

"Good," Phoenix said, turning back to Warlord. "We'll take the Juggernaut, and the Enduros can be on point and rearguard."

"Thought you'd say that," Warlord replied before turning away and speaking into his microphone. "Roll 'em out."

Phoenix couldn't help but smile when the Juggernaut exited *Blood Sky's* main cargo hold and pulled up onto the dock near the family. From the flight deck, two pairs of Enduro Mark I's followed by two pairs of Mark II's flew down to position themselves in front and behind the behemoth of a vehicle.

The Juggernaut was the first and the favorite of Phoenix's personal elite ground transportation. It doubled as a luxurious ride and a rolling fortress. It was a glossy dark-blue version of the Gurkhas' armored police transport, with several engine modifications and a luxury package upgrade for the interior. It seated six passengers in the rear cab with various weapons built into hidden compartments. Sometimes he drove it by himself, but on most occasions, he was driven by his protection team. It was scheduled to be the first of *Blood Sky's* vehicles to have Talon's newly invented SPEX lenses embedded into all the windows and mirrors.

As the command team, each member of the Medjinn family was assigned an escort. Talon always requested Falcon but was denied. Phoenix liked to match his escorts' gender with that of their principal in case accompaniment into the bathroom was required. Falcon led the protection team on the Enduros, so she was never an option for a personal escort. Talon's second choice was always Hawk because he worked well as a team with Eagle, who was Phoenix's escort. Because Hawk had law enforcement experience, particularly as part of protective details for visiting politicians, he was the most likely choice for Phoenix's son. Eagle was Phoenix's first choice because he was tough and scrappy in a fight. Eagle's loyalty to Phoenix was unparalleled by any crew member who didn't share his bloodline.

Jet, a Vietnamese martial artist and kickboxer, was Kite's escort of choice. Jet was second in command of the female infiltration team that she and her cousin, Nitro, called the Blood Sky Ninjas. Phoenix had rescued Jet and Nitro while raiding a slave barge. Some slavers were in the process of raping them when Phoenix and his team arrived to free the prisoners. In a fit of rage, Phoenix beat their rapists to death with his bare hands. Jet and Nitro decided to stay with *Blood Sky* after they recovered. They wanted training, so they would never be helpless again. Phoenix and Warlord trained the cousins to be assassins and sent them to a connection in Shangri–La for continued training in the art of ninjutsu. Jet became the trainer for *Blood Sky's* infiltration team while Nitro accepted the leadership position. Jet was ruthless and the perfect protector for Phoenix's daughter. Kite enjoyed Jet's feisty, vivacious personality. She had always been more talkative and outgoing than her sister.

Swan preferred as little contact with adversaries, and people, as possible. So, she welcomed Tiva for her protection. Tiva "Toa" Sefo was a robust, curvaceous woman with black curly hair and a beautiful bronze complexion. She was extremely intelligent, but she also had a mean temper and Samoan strength that made her a brute on the battlefield. Introverted by nature, she had the same preferences for social interaction as Swan did: the less the better. They spent most of their time together on and off the ship.

Warlord was the most dangerous person on the crew, so it seemed like an oxymoron for him to travel with a protector. However, to appease Phoenix and follow protocol, Warlord always had John "Slyder" der Sluys Veer escort him. Slyder was a muscle-bound Caucasian brute with tanned skin and a bald head. His graying mustache and goatee added to his menacing expression. Because his presence and words were intimidating, the two of them together convinced most people to think twice before starting a confrontation. This saved Warlord from getting arrested for blowing his crazy temper.

Apache stepped out of the Juggernaut's driver's seat while Toa exited from the passenger side of the large vehicle. Jet, Hawk, Eagle, and Slyder were sitting on the older Mark I Enduros wearing matching *Blood Sky* formal dress suits, which were used during protective escort details. Falcon, Raptor, Condor, and Vulture remained seated on the four Enduro Mark IIs wearing their tactical "Air Force blue" flight suits and helmets.

"Roll out!" Warlord ordered before climbing into the Juggernaut's rear cab. Talon was already in the back seat with Phoenix, Kite, and Swan while the others spread out to prepare their assigned vehicles.

The convoy moved forward with the Juggernaut in the middle, four Mark I's immediately in front and behind the Juggernaut, two Mark IIs in the lead, and the last two positioned in the rear. Two police motorcycle cops were in front of the motorcade with one tactical police Ripsaw wheeled tank following behind. It was the standard police motorcade escort that the messenger had mentioned. The few countries that graced *Blood Sky's* commanders with such VIP treatment handled it in different ways. In New America, Phoenix had seen such vehicles escorting official limousines, but this was the first time they had escorted him or his crew.

The motorcade caught the attention of everyone they passed as it traveled through downtown Manhattan City, especially with the flashing red-and-blue lights in front of them, clearing the way.

In the grand lobby of the Capitol building, relocated to One World Trade Center after the Vapor Incursion of 2029, Zara was steering Neil Torres in his wheelchair with Jun walking beside them. The lobby was filled with reporters who were forced to remain behind barriers manned by soldiers.

"Jun, you look nervous. What's up?" Torres asked. She remained at his side walking in an almost protective manner. "This is just a congratulations thing."

"I know, Neil, but I get a bad feeling when I go to these."

"But you're Senator Gash's personal assistant. You go to Senate meetings all the time," Torres stated.

"Are you sure it's not because of who'll be there?" Zara asked, smiling at Jun.

"Why? Who's going to be there?" he asked. Jun gave Zara a sharp glare, warning her to remain silent.

"The emperor of my country is rumored to be here today." Jun's answer seemed to omit the true reason for her nervousness.

"Yeah, right! Why would the emperor of Shangri-La be invited to a Senate meeting?" Torres asked. "Especially one where they may talk about details of the rescue?"

"That's what we're trying to find out." Zara said, glancing at Jun.

"Does Emperor Li Jaw-Long make you nervous?" Torres asked Jun as the three of them approached the security manned turnstile. Jun took a deep breath.

"Let's change the subject please. We're here." Jun she said as they approached the entrance, handing their identification badges to the military personnel at the door.

Shogun Kenji was a proud man of honor and an excellent teacher of combat and strategy, especially when it came to Bushido, the way of the warrior. As he sat next to Emperor Li Jaw-Long, he reflected on his current position of honor and pride, having followed in the tradition of his forefathers by becoming the general to a world leader. But the emperor was so much more than the ruler of Shangri-La; he was also Kenji's friend. He had a great deal of respect for Li Jaw-Long when he came to Japan to learn Bushido from Kenji, who at that time was considered a young master of sword techniques throughout Tokyo. He knew it took a lot of courage for a man born in China to come to Japan to learn a particular art of combat. Kenji's respect for Li grew quickly into a mutual appreciation for each other's culture and solidified in friendship. When the Vapor Incursion wiped out most of Japan, leaving only a few villages on Mount Fuji, Kenji feared that his culture and his people would eventually be lost in history, that is, until Li Jaw-Long approached him with a grand idea to restore Asia's various cultures before they faded away. Kenji had been at Li Jaw-Long's side ever since.

Now Kenji was sitting next to his emperor and friend in the newest invention from Shangri-La, the sleek hover limousine. Although both men traveled around Shangri-La in the vehicle often, this was the first time it had been seen outside of Shangri-La's borders. When Kenji asked why, Li Jaw-Long said he needed to make a statement.

The vehicle had a beautiful interior with soft Burgundy colored leather seats and rose-gold trim. Even the monitors embedded in the seats in front of them were covered in Burgundy leather and rose-gold piping. Li Jaw–Long watched the Global Comtext broadcast to learn more about the situation they were approaching. Kenji listened while occasionally looking out the window at their surroundings.

"We're here outside the Capitol building in Manhattan City attempting to capture a few visitors entering for the Senate meeting, which has been closed to the public and to the media." a female Chinese reporter in a fashionable red business suit said. Kenji had seen her before covering various crises and controversial situations in different countries. Now she was standing outside the Capitol building with approximately one hundred other reporters.

"She is very popular with the Asian demographic in New America," Li Jaw–Long said.

"My sources have confirmed that there will be a discussion of the recent abduction and rescue of two regional senators and their administrative entourage during today's meeting, but that is all I have been able to confirm." she continued. Kenji found her attractive but not beautiful or glamorous. He was put off by media personalities and women in general who paid more attention to their looks than to themselves as people, which was not the case with this reporter. "We have also learned that some members of the vice-presidential council arrived in the building earlier this morning, but we don't know if they will be attending this closed–door meeting."

Kenji turned away from the monitor and looked out the window as they passed police blockades, an indication that they were getting closer. "We're almost there." he said to the emperor. Kenji returned his focus to the monitor as the woman in red continued speaking.

"One entourage of individuals that we could not identify arrived only moments ago, but the military prevented us from speaking to those who were escorted into the Capitol building. As usual, the bodyguards who remained by the vehicles had no comment."

Li Jaw–Long watched the broadcast cut to a shot of a large military-style assault vehicle accompanied by two different types of flying motorcycles parked in front of and behind the large dark-blue SUV. Kenji was impressed with the vehicles' appearance.

"We're here." Mei–Ling said from the front passenger seat. Kenji was accustomed to sitting in her position when they traveled, but for the security of identity, Li Jaw–Long insisted that Mei–Ling take the role of head of security in a manner that would seem normal in New America.

"This is unbelievable!" the Chinese reporter exclaimed. "A hovering limousine has just arrived with an official police escort. We don't know who is inside, but they must be extremely important. This is J—"

The emperor turned off the monitors, and they looked out the window at the crowd of reporters, which had been cordoned off into one section of the police–controlled sidewalk.

Mei–Ling stepped out of the front passenger seat of the pearl-white limousine, which had arrived with two Manhattan City Police Ripsaw street tanks after the convoy had parked in front and behind the sedan. Her face was expressionless as she watched people stare at the limousine, which not only had a stunning paint job, with gold and red trim accenting the vehicle, but was the only advanced-design limousine that hovered above the ground and was silent on its approach, other than a mild humming sound.

Mei–Ling was calm as she surveyed the area and the path between herself and the front door where formally uniformed New American Marines were posted as sentries. The reporters and photographers pushed and shoved to get to the front of the stanchions, so they could catch a glimpse of the first hover limousine known on the planet. While other hover vehicles existed, they were often bulky with the need for extended propeller wings, which prevented them from traveling through most city streets. The limousine had the streamlined shape and width of a regular luxury sedan, only it had the ability to hover at different elevations over any surface, including bodies of water. Mei–Ling was used to the attention, but bringing the car to New America for the first time brought a higher level of satisfaction because she resented the country, which did not treat her to her liking as an Asian American.

Even though the reporters and civilians were kept at least one hundred feet from the carpeted path that the limousine's passengers walked from the curb to the building, they pushed and shoved as if they would be able to get closer. Even the police and military officers who were present to keep civilians from getting too close could not resist turning to look at the mechanical wonder.

After confirming that the area was safe, Mei–Ling tugged on her corporate vest and pantsuit to straighten her appearance, then turned with a stern expression to the Asian protection team and instructed them to ready themselves. The four average-size Asian protectors in burgundy business suits moved in unison at the command of the ponytailed Chinese woman in her early thirties. Although petite in stature, she was clearly in charge of the security detail.

Mei–Ling focused her attention on everyone around her as Emperor Li Jaw–Long stepped out of the rear of the limousine as it continued to float approximately eighteen inches above the street. Immediately after the emperor exited the vehicle, his most trusted friend and military leader, Shogun Kenji, followed. Emperor Li Jaw–Long was a well–built, clean–shaven man with closely cropped hair and wise eyes. His mere presence exuded power, leadership, and honor. Even without his protective entourage, he was easily identifiable as a man of purpose and destiny.

Shogun Kenji stood at the emperor's side like the warrior that Mei-Ling had always known him to be. Everything about him projected a sense of battle readiness, from his tanned, leathery skin and strong stance to his hardened gaze and lightning-fast reflexes. His hair was longer than corporate standards. Coupled with his facial hair, it was clear that he was not a man who abided by the rules of politics or corporations. He had been Mei-Ling's mentor in life and martial arts since she was able to walk. For Mei-Ling the Japanese general was more than the leader of the emperor's army. He was like her uncle.

A subtle head turn registered Kenji's acknowledgment that the unnoticed Asian protection team was already out of the standard SUV that followed the royal limousine, standing in position ready for the procession.

Mei-Ling surveyed the area with the eyes of a trained professional protector before signaling to the emperor and Kenji that they were clear to advance and for the protection team to move alongside without crowding the pair.

Walking at Emperor Li Jaw-Long's side, Mei-Ling and Kenji joined the emperor in noticing the customized blue battle vehicle and the flying bikes parked in front of the building. The emperor stopped for a moment, Mei-Ling and Kenji pausing as well.

"Our advance team reports that they belong to the merchant captain, Phoenix." Mei-Ling said, unimpressed by the attention that the vehicles brought to the emperor.

"Impressive vehicles." Li Jaw-Long said, glancing at Kenji before continuing toward the front entrance.

"The man comes to a political meeting with war machines,"

Mei-Ling blurted. "Only a criminal comes to a meeting like this looking for a fight."

"That may be true, but a true warrior comes prepared for one." Li Jaw-Long replied, smirking at the sight of the Juggernaut.

"Your majesty, are you saying that you feel this merchant is a warrior?" she asked, having little knowledge of Phoenix's reputation. She saw Kenji smile slightly, but did not ask for a reason.

"I'm not saying that." The emperor smiled back at Kenji as if they shared a secret. "Like you, I have heard of his recent reputation, and we both know that reputations and rumors can often be muddled and twisted based on improper interpretations."

Mei-Ling nodded, then returned her focus to the reporters who had been sectioned off in an area of the sidewalk that they were approaching. "Your majesty, you said you wanted to make a statement to the press." Some of the reporters were recording the hovering limousine while everyone else was getting rare footage of the emperor of Shangri-La on New American soil. "Is that still your plan, or did you want to go directly inside?"

The emperor turned from the *Blood Sky* convoy to stare at the horde of reporters, all of them calling out the emperor's name in a desperate attempt to get an interview with the reclusive nation's leader. To gain access to the area, all of them had passed an extensive background check, so Mei-Ling was not concerned for the emperor's security, although she knew that Kenji would never allow that to lower his situational awareness. Mei-Ling watched and waited patiently as the emperor looked at the many faces in the crowd of reporters, wondering about the purpose behind his visual search.

～

Jiayang had been following Emperor Li Jaw–Long for years. As a Chinese reporter in New America, it was no surprise that she would be assigned to any case where he may be involved in the hope that her broadcast would get the upper hand over other media companies that had not hired an experienced Chinese broadcaster who had her finger on the pulse of the Asian community globally.

While Emperor Li Jaw–Long seldom allowed his rare public appearances to be announced, Jiayang always seemed to be at the right place at the right time to capture still images and footage of the emperor as he was entering or leaving an official building. To her knowledge, this was the first official public appearance he had made in New America since it was announced that Shangri–La existed. Abroad, he had always been photographed with the stone–faced Japanese general and the stern, impassive Chinese woman, always with her hair in a long ponytail, which was cause of great curiosity. The few times the emperor had been identified in the media, the Chinese woman was always at his side. The emperor made it a point never to introduce her in any way, but her expression and her body language showed extreme loyalty to their nation's ruler.

After locking in on one of the reporters, the emperor approached the press area. The reporters became even more anxious, like a pack of puppies at feeding time. The stern young woman and the Japanese general stood close to Li Jaw–Long while the Asian samurai in matching blood–red business suits formed a protective outer perimeter around the trio.

"I will only accept a few questions, so if I select you, be sure to make your question worthy of an answer. Be wise with this opportunity," the emperor said to the gathering while media drones with cameras flashed above the men and women with microphones and cell phones in hand. Many reporters yelled over the others in the hope that the emperor would recognize them. He scanned the group directly in front of him. Jiayang was not in the right position, but she had intentionally worn a red business suit to help her stand out against the typical gray and black attire worn by the other journalists. She also knew that in Chinese culture, red symbolized luck and prosperity. For those two reasons, she hoped her outfit would catch the emperor's gaze.

The emperor focused on a white man in his thirties who raised his hands, calling on the emperor.

"What is your question?" the emperor asked.

"John Turner of the National Broadcast Network, Emperor Li Jaw-Long," the polished reporter announced, feeling confident that he had been selected. "Are you here at the Capitol today to be a part of the meeting with the Senate Committee involving the recent rescue of New American citizens in the Middle East?"

"My business here at New America's Capitol building is my concern," the emperor replied with a calm smile. "It is a large building, and I can assure you that several meetings will be transpiring this morning. Who else has a question?" he asked, obviously unimpressed with the question choice that Turner selected. This gave Jiayang an opportunity to maneuver a little closer, skillfully ducking under the raised arms of men who were taller than her.

Li Jaw-Long turned to focus on a tall, lean Black man with slightly graying hair who was standing on the opposite side of the press gathering. The emperor pointed to the man, and everyone else fell silent.

"Your Imperial Majesty, Henry Royal of the American News Channel," the man said. "Your majesty, when do you plan on opening your borders to non-Asians, so we can have a tour of the island?"

The emperor smiled slightly. "Good question, but it's not one that I will answer today. When I am prepared to open our borders, you will be one of the first on the list of invitees, Mr. Royal."

The emperor searched the crowd once more and finally made eye contact with Jiayang. She tried her best to appear regal and patient, not pushy like the other hungry, shark-like reporters. She smiled when she caught his attention, her hand raised. It seemed her choice of clothing had paid off.

"You in the red business suit. Your question?" the emperor asked. His expression was blank, but his stare was somewhat softer than before. She stepped to the front of the crowd, respectfully stopping at the metal barricade.

"Your Imperial Majesty Emperor Li Jaw-Long, I am Ms. Jiayang Chu of the Asian Daily Report."

"Yes, what is your question, Ms. Chu?"

"Your majesty, the flags on your sedan resemble a combination of the flags of Vietnam, China, Japan, and Korea," she began in a commanding yet pleasant tone. "How does this compare to the negativity that has been in existence between the Chinese and the Japanese for almost two hundred years? Do you believe the Chinese and the Japanese people can live in unity and peace, as your flag suggests?"

The emperor raised one eyebrow. Shogun Kenji looked away from the masses for a moment to observe Jiayang before turning to the emperor, who was watching him.

"The world has changed, Ms. Jiayang Chu," the emperor began as he stepped closer to the reporter, who had a noticeable Chinese accent. "Several years ago, most of China was turned into an uninhabitable radiated region due to nuclear attacks. Japan, Korea, Vietnam, and most of the other Pacific Rim countries were also altered, submerged and gone forever after the Vapor Incursion devastated the planet, followed by the Blitz War. For many of us, all that remains of our individual Asian cultures are the people who survived these natural and manmade disasters. The Chinese can continue to hate the Japanese for what happened a long time ago, or they can forgive and move on to allow healing to begin."

"Do you expect the Chinese to forget what was done to us, your majesty?" She asked, sounding offended at the nonchalant suggestion to move on.

"I did not say, 'forget,' Ms. Chu. We will never forget," the emperor replied. "Just like the Jewish people will never forget how the Nazis jailed, tortured, and experimented on them in prison camps until they died or how Black Americans will never forget how their ancestors were kidnapped from the African continent to become slaves in a foreign land, where they were raped, tortured, and treated like beasts of burden while not being recognized as human beings in the country where they were born even generations after the fact."

Royal, Turner, and several other reporters became ashamed and filled with remorse at the history lesson being presented. Kenji's expression hardened, which was difficult since his usual expression was one of granite.

"Let's talk for a moment about this country, New America," the emperor continued. "My mother was from Vietnam." He paused to let his words sink in, knowing that some of the reporters were broadcasting live across the country. "American soldiers came to my mother's country and raped young Vietnamese girls and burned their homes. They killed them even though these women and children were not soldiers.

"I spent my adult life here in New America and have been told to my face that the Vietnamese were the dogs of the Asian people. This was said to me and my mother by a Cuban man in this country. Yet here I am, and here we are, in New America where many cultures coexist."

"Your majesty, are you saying that you believe that Shangri–

La is one of the first steps toward peace between China and Japan?" Jiayang asked.

The emperor paused as he realized the trap that this clever woman was staging for him. "I believe that peace between these two nations began long before 2029, even though some choose not to accept it." He smiled slightly. "Have you ever visited Japan, Ms. Chu?"

"Yes, I have, your majesty, as a teenager."

"Were you mistreated while you were there?"

"Not at all, your majesty. I found the Japanese to be very polite." Jiayang stated, glancing at Kenji.

"That is the beginning of which I speak," the emperor explained. "Shangri−La was not created to solve an existing problem, nor does it exist to rectify feuds of the past. Shangri−La was created and developed to provide a peaceful alternative to previous conflicts. It is a place where all Asians can come together and choose to survive in peace and harmony, putting aside our differences to achieve greater goals as one body of people, one united culture. Like New America where Blacks and Whites coexist here with other cultures and races, Shangri−La is a place where all Asians can come if they choose not to remain in what is left of their ancestral countries."

"I see, your majesty. That is very noble." Jiayang bowed to show her respect for Li Jaw−Long's answer.

"It's more than noble, Ms. Chu. It is productive." The emperor turned to gesture to his hovering limousine. "That car is a product of combined ingenuity. Japanese and Chinese engineers built this advanced vehicle based on a Korean design."

"Sounds like a paradise too good to be true, your majesty." Jiayang said, smiling.

"It is real. Would you like to see it?"

Jiayang looked surprised and flattered. "Your majesty, you would give me the honor of being added to the list of those invited when Shangri-La's borders are finally opened to the world?"

"Not at all, Ms. Chu," Li replied. "I'm saying I have different Asian nationalities in positions of leadership in Shangri-La. I have also been monitoring your media broadcast for several years, and you have never failed at being honest and unbiased with your research and presentation. Would you, as a Chinese media celebrity, be offended to be around Japanese-born citizens such as my trusted military leader, General Kenji here?"

Jiayang looked at Kenji, who bowed slightly in her direction.

"No, your majesty, I would not be offended at all." She did not hesitate, as many had expected. She was an experienced investigator and had learned enough about the emperor to know that he made no decisions without thinking things through and doing a thorough investigation. She smiled at the notion that her years of broadcasts had become a visual resume to him.

"Then I want to present you with an offer." the emperor continued. "After you have completed your news segment on me today for your employer, the Daily Asian Report, come to Shangri-La and become the head of my country's media network." The other reporters all fell deathly silent. No one had expected such an impromptu offer.

"Today, your majesty?" Jiayang asked, startled.

"After this meeting I will attend to other business for the day, then my ships will sail back to Shangri-La after sundown. If you want the job, come to the Manhattan City Harbor by dusk for boarding."

"Are you kidding, your majesty?" Royal asked with a smile that showed that he was extremely happy for the opportunity that he was not offered.

"I seldom joke, Mr. Royal." the emperor replied, then turned back to Jiayang. "Help me continue the healing process between our Asian people, Ms. Chu. Help us start our own broadcasting network in Shangri-La." He paused for thought, then decided against saying anything more. After a quick smile, he turned to go into the Capitol building, leaving the reporters to yell their questions in the hope that he would give them a chance for an exclusive. Jiayang stared at the emperor and his entourage in stunned silence, her fellow reporters pummeling her with a barrage of questions that she did not answer.

16

THE SENATE MEETING

~

Phoenix was led into the Senate chamber of the Capitol building. At the end of the room was a high stand where the chairperson and VIP members of the Senate sat. Behind the stand was a large screen that displayed whatever senator was currently speaking. In front of the stage were multiple tables where senators from across the country normally sat. Above and behind him was gallery seating, normally reserved for reporters, but instead his family members and their entourage were taking their seats. No press was allowed inside, and Phoenix mentally groaned at how much the paparazzi were going to hound whoever came out the Capitol building afterwards. He was relieved, but he couldn't help but wonder if this was to keep his former identity classified or because any discussion of his involvement would be classified and give the government the opportunity to take credit for the rescue.

New America's government had undergone significant changes after the Vapor Incursion. The title given to the thirteen secretaries who were formerly of the US Cabinet was changed from "secretary" to "senator." Due to the immediate focus on defense during the Blitz War, the title of Senator of Defense was upgraded to Vice President of Defense, bringing the Cabinet down to twelve members. Originally, one senator governed each of the five regions of New America: Eastern, Southern, Central, Northern, and Western, which were how the islands of New America were divided. Eventually, as the population increased in New America and business and the economy began to be restored, the workload for such large regions was too much for one person, so it was decided that two senators should govern each region, the more experienced being the senior senator, and the auxiliary being labeled as the lieutenant senator of the region. In the end, there were a total of twenty-two senators in New America.

Phoenix was somewhat relieved to know that his presence and participation would only be a footnote in the meeting because it confirmed that he would not have to be in attendance for the entire time. He hated political meetings where everyone felt the need to speak even if they had nothing of importance to say. He was directed to take a seat at a guest table facing the senatorial tables. He noticed a small camera was attached to the desk and facing him, no doubt to put his face on display if he had to speak.

As senators filed into the chamber, Phoenix looked back to confirm that his family and crew were settled comfortably, sitting in the upper gallery, but he was surprised to see the emperor of Shangri-La and two others sitting in the gallery among other esteemed guests.

A door swung open, and Vice President Harp and Commodore Ward entered the chamber, taking a seat in the VIP section flanking the chair's seat, immediately followed by Senior Vice President George Mason and Vice President of the Department of Justice, Stanley Clayton. While Phoenix knew little of what went on in Senate committee meetings, he thought it was unusual for more than one vice president to be in attendance, not to mention a few high-ranking officials from New America and Shangri-La.

As Harp took her seat, she scanned the room, freezing when she locked eyes with Phoenix. She was confused at first, but when she recognized him, she glared at him as if wondering why he was there. Phoenix wasn't a public figure; therefore, the only ones who could connect his face to the name were his crew and those he rescued. However, now Harp knew as well.

Senior Senator Thomas Lynch, a stocky older man with graying hair and a stubborn personality, approached the chair's seat. As he sat down, the screen behind him activated to show his face. The other senators quickly faced him as he cleared his throat into the microphone. "The Senate committee meeting will now come to order," he declared.

Phoenix's face was expressionless as Lynch did a roll call of the other senators. The fact that two of Phoenix's old nemeses were present concerned him. He did not stare directly at Vice President Harp or Commodore Ward, but he made sure he monitored their movement in his peripheral vision at all times. Being the only military personnel in the room, Phoenix knew that Ward was not there for anything that Phoenix would consider good, and Ward's expression confirmed it. To his surprise, no one else seemed to be surprised at Ward's presence in the meeting.

"First of all, I would like to congratulate and thank Senators Gash and Kopensky for joining us today. As we all know, you two have only just been rescued, and you could've been excused from this meeting after dealing with such an extraneous ordeal." Lynch waved a hand at Kopensky and Gash, both still showing signs of facial healing.

Kopensky leaned forward toward his mic, and the screen

behind Lynch switched from the chair to Kopensky. "It was our honor, Mr. Chairperson."

Nodding, Lynch adjusted the papers on his desk. "Captain Phoenix, we have a lot on our agenda, so I thought we would begin with the topics that involve you, so you can be on your way."

"Thank you, Senator Lynch. I appreciate that." Phoenix responded, not a fan of his face being immediately plastered on the large screen for all to see.

"I read the debriefing notes from Senator Kopensky, Senator Gash, and their staff. I have to tell you, Captain, that was a remarkable rescue operation." Lynch said while looking over the papers before him. Phoenix recalled from previous interactions that Lynch preferred printed documents, enjoying the feel of real paper in his hands.

"Thank you, sir." Phoenix said, bowing his head slightly. He caught a smile from Kopensky and Gash. He glanced back at the audience gallery and saw that Torres, Zara, and Jun were smiling as well. He also caught Jun staring at the Shangri–La emperor with an unreadable expression on her face. The emperor did not seem to notice her gaze, instead focusing on the Senate meeting like a chess master in a competition. Phoenix wondered if the emperor was always so intense during such meetings or if he was anticipating something.

Phoenix's eyes swung over to the young woman on the emperor's right. Mei–Ling, Shangri–La's head of security, was returning Jun's stare, neither of them betraying their thoughts or emotions. For some odd reason, Phoenix had a feeling of familiarity as he watched the two. He quickly looked away as Lynch cleared his throat.

"Captain Phoenix, we are looking forward to having you join us at a victory gathering that President Bennett is holding for our rescued senators and their administrative group. President

Bennett would like to award you with a medal for your bravery."
Lynch's announcement was met by applause from everyone
except Commodore Ward, who frowned at Lynch. Curiosity rose
in Phoenix's mind as he wondered what was the purpose of his
presence if it made Ward so upset.

"Thank you, Senator Lynch. I would be honored." Phoenix
replied. Phoenix was polite but unmoved, as he already had
more than a few medals collecting dust in his trophy cabinet
under his birth name. The pieces of metal meant little after his
government betrayed him.

Knowing that Harp and Ward would not have been present
for a congratulatory meeting in his honor, Phoenix concluded
that their purpose would be revealed before the actual award
reception.

"Unfortunately, there were a few anomalies that the rescued
senators and staff couldn't explain, so we hope that you could
help us by filling in the gaps," Lynch said peering over his
reading glasses at Phoenix.

"Okay," Phoenix replied.

"Captain Phoenix, this is Commodore Reginald Ward,"
Lynch gestured to Ward.

Phoenix nodded slightly in recognition.

"Commodore Ward's team was assigned to locate the
kidnapped senators and perform the rescue operation."

"I see," Phoenix replied. "In that case, Commodore," Phoenix
said, turning to look at Ward directly in the eye, "you're
welcome."

The audience chuckled. Phoenix expected Lynch to reprimand him, but he simply smiled. "Commodore, you are free to
ask your questions." Lynch stated.

"For the record, you show yourself as a captain. How did you
earn that rank?" Ward asked, clearly seeing himself as witty.

"Anyone who is the owner of a ship with a crew of more than

three has the right to call themselves the captain of said vessel," Phoenix replied. "Are you not familiar with maritime law, Commodore Ward?"

"Of course, I am." Ward replied.

Kopensky stared at Phoenix in an attempt to signal him not to provoke the military leader in an open forum, but Phoenix ignored his friend.

"Vice President, Department of Homeland Security, Karen Harp." Harp said, identifying herself for the record. Phoenix knew that she remembered him, but she had to maintain the illusion of being neutral to those in the room who knew nothing of their history and previous encounters.

"You have the floor, Vice President Harp." Lynch acknowledged.

"Captain Phoenix, how exactly were you able to obtain the whereabouts of the kidnapped senators before Commodore Ward?"

"Skill." Phoenix replied, eliciting more laughter.

Emperor Li Jaw-Long watched each person who spoke on the large viewing monitors mounted on the wall high above the senators. He seemed to be studying their expressions, not just listening to their words.

"Captain Phoenix, this committee is not here for your entertainment!" Lynch scolded. "Now, we ask that you answer the question directly."

"My apologies, Senator Lynch." Phoenix took a deep sigh, then turned to Harp, who had a smug expression on her face. "The intelligence that allowed me to obtain the location of the senators' party is classified."

"Classified?" Harp exclaimed, appalled. "Captain Phoenix, may I remind you that I am the vice president of Homeland Security and hold one of the highest levels of clearance in the United States of New America?"

"There's no need to remind me, Vice President Harp. I am well aware of your title and the security clearance that goes with it. But as you may or may not realize, I am not a citizen of New America, so I do not answer to the rules and regulations of New America. What I deem as classified on my ship does not relate to the levels of security clearance in this country."

"Your ship is in New American waters." Commodore Ward stated.

"It wasn't at the time that I gathered the intel or performed the extraction." Phoenix replied.

"Are you aware that by withholding this information, which could interfere with our investigation, that you leave us only two conclusions?" Harp asked. "Either you were secretly trading with our enemy at the time of the assault, which placed you in the vicinity of the abduction, or you were directly involved with the abduction itself."

"First of all, I have no involvement with any investigation you are conducting," Phoenix replied. "My role in all this was simple. I rescued New American government personnel from hostile territory and returned them home safely, at no charge to the New American government, I might add. That's it. Second, those aren't conclusions; they're assumptions."

"Be that as it may, the options still stand as the only possible explanations." Harp said.

"So, either I was coincidentally trading with the insurgents at the time of the kidnapping, or I ordered my so-called army of terrorist insurgents to snatch the senators and beat the shit out of them, all so I could swoop in and kill the thugs I hired to, what, look good? Is that your theory, Vice President Harp?"

"You said it, Captain Phoenix." Harp smiled. "If you choose not to disclose how you obtained this knowledge, we may be forced to arrest you for suspicion of abduction and terrorism."

Phoenix sensed Warlord tensing in the seat behind him.

Phoenix made a subtle hand gesture, instructing Warlord to remain calm.

"Just so that I understand you correctly, you brought me here under the guise of showing your appreciation for rescuing the senators and their staff, but because I won't tell you how I did it, you're going to accuse me of a crime and arrest me, with only your assumptions as evidence?" Phoenix's eyes were hard and cold as he summarized the obvious. "Is that the stand you want to take, Vice President Harp?"

"Absolutely not!" Mason interjected, forever the voice of reason. "Captain Phoenix, we are eternally in your debt for this amazing rescue, but please understand that Vice President Harp is just trying to be thorough and eliminate all possible foreign or domestic threats."

"I understand, Senior Vice President Mason, but since this happened outside of New American borders, wouldn't this fall under the oversight of the vice president of the CIA not the DHS?"

"For your information Phoenix, once New American citizens are involved, the DHS has every right to take an active part in any investigation or solution in bringing our people home." Harp said.

"This is correct." Mason agreed, bringing the conversation back to the original topic. "But I must agree with Vice President Harp's path of questions. It's vital that we bring to light any and all possible threats to our country's security."

"I completely understand, Senior Vice President Mason, but I still cannot answer the question, sir." Phoenix said, his tone full of respect.

Harp smirked. "Then we have no choice but to—"

"It was me!" Kopensky shouted.

Phoenix frowned at Kopensky, warning his friend not to disclose the tracker enzyme.

"Please explain, Senator Kopensky," Lynch said.

"Less than a year ago, Captain Phoenix was commissioned as an outside contractor to create an undetectable tracking system. I volunteered to be the test subject, and I was using it when I left the country."

"Why would you do that?" Lynch asked. "We have our own concealable tracking devices."

"Yes, Senator Lynch, and those trackers were easily located on our bodies and destroyed before we were removed from the attacked location." Kopensky explained. "I agreed to Captain Phoenix's version because it is not a device or a micro−machine. It's an enzyme that goes into the bloodstream."

"What?" Harp was caught off guard, focusing on the secret, not the result.

"When Captain Phoenix heard that we were abducted, he activated the tracker so that he could find me, thereby finding all of us." Kopensky explained. "Because I agreed to the experiment, all of our lives were saved."

Phoenix kept his face expressionless, knowing everyone in the room was looking at him, waiting for a reaction that he refused to show.

"Is this true, Captain Phoenix?" Harp asked, her eyes narrowed with suspicion.

"Are you questioning the statement of an American senator, Vice President Harp?" Phoenix replied.

"Of course not!" Harp said, upset that the inquiry had taken an unexpected turn.

"Senator Roberta Blander here." Her image replaced Harp's red face on the screen as she leaned toward her microphone. "Captain Phoenix or Senator Kopensky, can either of you tell us why we were not made aware of this tracking system?"

"It's still in the testing phase." Phoenix explained.

"I object to this!" Harp exclaimed.

"Vice President Harp, this is not a hearing, and no one is on trial today, so you can't officially make an objection." Lynch stated.

Harp huffed before regaining her composure. "How can a senator have a tracking system on his person and the vice president of Homeland Security know nothing about it?"

Phoenix and Kopensky looked at each other, both of them trying to come up with an answer that would not lead to more questions.

"I was made aware of it in its early stages."

Phoenix and Kopensky did well to hide their surprise at Mason's comment.

"You knew, Senior Vice President Mason?" Harp's eyes shifted suspiciously between Phoenix, Kopensky, and Mason. Phoenix and Kopensky instinctively took slow sips from their water glasses, buying time for thought and hiding their surprised expressions.

"And I sanctioned the testing." Vice President of the Department of Justice, Stanley Clayton said while twiddling with his pen on the table before him.

Talon let out a choked cough. Phoenix glanced back, catching Emperor Li Jaw–Long's amused expression, seemingly pleased at the display before him.

"I see," Harp said with a sigh. "Well, if Senior Vice President Mason and Vice President Clayton were aware of it, I suppose there's not much more to be said on the subject." Her body was so tense that everyone could see the muscles in her neck on the screen.

"Senator Wendy Archibald." Wendy announced as she adjusted her position in her seat. "Captain Phoenix, good morning." she continued with a pleasant smile and comfortable familiarity.

"Good morning, Senator Archibald." Phoenix replied,

smiling back.

"On a lighter topic, Blood Sky is your ship, Captain, correct?"

"Yes ma'am."

"Can you tell us what exactly is the purpose of Blood Sky? There have been so many rumors, and this is the first time we've had the opportunity to ask you directly, as you are the captain." Her voice was pleasant and welcoming, like an old friend.

"Not a problem, Senator Archibald," Phoenix replied. "Blood Sky is a merchant ship that has become a haven for people who lost their residence after the devastation and the wars that started in 2029. For the last thirty years, people who lost their homes and countries decided to make attempts at life on the open sea in order to survive. Blood Sky helps such people from time to time."

"I've heard that Blood Sky is a pirate ship and a warship," Blander interjected, eager to bring negative rumors to light. "Is that true, Captain?"

"Not at all, Senator Blander," Phoenix replied pleasantly. He could be very charming when the situation required it. "Blood Sky is neither. Blood Sky transports merchandise and sometimes people from one place to another."

"Not a warship? Then how do you explain the heavy artillery on your ship?" Harp asked.

Phoenix smiled. "That's easy. Blood Sky was originally built as a prototype destroyer that I purchased and bartered for in exchange for services rendered." He glanced at Emperor Li Jaw–Long, but the man's expression showed no sign of agreement or denial.

"You're saying that those weapons are nonfunctional?" Ward inquired.

"I didn't say that." Phoenix replied. "Yes, we have weapons onboard. As a merchant–transport ship, we have a right to protect our crew, passengers, and cargo according to maritime law. We defend ourselves from pirates." Phoenix smiled confidently at Ward.

"Then you wouldn't have a problem with a New American science team getting a tour of your vessel to examine the rumored advanced technology that you have, would you?" Harp asked.

"Of course I would," Phoenix replied. "That's like saying that the military has the right to walk into your house and demand your grandmother's recipe for sweet potato pie." He paused as several people in the audience chuckled. "Blood Sky is a privately owned and operated ship governed and protected by maritime law. It cannot be boarded without confirmed authorization from the captain unless documented cause can be presented. Do you have a justifiable cause, Vice Present Harp?"

"No." Harp replied, her voice just above a whisper.

"Then you would need a personal invite from the captain, and I wouldn't expect that any time soon."

"I have heard that you are a mercenary and a smuggler," Ward said, leaning forward as if this would make his point clearer. "Your ship is now docked in our harbor. This would give us cause to investigate it, looking for illegal substances."

"Per maritime law, you can only perform a search of Blood Sky if you are able to prove that we have smuggled something to or from New American waters. Although we are docked here, we have not dropped anything off that did not go through customs; except of course, government employees." He smiled broadly. "Do you have evidence that Blood Sky has been or is being investigated for smuggling?"

"No." Ward answered.

"Are you going to investigate every ship docked in the harbor? Because I believe Shangri–La's helicopter carrier is docked in the harbor right next to Emperor Li Jaw–Long's beautiful luxury super yacht." Phoenix said.

"No." Ward responded, casting an uncomfortable look at the emperor, who stared back at Ward.

"Now, if the government staff themselves are illegal or were smuggling contraband," Phoenix said, "you would have to check with them on that matter. It's still not a Blood Sky issue."

"I assure you, Emperor Li- Jaw-Long, we have no intentions of—"

"Then can you tell us what's the difference between a transport ship and a smuggler's ship?" Harp asked, interrupting Ward's unnecessary apology.

"Yes, I can." Phoenix leaned into his microphone so that his next word echoed throughout the room. "Cargo."

Phoenix waited a few moments for the snickers in the audience to die down. "But to alleviate your concerns, I assure you that we are not smugglers. You have my word on that."

"Since you were once a member of the former United States military, you and all that you possess should fall under New America's government policies." Ward said, causing some of the senators to murmur quietly, unaware of Phoenix's past.

Phoenix stared at Ward, his face expressionless. Those who knew of his previous identity knew that his former self had been reportedly killed in action during an unsanctioned mission. Only a handful of people had the authorization to know that Alexander "Thor" Medjinn had been ordered to go along with the reports of his demise to save face for New America's government and prevent an international war. He and his team were scapegoats, but he suppressed his bitter feelings on the matter and focused on answering the question in a way that did not jeopardize the secret that he had kept for so many years.

"Commodore Ward, are you intending to discuss any involvement I may or may not have had in the past with the New American government that would probably be deemed classified information in a semi public forum?" Phoenix asked.

"Excuse me?" Harp replied.

"Discussing classified information in the presence of unauthorized individuals is a breach of security, which I believe could get you arrested for treason." Phoenix pointed out.

Harp was about to respond when she saw Clayton shifting in his seat while watching her intently. She decided to remain silent when she saw Emperor Li Jaw-Long and others staring at her.

"How do we know you didn't steal the advanced technology that you have on your ship?" Ward asked, avoiding the nearly treasonous subject.

"You don't," Phoenix replied. "But since it's more advanced than anything you have, I obviously didn't steal it from you, so no crime there."

"How do you know it's more advanced than anything we have?" Ward asked, confident of catching Phoenix in his snare.

"Because you and Vice President Harp just said that it's advanced." Phoenix's words and look of baffled innocence sent the audience into an explosion of laughter. Lynch waited for the murmuring to stop before he spoke. He knew that although Phoenix's tone was condescending, the captain had a valid point.

"Undetectable body tracker," Lynch said while skimming through his papers. "Fancy flying motorcycles that can outmaneuver attack helicopters. A helicopter that seems to be invisible in the night. This is all from the debriefing notes from Senator Kopensky, Senator Gash, and their aides as firsthand witnesses to these items." Lynch chuckled to himself. "This is damn impressive, Captain!"

"Thank you, Senator Lynch." Phoenix nodded in acceptance of the compliment.

Ward turned to Harp, but she shook her head slightly,

signaling for him to discontinue his unsuccessful verbal attacks. Ward chose stubbornness over obedience.

"How do we know that you didn't steal the technology from someone else?" Ward pressed, barely restraining his anger.

"Commodore Ward," Lynch warned, "you're starting to repeat yourself and waste the Senate's time."

"It's okay, Senator Lynch," Phoenix said, then turned to Ward. "My son and his team of young engineers create all of our technology."

"Your son?" Ward snapped.

"Commander Talon, Blood Sky's chief science officer." Phoenix gestured to Talon, who was seated in the gallery behind him. Talon raised his hand politely.

"Him?" Ward frowned. "He's a kid! There's no way he can create advanced technology."

"Genius has no age limit. Neither does stupidity." Phoenix winked at Ward.

"You can say whatever you want, but where's the proof?" Ward snapped.

Before Phoenix could answer, he heard a harsh whisper behind him. Swan had grabbed her brother's hand in an attempt to prevent him from responding, but he went ahead anyway.

"Here's one of my creations," Talon said while revealing the SPEX prototype eyewear.

"Very cool, kid." Ward chuckled, looking around for others to join him in his attempt to mock the young engineer. "You reinvented ski goggles."

Talon responded to the grins around the room with a smile of his own. "You're right, Commodore. In regular mode they are just goggles against the sun, but if I switch them to X-ray mode..." Everyone watched as Talon put on the SPEX, then pressed the button on the side, turning the lens to a slate gray. "I can now see that you and Vice President Harp's heart rates are over a hundred beats per minute, extremely high for two people sitting at a table, and faster than anyone else on the panel. That usually means that you have been exercising recently, or you're nervous about something."

"Yeah right! You're guessing, kid." Ward said in disbelief.

"With a minor adjustment, I can see that Senator Lynch has three gold screws in his left shoulder, probably from some sort of reconstructive surgery." Talon said. Everyone looked at Lynch for confirmation.

"He's right!" Lynch said with a surprised but amused chuckle. "They put in titanium ones when I was a teenager and then had to replace them with gold ones after the titanium ones dissolved in 2029."

"You read his files or something!" Harp shouted, leaping to her feet. Talon turned to her and smiled.

"With another slight adjustment that reduces the intensity, I can also see that you, Vice President Harp, are wearing provocative undergarments." Talon raised his eyebrows with surprise. "Red lace with garter belts."

Harp wrapped one arm across her chest and the other across her pelvic area and plunked back down into her chair, embarrassed. Kopensky and Mason looked down to hide their amusement, caught off guard from Talon's statement.

Kite and Swan hit Talon from either side, causing him to suddenly remove the goggles and return to his seat. Phoenix looked back at Talon with no expression. He found his son's actions inappropriate and disrespectful, but considering the target, Phoenix was not as upset as he would have been otherwise. Warlord, on the other hand, couldn't keep the huge grin off his face. When Harp saw the giant smiling, he winked at her. She looked away, disgusted.

"Impressive, Captain!" Lynch said with hesitation in his

voice as he looked at Harp, a barely detectable smirk on his face. "Young man, may I examine those goggles?"

"No!" the female senators said in unison.

"So," Gash began, still smiling at the abrupt outburst but attempting to change the subject. "What would it take for us to have the technology to make those goggles, Captain Phoenix?"

"Classified!" Warlord blurted. Gash looked up, startled at the deep, bellowing voice. Warlord simply winked at him, relaxing Gash's fears. Gash smirked, understanding that this was one of many secrets that would not be revealed until Phoenix decided the time was right.

"That's one of many prototypes. Commander Talon brought it today, at my request, to show Senator Kopensky." Phoenix replied.

"How long before they're out of the testing phase?" Gash inquired.

"Classified!" Talon said at the same time as Warlord, Kite, Swan, and Phoenix. Wendy, Kopensky, Mason, Gash, and Clayton all smiled at their unified reply.

17

A LACK OF HONOR

~

E mperor Li Jaw-Long was led into a room with antique oak wood furnishings set up in a corporate lounge design. He was escorted by Mason, whose face was grim. The emperor stopped when he saw CIA Vice President Robert O'Leary already seated inside the room. He signaled for Shogun Kenji and Mei-Ling to remain behind. The two stopped abruptly. Mason was already inside, and he closed the door behind the emperor.

"I expected to see you in the Senate meeting, Robert." Li Jaw-Long began as he approached the comfortably plush seating area. O'Leary was sitting at his designated seat at the head of the coffee table, leaving Li Jaw-Long and Mason the option to choose either sofa. Li Jaw-Long had known O'Leary for years and found it typical that he would demonstrate "alpha male" qualities by making sure he was seated at the head of the table for their discussion.

"I don't go to Senate meetings, Li." O'Leary explained as the emperor chose one of the sofas. "I only watched it on the monitors from here because I knew that you were there."

Mason sat on the sofa opposite Li Jaw-Long and smiled cordially. "May we ask why you decided to attend today's meeting?"

The emperor watched O'Leary for a moment before turning to reply to Mason's question. "I would think the answer is obvious, George." His posture was upright and erect. O'Leary was a trained profiler who had attended many meetings with the emperor over years. Judging from the emperor's body position, O'Leary knew that Li was not relaxed.

"Please tell us, so there are no misunderstandings." O'Leary stated.

"We had an agreement. You broke that agreement, and I am here to learn the details behind your actions."

"Li, we agreed to allow a representative from Shangri-La to intern in our government for four years, so your new nation could learn the politics of our country from the inside." Mason stated.

"And in turn you agreed to maintain a close relationship between our nations for decades, growing together as allies." O'Leary added.

"And it was understood that I did not want this representative placed in any danger. She was only to be in a position to observe how New America handles trade, negotiations, and other political affairs."

"Li, how could we have known that the convoy would be attacked?" O'Leary asked.

"You couldn't, Robert. That's my point. There was no way you could have guaranteed her safety; therefore, the representative should not have been placed in a position where she would be on foreign soil less than one hundred and twenty miles from a country that opposes your own. That, in my opinion, is too close for comfort."

"The threat assessments were very low." O'Leary explained, attempting to defend the decision.

"Oh? Then why was there a need for military escort if there was no threat?" Li stared at the Americans, awaiting an answer that neither could give.

Mason sighed, surrendering to the error in judgment. "We apologize."

"To make matters worse, you invited the man who rescued my representative and your senators to a congratulatory ceremony, only to subject him to persecution and accusations." Li scolded, his tone growing increasingly harsh. "I'm impressed that he remained long enough to receive a medal after such an insulting display. Tell me, Robert, is it your country's practice to strike someone immediately after kissing them?"

"No, it's not," O'Leary replied, withering under Li's hardened stare.

"This is not how I would expect a hero to be treated." Li stated as he stood up. Mason was surprised at the abruptness of his action but stood as well. "This is not the behavior that Shangri–La should be in alliance with." At those words, O'Leary stood as well.

"Wait, Li! Are you saying that you're canceling our alliance agreement?" O'Leary asked.

Li looked from O'Leary's stony face to the compassionate expression in Mason's eyes. His first thought was if he said yes, they would find a reason to arrest him while he was still on New American soil, as they had attempted with Captain Phoenix. He considered that was his anger speaking, though. He could see that Mason could not understand that O'Leary's level of comfort was due to over three decades of them doing business together, though there was no formal record of such dealings. Besides, there was a reason why Li had brought a helicopter aircraft carrier to accompany his private yacht. Caution was most prudent in times such as these. Li took a moment to compose himself before answering the question.

"No. I am emotional at the moment. Emotional and disgusted. It is never wise to make decisions in this state of being." he said with a kinder, understanding tone. "All will remain as we agreed. I will speak to my representative to make sure she is willing to continue forward, then I will return to Shangri–La and consider our options."

"Thank you, Li." Mason smiled politely, unhappy at how quickly the situation had nearly exploded. "And I apologize again for what took place today."

Li walked toward the door with Mason at his side. O'Leary remained a few steps behind them, assessing the situation as he walked. Before exiting the room, Li turned to face Mason.

"You are the senior vice president, in charge of all vice presidents, am I correct?" he asked, though both men knew he was already aware.

"Yes," Mason confirmed, sounding wary of the question.

Li turned to look at O'Leary. "And you, Robert, are in charge of all international affairs, correct?"

"You know I am, Li."

"Then it is my advice that you both should work together to get better control of your vice president of Homeland Security. She is becoming like a spoiled child in a house with no adult supervision, or an untrained dog that does not know its place in the presence of its master."

"We will be speaking to her today." Mason assured him, blushing slightly.

"I can promise you that!" O'Leary said, not taking kindly to the verbal scolding due to his colleague's actions.

"That is good." Li said, nodding. Then his face hardened into that of a dangerous warrior. "Keep your bitch in her place, or she will try to bite the wrong master one day, and you will be held accountable for her actions!"

He did not wait for a response before leaving the two men.

O'Leary paced angrily after the emperor left.

"What are you thinking?" Mason asked.

"Who the hell does he think he is, calling a vice president of New America a bitch? That son of a bitch has no right to tell us how to run our people!"

"No, he doesn't, but you know he's right. Karen made us look bad out there today." Mason was more frustrated at the overall situation than at Li's attitude.

"I know he's right!" O'Leary admitted. "It just pisses me off that he had to be there to see it. What the hell was she thinking, using the Senate meeting for her damned advanced technology agenda? She's going to put this country in a position we won't be able to pull away from."

"I know. She means well, but she can't see that she's doing it all wrong." Mason said. "She's allowing her hatred for one man to change her view of the big picture."

"What do you mean?" O'Leary asked.

"Come on, Bob," Mason said, exasperated. "The emperor of Shangri-La pulls up in a hovering limousine with no visible sign of propulsion, and she's trying to frame Phoenix on some bullshit charge just to harass him for technology. The one with the most advanced technology in the world obviously just walked out of this room."

"You have a point, George," O'Leary agreed. "That's why I want to keep Shangri-La as our ally. We can't afford to have them as an enemy. We would all love to have the best toys on the playground, but trying to take them from everyone else by force is not how we do it anymore."

Mason shook his head. "No, no it's not. That was the former

leadership during desperate times, and she knows that! We need to keep her in check before this gets completely out of hand. Now I have to wait a week to let Li calm down before seeing where his head is with our future trade plans. At least Shangri-La wants what we want, and they're willing to go about it the right way."

"What does that mean?" O'Leary asked.

"Kris told me that Jun asked Phoenix if he would be interested in selling the plans for those flying battle bikes. Then Li came here, and Karen tried to claim them like we have a right to them." Mason spoke with more composure, having released his frustration out of his system.

"Yes, you're right, George. She's got it out for him. She won't let the past go."

"Or it's something else."

"Whatever it is, we need to talk to her today!"

"Okay. I have a quick meeting with Stan and Kris, then I'll meet you in your office." Mason said, looking at his watch.

"Yes, and try not to make it look so obvious next time."

"What do you mean?" Mason asked.

"You know damn well you didn't know anything about any tracker until today." O'Leary snapped. Mason said nothing, just stared back at O'Leary. After a moment of silence, O'Leary smiled, "But I give you points for backing up each other's bullshit."

Mason smiled slightly on his way out.

18

OUTDOOR BRIEFING

∼

T he *Blood Sky* team looked grim as they walked out of the Capitol building . Once they were far enough away from the entrance to be free from prying ears, Phoenix halted the group. The protection team surrounded their principals, facing outward and monitoring to make sure no one was listening.

"Okay, now's the time to say what's on your mind," Phoenix said as they stood in a semicircle facing one another.

"That could have gone better." Swan said before letting out a deep sigh.

"Dad," Kite began, her brow furrowed with frustration, "I don't understand. Why were you trying to piss her off?"

"You don't know what you're talking about." Warlord replied. "Your father was working on a strategy."

"Can we talk about this in the Juggernaut?" Talon asked.

"We're fine here." Phoenix said, staring at their surroundings. He wanted to be standing right where they were. He was looking for something that only an outside vantage point could provide.

Phoenix took a deep breath of fresh air while he looked away from his family to gather his thoughts. He noticed the Shangri–La emperor and his entourage exiting the building with Jun Li. She was walking beside Mei–Ling, comfortably close to the emperor.

"Strategy?" Swan turned to Warlord, surprised at his comment, practically ignoring her brother's interjection. "She's the vice president of the Department of Homeland Security!"

Phoenix took note that Emperor Li Jaw–Long, Mei–Ling, Kenji, and Jun had gathered in a formation identical to his family's own.

"Do you realize how much trouble she can make for us, Uncle Aaron?" Kite hissed. She and Swan were playing off each other's feelings, as always. It was the invisible gossamer thread that always seemed to bind the twins together.

Li, Mei–Ling, Jun, and Kenji stood near the limousine speaking quietly to one another. The police and the military had fortified the physical barricades, assuring them that no one was standing within earshot.

"You wanted to see me, your majesty?" Jun asked, bowing. The emperor regarded her for a moment before speaking.

"Yes," he began, speaking in the coded language of Shangri–La that was rarely spoken in public outside of their country. "I'm glad that I can finally see in person that you have not been seriously harmed." he said, concealing his true emotions.

Jun looked around at her surroundings outside of the protection perimeter before responding. Reporters were still recording everyone who exited the building, so they had to keep up appearances. Finally, she bowed again. "Thank you."

The emperor smiled pleasantly for a moment and then

frowned. "I have concerns regarding the Americans' display of loyalty in the presentation I witnessed today. It was disgraceful."

"Yes, your imperial majesty." she replied. "I was not expecting that. I am ashamed you had to see it."

"Jun, if this is how they treat the man who rescued their politicians, how can we trust them in future dealings with Shangri-La?" Mei-Ling asked.

"They're not all like Vice President Harp." Jun said.

"We can see that," Kenji said, "but this is just one of many concerns."

"What are the other concerns, Shogun Kenji?" Jun asked, though she realized that no one would agree with her assessment. Only she had spent time living and working with the New American government staff. Her greatest fear was that the situation would end negatively for her and her country.

"They are divided as a leadership group." Kenji said with disappointment. "They invited our emperor to this meeting because you were involved in the abduction, and instead of us witnessing a ceremony of gratitude, we witnessed a disgraceful display of disloyalty to a man who was apparently once one of their own. There was no honor in what we saw from the Americans today."

"I now have great concern for your safety in this country, Jun." Li admitted as he stared into her eyes. She knew he had already made his decision, but she decided to protest anyway.

"Your majesty, this is not the usual behavior of the American Senate." she said, unable to keep the desperation out of her tone.

"It no longer matters." Li replied. "You are to resign from your position in New America, effective immediately. You can tell them you are distraught from the hostage situation."

"Yes, Father." Jun whispered, sadness in her eyes.

Jun knew that it was the right decision and had foreseen this happening from the moment she was rescued. Her life in New America was at an end. She had learned so much and become accustomed to the American way of life. In New America she was a regular person. She could travel and socialize like normal people. She enjoyed the freedom, but soon she would resume her identity on the secluded island of Shangri–La as the daughter of the nation's emperor.

Kenji gazed at his surroundings, allowing a moment to let the decision sink in. He stopped to look at Phoenix, who was watching them.

"What about Phoenix?" Kenji asked. The emperor turned to look at Phoenix and the rest of the *Blood Sky* team.

"There seemed to be a lot of tension surrounding Captain Phoenix today, and it all came from Vice President Harp and the commodore." Li said. "Although the senators seemed to be focusing on the good deed he did, the other two continually pressed their suspicions to implicate Phoenix in something criminal. It was a bullying display of their political power against a man who should be regarded as a hero."

"Yes, father, I noticed that too." Mei–Ling agreed.

Jun glanced at her younger sister, annoyed that she felt the need to speak when she knew as well as Jun that their father preferred silence as he weighed various scenarios in his mind.

"They lost today, but the commodore did not accept defeat easily, and as a military man, it's probably that he will try again when the situation is in his favor," the emperor said, turning to look at Kenji as if in confirmation.

"That will not be in a meeting room." Kenji stated. "He will likely attempt to challenge Phoenix again in a place where politicians can't interfere. It will probably be after they leave the harbor, so they can reduce negative feedback from citizens of the island or the media."

"As a military leader, that's where he's comfortable." Mei-Ling added.

"Yes," Li agreed, nodding. "I believe Captain Phoenix's life is in danger."

Jun could not explain it, but those words gave her a nervous feeling deep within. Like her father, she did not like it when people were bullied. Although Captain Phoenix had demonstrated that he could handle almost anything that came his way, Jun didn't feel comfortable just watching from the sidelines.

"I agree, your majesty." Kenji replied.

Li returned his attention to Jun. "Does he trust you?"

Jun glanced at Phoenix and then back at her father. "He doesn't know me very well, but I believe he will trust me if I give him reason." She wasn't sure if she was speaking from observation or from personal desire.

"Very well." the emperor said. "Once we board Knight Spear and are out of New America's territory, I want you to take Black Arrow and your escorts to Blood Sky."

"Your majesty?" Jun was shocked. She knew he would use her to contact Phoenix, but she hadn't expected him to do it so openly.

"If my royal airship is visiting Blood Sky as a guest, the New American government would not dare to take aggressive action against Blood Sky or its crew without risking repercussions from Shangri-La." the emperor explained.

"Very wise, your majesty." Mei-Ling bowed and smiled at her sister. "Your presence on the ship will protect the crew of Blood Sky."

"Ask Captain Phoenix to allow you to remain on the ship until it has cleared New America waters." the emperor added.

"Yes, your majesty, but won't it look suspicious to him?" she asked.

"Be honest with him. Tell him I would take it as a personal favor if he allowed you to carry out this assignment."

"Yes, your majesty," she responded with a more pleasant expression. "May I be permitted one detour before I resign my position here?"

"Where?"

"Reconnaissance on Karen Harp. I believe there is more to her actions today than what she said in the meeting." Her brow furrowed in determination. "If I'm caught as a government employee, my security clearance will justify me being in the building. But after I resign, they'll take my badge, and I won't have the free access I have right now."

"Permission granted." the emperor agreed, nodding at Kenji. He removed a small case the size of a checkbook from his inner suit pocket and handed it to Jun.

"Attach the adhesive patch to any material. It has a range of approximately five city blocks. The patch will dissolve in approximately twenty hours after being applied. Then the untraceable signal will end."

She opened the thin box and stared at the flat, transparent circular object inside as well as the skin-colored wireless earpiece beside it.

"Thank you, Shogun." She bowed slightly before closing the box and putting it in her pocket.

"You have until the end of the day to learn what you can about Harp." her father said. "Then you are to return to the yacht, so we can leave this country, hopefully for good. We leave at sunset."

"Yes, your majesty." Jun bowed. "Thank you, Father."

～

Phoenix watched Jun as she bowed to the emperor before turning and walking back toward the building's front entrance.

"And why show them the goggles, Axel?" Swan demanded.

"Because Dad told me to." Talon said.

"But why, Daddy?" Swan turned to her father, but he was busy watching as Emperor Li Jaw-Long and his companions returned to their deluxe limousine as it hovered above the street. The emperor altered the tint on his window from dark to clear, so he could meet Phoenix's gaze as the limousine and its police escort drove past, lights flashing. Li Jaw-Long shook his head so slightly that only Phoenix picked up on the movement. His expression did not change as the Shangri-La royal vehicles drove into traffic with the nation's flag on each front fender.

"Because I had to see what we were up against." Phoenix replied, finally turning back to face the others.

"And did you?" Swan challenged. He gave her a stern look in response to her disrespectful tone. Swan backed down and looked away.

"Yes, I did. I'll explain on the way back." Phoenix stated.

After climbing into the rear of the Juggernaut, Phoenix looked out the window and saw that Jun was standing at the entrance to the building, watching until the *Blood Sky* entourage drove away from the curb. He was troubled as he watched the pedestrian crowds of downtown Manhattan City out the window. With the police escort in front, the *Blood Sky* convoy moved through the streets at a steady pace, their lights flashing as they traveled back to Manhattan City Harbor. Kite finally broke the silence.

"Dad, what's going on? What happened back there that we didn't see?"

"We need to leave York Jersey as soon as possible," Phoenix said.

"But why?" Swan asked, clearly frustrated. "We just got here! I thought we were going to stay for a few more days."

"Do you think it was a coincidence that we were invited to an opportunity for congratulations that turned into an impromptu trial?" he asked.

"Yeah, Ward and Harp came there to arrest us on the spot." Warlord said.

"Or at least board Blood Sky." Phoenix remarked.

"Why?" Talon asked.

"They're looking for advanced technology, like they said." Phoenix sighed. "Harpy has always had a weakness for having the best tech. She claims it's to keep New America on top, but I think it's vanity driven."

"Always?" Swan asked. "You know Vice President Harp personally?"

"Professionally." Phoenix corrected. Warlord stared at his cousin, eager to reveal the truth that Phoenix had withheld for so long. Phoenix saw it in his eyes and gave him a subtle nod of approval.

"She's the reason why we can never use our real names in public anymore," Warlord said bitterly, "why we had to become ghosts without a past." Warlord had told Phoenix on many occasions that his children had a right to know the truth, but Phoenix had become so accustomed to keeping government secrets from everyone, including his family, that he had Warlord promise to keep his trust. However, with them having to leave the country of their birth again, for God knew how long this time, Phoenix finally yielded and allowed the giant to speak on the matter.

"I'm confused," Kite said, a troubled frown on her face. "I thought that was because you survived a mission that should have killed you."

"Harp ordered the mission." Warlord explained, his voice

filled with resentment at the memory. "When things went sideways, she decided that New America should disassociate itself with the mission. Then to wash her hands of everything, she announced to the world that we were KIA."

"Killed in action?" Swan asked in surprise. Phoenix felt her eyes on him as he continued to look out the window. He never stopped listening to the conversation, but he wanted to enjoy the sights of the city he loved so much. He thought back to his youth and the flourishing city of Manhattan prior to 2029. He often reminisced about those times. He was fascinated at the fact the Hudson River was gone, and the bridges and tunnels that had connected old New Jersey to New York City were no longer needed, as it had all become one landmass. He accepted with a heavy heart that to protect his family and crew he had to make yet another decision that they would find unfavorable.

"She conveniently forgot to mention that she sanctioned us to be in that particular foreign territory." Phoenix said. "We found out later that Harp was told specifically that New America was not authorized, but she sent us anyway. To her we were expendable weapons."

"She had us steal their technology and had us believing we were the heroes, but we came out as the bad guys," Warlord said. "Stealing technology. Sound familiar?"

"She's nothing if not consistent." Phoenix said, chuckling sarcastically.

"Consistently dangerous!" Warlord said.

"And she has the title to take everything from us if she can find a legal reason." Swan realized.

"Only in New America." Talon pointed out.

As if on cue, Phoenix reached for his cell phone just as it started buzzing. The others looked at him with puzzled expressions. As far as they knew, everyone who had Phoenix's personal cell phone number was in the Juggernaut at that moment.

"Is that Blood Sky?" Warlord asked.

"No, it's a text from Kris." Phoenix said while looking at his phone.

"What does it say?" Swan and Kite asked at the same time.

Phoenix looked up with a disturbed expression. "'Get out' in all caps."

Warlord immediately keyed up the vehicle's communication transmitter.

"Blood Sky, Warlord."

"Go with your traffic, Warlord." Athena replied.

"Per the captain, recall all crew members from shore leave, and prepare for immediate departure once everyone's onboard."

"Roger that, Commander." Athena confirmed. "Blood Sky out."

Swan sank in her seat as Kite turned to Phoenix with a worried look on her face. As Phoenix stared out the window, he realized he wouldn't be seeing that familiar scenery again for a long time.

19

OUR ALLIES, THE ENEMY, AND A SPY

～

Deck Chief Marcus Medina stood at the entrance to *Blood Sky's* main cargo area as crates were brought in one at a time. When his cell phone rang, he answered it, somewhat frustrated at the interruption.

"Medina."

"Marcus, the captain is on his way back, so make sure there's room available for immediate loading of the Juggernaut." Athena said. "He's ordering an immediate recall of all crew on leave. Have someone recall your team while you finish your loading."

"Roger that, Athena." Medina disconnected the call as two wooden crates were brought up the ramp. He sighed deeply and then resumed his duties.

"Last-minute arrival, Chief." the deckhand steering the first pallet jack said from the controls.

"What is it?" Medina asked as he peered around the crate.

"I don't know, but there's two of them." the deckhand replied, speaking in an Australian accent.

"They're not on my list."

"That's what I told the delivery truck, but they said it was a rush from the Capitol."

Medina found a shipping label attached to the side of one of the crates with a note inside. "It says, 'Captain Phoenix, sorry for the late delivery, I had a hard time finding enough wine for your entire crew. Here are two crates of red and white wine as a show of our appreciation. Thank you for saving our lives.' It's digitally signed by Senator Chadwick Gash." Medina looked up at the deckhand, who was already smiling.

"It's about time somebody gave us some proper love, mate!" the deckhand said.

"Open it." Medina ordered.

"But it's from a senator, Chief." the deckhand responded cautiously.

"It doesn't matter. SOP states all shipments not preapproved get checked."

"Yes, Chief." The deckhand began prying the crate open. Medina smiled at the rack of red wine at the top row of the case, each bottle surrounded by soft synthetic straw-like material.

"Wifey's going to love this!" Medina smiled as he grabbed a bottle by the neck and looked at it.

"I wonder when the cap will let us drink it."

"Probably after we're out to sea." Medina said. "He's ordered us to rush all cargo loading, so we can leave as soon as everyone is back from shore leave."

"Is there trouble?"

"You know they don't tell me anything." He put the bottle back in its slot in the rack and scanned the label to confirm that it was actually from Senator Chadwick Gash. "Confirm the other crate is white wine, and I'll add it to the cargo manifest."

"Yes, Chief."

Vice President Harp stood in the reception area giving her official take on the events of the meeting to a small gathering of reporters. She, like the reporters in front of her, knew that most of the information discussed in the meeting was classified, so she was careful not to disclose too much. News media celebrities Henry Royal and John Turner were among the many recognizable faces that Harp saw in the gathering of the elite press team from various news broadcast companies. Although Henry Royal had managed to maneuver his way to the front, Harp ignored him in favor of John Turner.

"The last question goes to you, Mr. Turner." Harp announced, frowning slightly at Royal.

"Thank you, Vice President Harp." Turner said with a smile as he stroked his blond hair like a model. "Can you tell us anything at all about the rescue of the senators and their party?"

"I can only tell you this," Harp said with a smile. "I'm proud to say that the senators and their administrative associates all made it back with a few minor bruises, but they are safe and alive thanks to the bravery of our New America Armed Forces and the leadership of the Vice–Presidential Council."

"You played a role in their rescue, Madam Vice President?" Royal blurted in surprise.

"Yes, I did. It was my colleagues and I who uncovered the plans to kidnap the delegate party, and it was our leadership that had a covert military strike team in the vicinity to launch an attack on those terrorists before it was too late."

"Then what caused the delay that allowed them to be captured?" Turner asked.

Harp's confidant smile faltered as she struggled to come up with an answer. "That was due to faulty civilian involvement, but we were able to adjust and find the hostages by using our advanced tracking system on the senators, which the terrorists were unable to locate. That's all I can say on that matter. No further questions."

Not wanting to be further confronted with questions that she was unable to answer or lie about, she turned to walk toward the elevators.

Suddenly, someone bumped into her, knocking her off balance. She turned, ready to reprimand her attacker, and found herself staring into the puffy eyes of Jun Li.

"Oh, I'm so sorry, Vice President Harp!" Jun said in surprise. "I should have been looking where I was going! I'm so sorry, ma'am."

"Miss Li, is it?"

"Yes, Madam Vice President." Jun said, sounding emotionally distraught as she looked up at the woman.

"It's okay. I understand. You've been through a lot." Harp replied. She glanced over her shoulder to see that news cameras and microphones were facing her interaction, trying to overhear whatever they could.

"I thought I had it under control, but I guess I don't. It keeps coming up in my mind at random times of the day." Jun said, fighting to hold back her emotional weakness. Harp smiled, knowing this would be the perfect opportunity for positive press.

"I'm so sorry, Jun. I can't imagine what you must be going through." she said, using a tone of comfort and support. "Why don't you ask Senator Gash for a few weeks off? Take all the time you need to take care of yourself after such a traumatic experience."

"Yes, ma'am, that's what I came back to do. I'm so sorry I bumped into you, Madam Vice President." Jun said with a slight bow and a sniffle.

"It's okay. Go and be safe." Harp said, resting a supportive hand on Jun's shoulder. Jun bowed again, then rushed down the hall wiping her eyes as if she was going to cry. She didn't bother to continue watching Jun. For her, the incident was over as quickly as it began. She adjusted her shoulder bag and resumed her pace to the elevator foyer.

Kopensky strode down the hallway, following George Mason and Stanley Clayton. The three men were the members of what Phoenix referred to as the Political Trinity, not because they were holy or religious men but because they were well connected, both to each other and everything within their leadership positions. The three men had a history together and a secret—and loyal—friendship with Phoenix.

Kopensky began his career in the Department of Transportation, where his genius at problem solving and increasing efficiency helped him rise quickly through the ranks. It didn't take long for him to be elected as the senator overseeing national transportation.

One of his early assignments was to join Mason in hand picking a commander to lead a team of specially trained combat personnel for highly classified non-military missions. He had no experience. Colonel Malo gave him candidates, and that was where he met Alexander Medjinn, who worked for an undisclosed, classified section of government but not in a military capacity.

They entered Clayton's office. He waited for the other two men to enter the office before closing the door.

"Now, do you want to tell me what the hell is going on with Phoenix?" Clayton snapped while walking to the far end of the office to sit behind his desk.

"That was Karen on another witch hunt again, Stan." Mason

began. "This time it's not Alex." Mason was the second and final interview that Alexander Medjinn had to do to secure the leadership position in this covert missions team. Mason had extensive experience and vast knowledge of politics, but he also had the advantage of working with covert civilian and military operations, such as the one that they had hired Medjinn to oversee. Mason looked at all options before making decisions or giving advice. When it came time to address areas for which he was unfamiliar, he was wise enough to know to hire experts in that field.

"I know what Karen was doing." Clayton said before turning to question him. "What was that crap about Phoenix installing a tracker in you? Was that the best you could come up with, Kris?"

"It's true, Stan." Kopensky said as he sat down in preparation for the lambasting that was about to follow. Mason and Clayton both looked at him in shock.

"But I thought you were buying time for Alex to come up with an answer," Mason said. "I had no idea that you were telling the truth."

"Why would I lie about something like that?"

"Kris, you let Alex experiment on you?" Clayton asked, stunned.

"No. He was the guinea pig, the first test subject, so I knew I wasn't a guinea pig, if that's what you mean. I looked at the test results and made a choice, one that saved my life."

"That was a huge risk, Kris." Mason said.

"Look, I trust him, and that trust saved not just my life but everyone else who was with me."

Clayton and Mason had been friends for years before meeting Kopensky. When Clayton broke off from the Senate circle to oversee the new government's military administrative branch, it skyrocketed his career into the office of vice president of the Department of Justice. He knew more about domestic military actions than even the president. Some said that Clayton was the most powerful man in the country because he headed special political and military operations that the president was not privy to so that the president could maintain plausible deniability in delicate matters if they were unsuccessful.

"So," Clayton began, pausing to think for a moment. "Alex and his crew really created an undetectable tracking device that's better than what we already have?" Clayton looked away then smiled. "That's genius! How does it work?"

"It's not a device. It's more like a serum. I don't get all the science behind it." Kopensky shrugged. "Tiny liquid molecules were injected into my bloodstream."

"That's it?" Mason asked, his face still showing concern. "How do you get it out?"

"From what I understand, I don't."

"What? Then what do we use to track you?"

"You can't. Only Blood Sky has the technology to track me."

"Well, I don't like that at all, Kris!" Clayton replied. "You realize we can't use this unless Alex gives us the equipment to track our people. We can't give Blood Sky, a non–American civilian ship, the only access to this tracking technology of our government leaders."

"Now you're sounding like Karen." Mason replied.

"Don't talk crazy, George! You know what I mean." Clayton stood up and began pacing before turning to the other two. "Karen does have a point though."

"Which is what?" Kopensky asked.

"Alex making all of these breakthroughs in technology and not sharing them makes it look like he's hoarding them for a power play later."

"Or he doesn't want us or anyone to get them and start another war." Kopensky said in his friend's defense. "You know he was always vocal about the fact that he felt we used our technological advantage to bully other countries to get what we wanted."

"Kris, are you saying you're OK with Alex being the only one with advanced weapons and technology?" Mason asked.

"You too, George?" Kopensky shook his head. "What about Shangri-La? The emperor showed up in a hovering limousine!"

"That's different." Clayton insisted.

"Why?"

"Because he represents a nation," Mason replied, "and Alex represents himself and a small crew on one ship."

"Think about this for a moment, Kris." Mason said. "One man with advanced technology, no national loyalties, and enough power could eventually take over the world. The only thing he would need would be an army."

"From what I can tell from the rescued senators' incident reports, Phoenix already has an army," Clayton said. "His Blood Sky mercenaries have beaten pirates better than most of our special forces personnel, and that's just the incidents that we know about. Hell, they took on a building filled with insurgents to rescue you, and they made it out without losing anyone."

"Then I really think you should be worried about Shangri-La, shouldn't you?" Kopensky asked.

"We don't know if Shangri-La even has an army or, if it does, what it's composed of." Mason stated.

"Which is my point, George."

"Emperor Li Jaw-Long is being handled by Bob. He has a personal relationship with the emperor. That's out of our hands," Clayton explained. "Alex is not."

"We have a personal connection to Alex that's more reliable than Bob's relationship with the emperor." Kopensky argued. "Doesn't that count?"

"You have a bond with Alex that's stronger than us, Kris. And until today, George and I had no idea that he was able to track your location to get you out of trouble."

"You two both know that Alex would never use his crew or his technology to go to war with everyone." Kopensky said. "At least, he didn't steal it like we used to. That's what instigated the last war. The whole fight for superiority and unconfirmed accusations got out of hand."

In the past they had all felt that when the time came, and Alexander Medjinn was ready for it, he would be perfect in the role that he hated most: political leadership. The way the other two men were talking about Phoenix now though, worried Kopensky.

Clayton continued to pace, deep in thought, and then stopped. "You know him better than we do." Clayton said, observing Kopensky's reaction as he spoke. "Can you say without a shadow of doubt that you believe he wouldn't use his technology against us or sell it to our enemies?"

"No doubt at all." Kopensky stared at Clayton without so much as a blink.

After a few moments of staring at each other, Clayton sighed deeply. "Let's say you're right. Who's to say that someone else wouldn't do it if they got their hands on that level of technology? And God knows what else Alex and his crew have thought up. You said that the things he let you and Chad see were only a small part of what his son might have developed on that ship." Clayton looked away, troubled.

"It's dangerous for a governing group not to have some sort of monitoring system in place for technological global improvements." Mason said.

"I'm just concerned that either way, whether Alex does it or someone else decides to grab it from him, if this gets out we may have just inadvertently made Blood Sky targets for every power-hungry, would-be dictator in the civilized world."

Mason and Kopensky nodded with mutual expressions of concern.

Harp stormed down the office corridor of the Capitol building. When she reached her office, she walked past the receptionist area, which was empty, before entering her office and closing the door.

Inside her conservatively decorated office, Harp dialed a number on her cell phone and then began pacing frantically.

"What the hell is going on?" she snapped into the phone. It was obvious that whomever she was talking to, she considered the person her subordinate, but in Harp's eyes, most people were her subordinates. "I told you I want that technology, not excuses!" Harp paced harder, practically stomping as she walked. She was not used to being turned down, and she hated it more because it was Medjinn of all people who had beaten and embarrassed her in front of her peers.

"You listen to me and listen well, you damn idiot! You told me that the Medjinn monkey has better weapons than anything I showed you, and I want them all! There's no way that that damn menace to society should be able to outdo New America! No way in hell! That bastard will probably sell his technology to the highest bidder or give a discount to his spear–chucking relatives!" Harp continued to pace as she listened to the voice on the other end.

In a parking structure near the Capitol building, Jun Li sat in her car alone. She had her earpiece in and was taking coded notes of everything she heard. She knew not to document anything on her phone or on a digital tablet that could be hacked, so she wrote everything down on a small notepad.

While Jun could only hear Harp's side of the conversation, she felt that it was enough to gather information that would be useful in the future. The angrier Harp became, the easier it was to hear what she was saying.

"Hell no, I don't believe his junior jigaboo son made any of those things! He's a fucking descendant of slaves and apes, for Christ's sake! They're not smart enough to make shit! But they might have kidnapped someone to duplicate the technology, either that or they stole it from somewhere else."

Jun stiffened, startled at the colorful racial metaphors that Harp was spouting. This was not the same woman whom she had known and respected professionally.

Harp continued to pace in her office while huffing and puffing her frustration into her phone. "And that overgrown junior tar baby is going to pay for embarrassing me in front of the Senate committee like that." Harp paused to listen to the person on the other end of the line. "What? Of course, I'm wearing red lace underwear, you dolt! Why else would I be embarrassed! You're a fucking moron!"

Harp sighed deeply and dropped into her office chair, mentally exhausted and frustrated. She was certain that a Black man couldn't have the ingenuity to create the weaponry she was seeking. No, Medjinn didn't have the mental capacity to do anything more than run around and shoot guns. She just needed a moment to gather her wits and calm down, but that was hard when her subordinates asked stupid questions.

"Of course, I already started my alternate plans! You think I'm just going to let that shit-skinned menace leave with weapons that New America could use? Just do your part, and don't fuck this one up!"

Harp disconnected the call. Her stress and irritation were so high that she could barely focus. After another moment of thought, she stood and grabbed her shoulder bag. "Ugh, I could use a good fuck!" With that said, she walked out of the office, turning off the lights as she went.

Jun's eyes widened in response to Harp's last comment. For years Jun had held Harp in high regard for, as a woman, having reached such a high position in New America's government. However, now Jun's opinion of Harp was forever marred. She realized this was not someone who should have such a powerful position as the head of Homeland Security, controlling espionage and military for an entire country. It was unfortunate that Jun could not inform anyone of her findings without admitting that she had been monitoring Harp's conversation.

Other than her family, there was only one person that she felt comfortable talking to about this new discovery. It was unfortunate that he was also the same person who was the target of this tyrant. Her father had been right again. New America was not what it appeared to be, and Phoenix was in grave danger.

20

OUT TO SEA

⌁

E mperor Li Jaw-Long watched from the deck of his super yacht as *Blood Sky* sailed away, leaving the Manhattan City Harbor. He had mixed feelings for the captain and the crew after what they had experienced earlier that day. He felt that it would be best if he remained silent on the issue and watched how things developed from the safety of his own country's borders, but part of him wanted to defend the valiant crew who had saved his daughter. As he heard a familiar car approaching, he decided that would be a solution for another time.

The driver of the limousine stepped out and opened the rear door, allowing Jiayang to step out with poise and grace. She was taken aback at the size of the luxurious multilevel black yacht with the large flag of Shangri-La on its bow. It was the *Knight Spear*, the royal transportation for the emperor and his family. Ms. Jiayang Chu paused to admire the legendary passenger vessel. She smiled when she saw the emperor standing in the bow, relaxed as he watched her.

Jiayang waited patiently as two crewmen removed her luggage from the limousine's trunk.

One of the men in the emperor's protective team was standing at the end of the gangplank waiting as the driver escorted Jiayang to the bottom of the ramp. The suited samurai gestured politely for her to continue to the ship, where she saw that Kenji was waiting at the opposite side of the gangplank.

Upon reaching the end of the ramp, she stepped onto the super yacht. The crewmen stood behind her with her luggage, waiting patiently. Kenji smiled pleasantly as she looked around.

"Allow me to be the first to welcome you to Shangri-La, Ms. Chu." Kenji said with the politest of expressions and a smile that she found surprisingly warm. She responded in kind, excited at the prospect of the new life that awaited her.

As the sun began to set, *Blood Sky* was exiting Manhattan City Harbor. A few crew members stood on the deck watching as the familiar harbor faded into the distance. With all that had happened, the crew had no idea when they would return to the shores of New America. What started out as a simple rescue mission had ended with each crew member saying goodbye to friends and family in their own manner.

The ship's combat training center was a small gym and lounge reserved for elite crew members like SOCIT, the Ravens, and the protection team. Nitro knew there was a question mark regarding who exactly was on the protection team and who were members of her Ninja team. She smiled to herself as she told them time and time again how the protection team was on an as-needed basis and always a combination of the three primary assault teams onboard, but many people still didn't get it.

A few members of the Raven team sat with her on the

padded mat as others worked out around them. It was a somber moment. There was little conversation from any of them as they all watched the view out the window. Finally, Raptor broke the silence.

"Somebody, say something!"

"Like what, Pops?" Deacon asked with frustration.

"Why did we all get pulled from a three–day shore leave? What happened in that meeting?" Raptor looked at Hawk and Eagle for an answer.

"Yeah, guys," Nitro said while returning to her stretches on the floor. "Did Phoenix tell you anything?"

Deacon stopped punching the heavy bag to wipe his face and listen as Hawk and Eagle dropped their weights to explain.

"Everything was going smoothly," Hawk began, choosing his words carefully, "until that red-headed VP of Homeland Security started up."

"Who?" Nitro asked. She didn't care much for politics, so the members of the vice presidential council were as interesting to her as instant pho in the supermarket.

"Karen Harp." Eagle said. The name meant nothing to Nitro, so she just shrugged and listened.

"Didn't Phoenix have some beef with her a while back?" Deacon asked.

"Yeah. She's the racist bitch who was dogging out a Dominican subcommander assigned to her but under Phoenix's command." Eagle explained, "Phoenix brought her up on charges, but because the guy didn't want to follow through with documenting all the things that Harp did and said, Harp got off with a warning."

"I didn't know that." Pops said, looking out the window at York Jersey. "But what's that got to do with us leaving?"

"In the meeting, Harp was trying to say that we're pirates or smugglers." Hawk replied.

"She wants to give the Senate a reason to board Blood Sky and take whatever tech she can get her hands on." Eagle added.

"How would that be legal?" Deacon asked.

"That was the problem." Eagle explained, "She was trying to tell the Senate committee that there was no way we could have known where Gash and Kopensky were unless we were the ones who snatched them and then played hero."

"The woman's crazy!" Hawk said. "She's really got it in for Phoenix. I could tell that she and her soldier–boy lacky were trying anything to take him down and us with him."

"Bitch can try!" Nitro blurted.

"I don't get it," Raptor said. "How does that red-headed vampire know what we have?"

"Senator Kopensky saw that the Senate was siding with Harp, so he told them about the tracking enzyme." Falcon explained. The others responded with a mixture of surprise and disappointment.

"Yeah, now they want it and probably anything else they saw while they were on the ship." Eagle added.

"Great!" Nitro sighed. "Now it makes perfect sense. We're leaving to make sure we're out of New America before Harp can figure out a way to make her search stick."

"Yes," Falcon agreed, nodding. "Once we're past the three–mile marker of New America's waters, maritime law takes effect and protects us from what Harp could have pulled off in the harbor."

"Dagnabbit! I really wanted to spend some time in the city!" Raptor grunted. Hawk and Eagle chuckled to themselves.

"'Dagnabbit,' Pops?" Eagle smiled. "Where do you come up with these words, old man?"

"Look it up and respect the classics, yah young Al Capone wannabe." Raptor snapped in his usual grumpy tone.

"Attention, Blood Sky crew. This is your captain speaking."

Phoenix's voice rang through the public address system of every speaker throughout the ship. Nitro continued stretching while listening to the announcement.

"Here we go." Deacon looked up at the speakers in the corners of the ceiling.

"It is unfortunate that you had to cut your shore leave short, but it was a necessary act to protect the safety and well-being of the crew and the freedom that we believe in." Phoenix paused for a moment. "We have set course for the Florida Strait and then the Central Ocean, where we will pick up our new assignment from Cuba, transporting grain and medical supplies to Brazil."

Nitro looked around the room as everyone's expressions lightened, and smiles broke out.

"We will make delivery to the government and be welcomed, as always, by the Brazilian residents. Then we'll celebrate!" A smile could be heard in Phoenix's voice.

Everyone in the room cheered.

Throughout the ship the sound of cheering could be heard. The celebration stopped abruptly when the announcement was interrupted when the strobe lights that were positioned near every speaker on the ship began flashing amber. Along with the amber alert flashes came the gradual pulsation of a siren.

In the combat training center, everyone in the room tensed up as they awaited the direction that was to follow.

"Action stations, action stations!" Athena announced over the PA system. "We have an amber alert! I repeat, we have an amber alert! An unidentified aircraft is approaching from the coast. All security and combat personnel, report to your action stations, and prepare for defensive maneuvers. Flight deck, begin preparing Lola for launch in the hangar bay. This is not a drill! I repeat, this is not a drill!"

Without another word, the crew members rushed off in different directions.

In the helicopter hangar bay, Swan began doing emergency flight check procedures while preparing *Lola* to be towed out onto the deck. Talon jumped into the copilot's seat to assist his older sister. Swan and Talon had been through many amber and red alerts, so they knew all the procedures and were able to complete them as a team faster than any other two pilots on the ship.

A few members of SOCIT joined them, placing guns onto their designated mounts in the cargo hold. They brought their duffle bags of gear into Lola in case an attack from land or another ship was imminent. Once Lola's rear gate began to close, the flight deck crew began pulling the helicopter out of the hangar bay and onto the large flight deck.

In the smaller portion of the hangar bay, the Ravens mounted their Enduros and moved into position on the secondary flight deck, ready to launch into the night sky and attack whatever was coming.

Warlord hurried to the farthest portion of the stern to look up at the sky. He frowned as the sound of an aircraft in the distance grew louder. Even over the sound of *Blood Sky's* siren, his keen sense of hearing was able to distinguish the approaching ship. He put on the prototype pair of the SPEX goggles and scanned the darkness between *Blood Sky* and the coast of York Jersey Island.

"I know that helicopter engine." he said in surprise. When he finally spotted it, he stared at the glossy black helicopter with an insignia on the nose. It was the flag representing the combined nation of Asian culture: Shangri–La.

"Bridge, this is Warlord," he said into his transmitter. "Are you seeing this?"

Phoenix sat at his desk while the amber alert siren sounded at a lower volume in his quarters. From his desk he was able to monitor the entire ship, including the exterior cameras that were focused on the approaching craft.

"Captain, Warlord." Warlord said through the radio. Phoenix pulled the small handheld cylindrical radio from its charger.

"Go, Warlord."

"Captain, the bridge has confirmed that the incoming aircraft is identifying itself as the Shangri–La imperial transport Black Arrow and is requesting to land."

"What are their intentions?" Phoenix asked while continuing to watch the incoming aircraft on his monitor.

"They say they have a delegate requesting an emergency meeting with you, sir." Athena replied over the radio. Phoenix watched as the helicopter stopped advancing and began to hover, no doubt at the direction of *Blood Sky's* bridge crew.

"Permission granted." he said dryly.

"Roger that, sir." Athena replied. "Permission to cancel the amber alert, sir?"

"Permission granted." Phoenix sat back in his high–back executive office chair as the helicopter resumed its advance toward *Blood Sky*. He smiled in admiration. He had not seen *Black Arrow* in a long time.

Once the alarm went silent, the deck crew towed *Lola* back into the helicopter hangar bay to make room on the flight deck for *Black Arrow*.

As the destroyer's floodlights shone on the descending helicopter, the national colors of red and gold with white frame trimming were now clearly visible on the black chopper. These were the national colors of Shangri–La, born from the unity of what used to be Vietnam, Japan, China, and Korea. SOCIT members were still on the flight deck in their civilian clothing but heavily armed in standby readiness.

When Manh and Alvin stepped out of the helicopter, they were wearing stylish blood–red business suits with thin armored vests beneath the blazers, disguised in a fashionable manner. The two Asian men had their firearms and bladed weapons holstered and sheathed as they looked around before signaling for the VIP passenger to exit the craft.

Talon walked onto the upper flight deck with Swan as the occupants exited the chopper. Warlord was already at the main flight deck and was standing by to receive the passengers. Falcon walked over to stand with Swan and Talon. They watched with surprise as Jun Li stepped out of the helicopter, greeted by Warlord with a smile and a head bow. Falcon smiled as she looked at Swan, unable to resist the obvious question.

"Talon, what's Miss Li doing on a Shangri–La imperial chopper?"

"I honestly have no idea," Talon replied, shaking his head in bewilderment.

"It looks like there's more to Miss Jun Li than we were told." Swan said, her face expressionless as she watched.

～

Phoenix continued watching his monitors, focused on Jun exiting the helicopter and being escorted from the helipad by Warlord. Phoenix was expressionless as he turned off his surveillance equipment, a three-dimensional image of a gold coin floating as it spun clockwise returning to the screen. A griffin was imprinted in the center of the coin on one side. Its wings were away from its body but not fully extended, as if it were ready to expand and fly at a moment's notice. It was a powerful-looking beast, even in its relaxed pose. The band that covered the outer edge of the coin displayed eight Greek letters, positioned in two groups of four. The first four letters were Alpha, Tau, Gamma, and Lambda. The next four letters were Nu, Upsilon, Iota, and Chi.

On the back of the coin was the image of the same griffin, only the wings of the mythical beast were outstretched while it sat perched on the coin's inner circle. Its front talons, back claws, and thick lion's tail rested comfortably over the ring. Behind the griffin was the top portion of *Blood Sky*, including its tall mast. Above its head and outstretched wings were the words "God Is with Us." These were the words spoken by the ancient Medjai tribes prior to going into battle or leaving their brethren.

At the top of the back side coin were raised letters that spelled "GRIFFIN OF MEDJAI." At the bottom of the coin below the griffin was the coin description "1 OZ * FINE GOLD * 999.9 * 2036." This signified the actual weight of the coin, the material the coin was made from, the coin's gold percentage, it's purity level, and the year it was pressed.

Phoenix stared at the image for a few moments, then bowed his head and closed his eyes, as if in silent prayer. When he opened his eyes, he kissed his fingertips, then touched the coin on the screen.

Jun Li's arrival and timing raised many questions for him. He was naturally suspicious of anything unexpected. He often received premonitions. For this reason there was little chance of surprising him. On rare occasions when he was taken by surprise, his personal radar became heightened, allowing him to be prepared for the worst-case scenario.

As he stared at Jun's image on the monitor, he found her to be an attractive woman who could easily seduce a man with simple words and the right stare. For that reason he felt the need to be cautious of her presence on his ship only hours after he had received a warning to leave the country.

Phoenix turned away from the monitor and looked out the window. Jun wanted to see him. He had not been alone with a woman since his wife. Although there had been potential suitresses, none held his interest long enough to make a difference. Now there was this woman. Kopensky had connected Jun to a woman who had visited Phoenix in his dreams from time to time. Were they dreams, premonitions, or the expression of a subconscious desire? Was Jun the woman from his reoccurring dream of more than ten years? Phoenix turned away from the window, deep in thought.

21

EMISSARY

～

"Come in." Phoenix said in reply to the knock at his door. When the door opened, Warlord stepped aside to allow Jun Li to enter.

Warlord flashed a smile at Phoenix as he closed the door behind him. Phoenix did not respond to his cousin's silent show of approval.

"It's bigger than I expected." Jun said while looking around Phoenix's quarters. Phoenix hid his amusement from Jun as he imagined Warlord's temptation to peek back in the room to find out what she was referring to.

Phoenix focused on Jun as she looked around the cabin, admiring the balance of modern technology with the antique warship's design.

"I had to cut away a few walls, but I figure since I spend most of my free time here, I should make it comfortable," Phoenix said. "The next one will be bigger."

"The next one?" Jun looked at him with a puzzled expression. "Do you mean the captain's quarters or the ship?"

He watched her for a moment, wondering how he should respond. "Are you asking as a member of the American Senate or as a representative of Shangri-La?" he asked. Jun frowned as he continued. "You're obviously more than a senator's staff member to have access to a foreign government's fuel-powered helicopter."

Jun merely smiled in reply as she walked around the room like a tourist strolling through a museum. It allowed Phoenix a moment to admire her beauty in silence. Although her hair was in one braid down her back, it was exceptionally longer than he expected, with the tip ending just above the small of her back. He was momentarily distracted at the estimation that her hair flowed past her waist when allowed to flow free. She stopped to stare at a gold mask that was positioned on a podium at the far end of the room. After glancing at Phoenix, she approached the artifact.

"This is beautiful." Jun said softly, as if a loud voice would damage the artwork.

"Thank you." Phoenix said as he walked toward her, smiling proudly at the artifact. Jun bent over slightly to examine the details.

"It looks Egyptian." she said as she continued to study the sculpture. "I studied ancient art, but I've never seen this piece before. Is it a complimentary rendering that was made for you?" Jun wondered.

He frowned in confusion. "What do you mean?"

"Why did you have it made to look like you? Is this how you see yourself?" Jun asked, scrutinizing the detail that went into the shaping of the face. The headpiece was adorned, and above the brow, it was striped in gold, sapphire, and black-onyx gemstones, which matched the necklace draped over the shoulders. A golden griffin sat proudly on the band above the forehead.

"I didn't have that made. I bought it from a collector. It's an authentic piece from a tomb in Egypt that was unearthed when the ground in the region shifted in 2029," Phoenix said, looking slightly offended and a bit perplexed at her comment.

"Then why does it look like you?"

"It doesn't look like me."

"Yes, it does." Jun insisted.

Phoenix looked at the golden head before focusing on her. "Are you trying to say that all Black guys look alike?"

"Not at all." Jun said, her eyes darting from the mask to Phoenix and then back again. "I think the resemblance is very strong. Who is he?"

"I was told that he was the first pharaoh of the Medjai nation. He reigned over ten thousand years ago, long before most formal religions."

"I was not aware that the Medjai had a pharaoh."

"A lot of people say that."

"And he had a griffin as a headpiece."

"Yes."

Jun smiled, feeling as if she had found proof in the mistruth in his statement. "The griffin is a mythological creature found primarily in Greece and Asia. Even if they did exist, there are no records to show that they were spoken of ten thousand years ago."

"No public records." Phoenix corrected.

Jun turned to look at him. "Are you saying this is from a collection that has not been made public?"

"I'm saying that archeologists base history on what has been discovered, right?"

"Correct."

"Just because something has not been discovered doesn't mean it doesn't exist." Phoenix explained, noting the deep thought in Jun's expression as she stared at him.

"What was his name?"

"The previous owner said his name was Pharaoh Kee."

Jun raised her eyebrows in surprise. "'Key' as in to access a locked door?"

"Kee, spelled K‑E‑E." He smiled pleasantly. He felt comfortable and somewhat relieved telling her about his history, even if she didn't realize that was what he was doing.

Jun turned her focus to the image of the coin on the computer screen behind him. He followed her gaze to see what had captured her attention.

"What's that?" Jun asked as she approached the monitor for a closer look. Phoenix gazed at the image, then back at Jun as she watched with admiration.

"It's called a griffin coin."

She shook her head. "I don't know this artifact."

"Because it's not an artifact. It was created recently as one ounce of solid gold currency."

"It has 'Griffin of Medjai' engraved on one side above what appears to be the top portion of a ship." Jun said while staring at the rotating image. "Is that your ship?"

"Yes. That's Blood Sky's mast."

"You designed this coin?"

"My daughter did."

Jun smiled slightly at the pride in his voice. Based on her reaction, he assumed that her parents had given her the same look when she presented her achievements.

"It also reads 'God is with us' above the griffin." She turned from the image to stare at Phoenix. "Are you religious?"

"I'm more spiritual than religious."

"What is the difference, in your opinion?"

"In my opinion? The older I get and the more I learn about life, the more I believe that religion is of man. That's why there are so many different religions in the world today. People conform the worship of God to their individual needs to amass followers."

"And spirituality?"

"Spirituality is the hard, raw facts. The basis of the belief that, above all else, there is only one true God, master of all things, whether you call him God, Allah, the Universe, or whatever."

"There's a lot more to you than I expected, Captain Phoenix."

"I'll take that as a compliment."

"You should." Jun said before turning back to stare at the image. "And the eight Greek characters on the other side? What do they represent?"

"They're not Greek. They're older."

"As you said during the tour." Jun recalled. "I assume you have proof of this?"

"Yes, but it's not something I want to discuss at this time."

"Can you tell me why this obsession?"

"What obsession are you referring to?"

"The red 'X' painted on your hull, which you said represents a group of warriors called the Kee. This pharaoh mask in your quarters that you say is the possible founder of these Kee warriors and ancient Medjai people from Egypt and Africa. Now this gold coin that has the word 'Medjai' on it and the same type of griffin that is on the mask along with 'pre-Greek' letters. What's this all about?"

Phoenix stared into her eyes, determining how much he should reveal to this stranger. His heart felt compelled to flood her with information about history, all he had learned, and his personal connection to it all, but his mind knew that it was not wise to do so yet. He would find a way to meet in the middle.

"Well, over ten thousand years ago, the Kee were all descendants from that man." Phoenix gestured to the pharaoh mask on display. "His bloodline became the greatest combatants in the world, sought after for battles, protection, and breeding. The Kee warriors are said to have given birth to the Medjai, who were a race of nomadic people from the Nubian sector of the African continent."

"This is new to me but very interesting," Jun said. "Please continue."

"The Medjai were a proud people known for superior combat skills and loyalty as well as creative and ingenious inventions. It's actually from the word 'Medjai' that 'magic' originated as a way of describing scientific discoveries and methods that other cultures couldn't understand."

"That I do remember from history." Jun replied.

"The Egyptian royalty was said to have commissioned the Medjai to protect their family and valued possessions. It is believed that the Medjai eventually faded out of existence for some unknown reason, like so many ancient cultures, but that isn't true. The truth is that the Medjai continued to travel the world, spreading their loyalty and beliefs throughout the nations, always helping those in need and protecting those who couldn't defend themselves. They just decided not to identify themselves openly. Over time the real Medjai people were no longer merely descendants from the Kee bloodline but included anyone who followed the teachings of the descendants of Kee."

"You mean a religion?"

"More like a cause driven by a code of honor, like the samurai of Japan."

"You're saying that the crew of this ship has taken on this noble cause of the Medjai?"

"In a manner of speaking," he said, nodding.

Jun stared into his eyes as if looking for a flinch or any other sign of his words being false. "Why not call the coin 'Griffin of Kee'?"

"Because no one knows what a Kee is."

"Then you could enlighten them."

"I don't want to. Instead, I use a less ancient name that is relatable to the same cause."

"I have many questions that I hope you will answer one day, but that is not why I boarded your ship, Captain."

"Why then?" he asked, welcoming the change of topic. His attraction to Jun had caused him to say more in a few minutes than he had told any outsider before.

"May I sit down?" she asked as she approached the sofa that faced the open door to the balcony.

It was his favorite seating area during rainy weather when he wanted a view of the outside. For some reason he had to fight the urge to inform her of this.

"I'm sorry. I don't usually entertain in here." he said, startled at how quickly he allowed his suspicions to overwhelm his hospitality. "Yes, please make yourself comfortable. Would you like something to drink?"

"Red wine if you have it, please." Jun said as she sat on the sofa. Phoenix noted signs of nervousness in her as he approached his small bar.

As he reached out for the bottle of wine, his mind flashed to the image of the cargo hold and two large wooden shipping crates. He shook the image out of his head and poured her a glass of wine.

"Is everything OK, Miss Li?" he asked as he extended the glass to her.

She looked into his eyes and smiled. "Jun please. I'll be fine. Thanks for asking."

"So, you were about to explain how a member of a US senator's office is able to have access to a foreign government's helicopter." he said, sitting on the chair across from her with a glass of ice water in hand.

"Zara and I resigned from our positions with the Senate after the meeting this morning." Jun began.

This was not the answer he was expecting. "Resigned?"

"Technically, yes." Jun stated. "Zara is on a leave of absence, so she can get government-protected transportation back to her country." He heard sadness in her voice as she said it. "Because of her title, it won't be an aircraft, but it will at least be protected by the military. Once she's home she'll send her official resignation."

"I see." He sipped his water. "She's not handling the abduction well. We expected that. You seem more stable considering everything that you went through." Jun gave him a shy look, then sipped from her glass.

"I distract myself with work." Jun said, her voice just above a whisper. He realized she was struggling to maintain a strong front in response to his mention of the topic, so he did not press the issue.

"Work? Is that why you're here?"

"Yes and no." Jun sighed. "I resigned today, effective immediately. I was really upset at how they treated you in the Senate committee meeting this morning after all that you had done for us."

"Thank you, Jun, but I don't think that it was a good reason to give up a promising career in government."

"I already have a career in government," she said, swelling with pride. "My government."

He smiled in realization. "That explains the dignitary transport on my flight deck."

"Yes. I was working for the Senate as an intern to learn New America's politics to help our two countries with trade in the future. It was decided that if I could spend a few years in government in New America, I would learn alternate ways of doing things and bring political variety and options to my country."

"Shangri-La." he confirmed as he stood up and began pacing.

"What's wrong, Captain Phoenix?"

"Are you here representing Shangri-La or New America?"

"Neither." Jun replied, looking a bit disappointed.

Phoenix watched her, puzzled. "I apologize, Jun. I don't mean to be blunt or rude. I'm still a little scorched from being the main course at that Senate barbecue this morning."

His analogy made Jun smile slightly, causing his expression to soften as well.

"You think I was sent here by my government? For what, exactly?"

"I don't know." He shrugged. "Maybe for me to form an alliance with Shangri-La now that it's gone semi-public that there's tension between me and New America?"

Jun watched him for a moment, curious and troubled.

My God, Phoenix thought. She had such an aura of beauty about her. It wasn't glamorous beauty that was restricted to her facial features. What he saw was a regal beauty in how she walked and spoke and even in the manner in which she sat on his sofa. She captivated him so much, he hoped it wasn't visible in his expression.

Jun stood up and stepped toward the door to the balcony, then turned back to address him. "Then you really know nothing about Shangri-La."

"You're right. All I know is what I've seen on the media or learned on my own."

"And what is that?" she asked, preparing for a negative response.

"Shangri-La is a very secretive place." Phoenix said as he stepped out onto the balcony, gesturing for her to do the same. She followed hesitantly. "It closed its borders to the general public not long after its existence became known, and other than trade agreements in the main harbor city, the country itself is locked down."

"Is that unusual? During the COVID-19 pandemic in 2020, all major countries participated in their own individual lockdown procedures to prevent the viral contagion from being imported from other countries. That lockdown lasted for years." Jun said.

"But Shangri-La didn't go into lockdown to prevent a pandemic, did it?"

"The purpose for a country to close its borders has always been to prevent something toxic from entering the country and infecting the nation."

Phoenix smiled at her wit. "And toxic invasions aren't always in the form of a viral pandemic."

"No, they are not," Jun admitted, restraining a smile. "Is that all you have learned?"

"Pretty much." he said, grinning. "As for your emperor, his history is a bit more public but not by much."

"Why do you say that?"

"Well, he's the only one who has attended political events as an official representative of your country. I think that's a strategic move because it minimizes contact, leaving no room for infiltrators in his young government. I hear he's an honorable man and extremely wise. Some say he's a tyrant dictator because he took advantage of the crippled countries of Asia and combined them for his personal gain."

"What do you think?"

"I think he saw an opportunity to unite a dying people in a manner that maintained the culture of Asians around the world. I think this is why he's made Shangri-La so private. He's giving his people time to reestablish themselves and rediscover their heritage. Without Shangri-La, the Asians who are scattered around the world would just become individual diasporas in the history books."

"Insightful."

"I've run into a few of his salvage operations, so from what I can tell, he has been collecting ruins from the bottom of the ocean off the shores of Old China and where Japan used to be to strengthen and possibly restore various Asian cultures. I think it's genius because your culture got hit the worst between the war and the natural disasters."

As he continued to speak, Jun looked out at the ocean and the night sky. "What wasn't buried by the earthquakes in Japan, Vietnam, and the Philippines was sunk by the floods and tsunamis. Now China and Russia have the largest sections of radioactive wasteland in the world, thanks to the Blitz War. Your culture wasn't prepared for that kind of devastation. None of us were. At least your emperor had the resources and the ingenuity to start rebuilding your culture before it became a footnote in history. What a great legacy."

"You seem to know more than you first admitted." Jun said, smiling.

"I'm only guessing based on what I see." He sat down, troubled. "I wish I had had the foresight at that time to save my country."

"New America didn't need saving."

"I wasn't talking about New America."

"You're not American?"

"I was born in Jamaica, West Indies." Phoenix said, his voice filled with hurt. Jun's expression became sympathetic. "If not for the height of the Blue Mountains, there would be no island of Jamaica left at all. Most of the island is now below sea level, the people on the island washed away by storms and floods. I'm told a few have gone back, but my home is no longer the flourishing country it once was. It is now considered one of the many needy islands in what's left of the Caribbean."

"I had no idea that you were Jamaican." Jun said with interest. "I don't hear an accent."

"My parents came to America when I was very young. My accent slips out every now and then, usually when I'm relaxed." He sighed. "Your accent is slight but hard to pinpoint as far as an origin."

"Like you, I was raised in New America. All my schooling was from California. I'm a mix of Chinese and Vietnamese, so people never guess my background correctly." Jun admitted. "Please don't take this the wrong way, but you don't look like the Jamaicans who I've worked with."

"My heritage is all over the place: Egyptian, Scottish, Apache Indian, and Arawak Indian, which most Jamaicans trace their lineage back to. There are other nationalities, too, but too small a percentage to mention."

"Egyptian. Is that why you have the mask?"

"Yes. Phoenix said, not wanting to divulge that his surname was a derivation of "Medjai" and that the mask was of his ancestor.

"Now I understand." Jun said, looking mildly startled. "Four different races and born in Jamaica. That's a lot."

"I guess, but when people look at me, they just see a Black man."

"People? You mean like Vice President Harp?" Jun said, sipping her wine. Phoenix offered a twisted smile, wondering how she knew that.

"Why would you mention her?"

"You're right about Emperor Li Jaw-Long." Jun said, avoiding the question.

"How so?" Although she seemed unwilling to answer his

question about Harp, he decided he would find a way to return the conversation to that subject.

"He was always a student of Japanese and Chinese culture and history. Because he traveled a lot he had firsthand experience in the smaller Asian cultures, like the Pacific Islands, Vietnam, Cambodia, Thailand, and so on. Some say he is a visionary because he was always prepared for a global disaster. He always said that it was written in our history; we just had to know how to read it."

"Your emperor's vision must be strong as a leader."

"Why do you say that?"

"It seems that your parents and many successful people of Shangri-La must have embraced the emperor's ideology and, like him, were prepared for it before it happened."

"Please explain." Jun narrowed her eyes in suspicion. "What do you know about my parents?"

"Nothing other than the fact that they are probably wealthy, based on the high-end stretch limousine that picked you up for shopping." Phoenix smiled. "Like the emperor, your parents must have realized that these times were coming. Unifying Asian cultures to reside on one island, named after the fictitious place of paradise and a retreat from the evil of the world? Shangri-La developed too quickly to have just been thought up on a whim. I think it was on someone's mind long before 2029. More than likely a group of someones."

Phoenix stared into her eyes, his slight smile genuine and ready to laugh with her.

"Wow, Phoenix!" She giggled to herself, taking another sip of the wine. She hesitated, then tilted her head back and drained the glass. "Uh, can I have more wine please?"

"Sure." Phoenix smiled. He knew she was deflecting the conversation to give herself a chance to collect her thoughts.

He stood, taking her glass and walking back into his quarters. When his back was turned, she looked away, fanning her face with her hand even though the night was cool. He watched her in the mirror at the bar and smiled.

"One day we'll have time to talk about culture and politics." she said when he returned, still smiling, carrying a full glass of wine in one hand and the open bottle in the other.

"Yes, I believe we will." Phoenix replied.

"But that's not why I came." she continued, pushing the glass of wine to the center of the table.

"Okay."

"Emperor Li Jaw—Long is having an appreciation celebration in your honor." she said, having trouble finding the words. Phoenix almost choked.

"Excuse me?"

"I've been sent here to invite you to a private dinner that my emperor is having, in your honor, to celebrate your heroism in rescuing me and the senators last week."

"I see." Phoenix watched the horizon, perplexed at the thought that Shangri—La was willing to give him a congratulatory dinner. He took a few moments to think, then turned back to Jun.

"Will you be there?" Worry suddenly filled her eyes, as if she was worried that he might refuse.

"When is he planning on having it?" Phoenix asked, wanting to stem her discouragement.

"He wanted me to tell you that he knows you're a busy man, so it will be whenever you can make time to come to Shangri-La." Jun paused, continuing to stare at him. "Will you be there?"

"Oh! Yes, of course! I'm sorry. Yes, I'll come. I have to pick up cargo in Cuba and make a delivery to Brazil, but after that I'm free."

"I can give you the coordinates when you're ready."

"I already have the coordinates." he said, smiling at her puzzled expression.

"Okay." She paused, deciding against asking how he had obtained that information. "The invitation is also for the command team that you had in the meeting this morning, and, of course, your usual escort team will be allowed to accompany you, but they won't be needed, I'm sure."

"Would the emperor find my escorts offensive?"

"He takes his protection everywhere, just like you."

"And you detoured from your trip back to Shangri-La to deliver this message personally?" Phoenix bowed slightly. "I'm honored, Jun."

Jun's smile faded, replaced with a concerned frown. "That's not the only reason I'm here. It's just the official reason that I will give if I'm ever questioned." she admitted before scooping up her glass and taking a few swallows of wine.

He watched with concern as Jun was obviously preparing to tell him something that was uncomfortable for her.

"Vice President Harp wants your technology," she said when she finally set down her glass.

"Oh." Phoenix sighed and smiled. "Is that all? Well, she made that very clear in the Senate meeting this morning."

"No, you don't understand." Jun shook her head, agitated as she searched for the right words.

Phoenix sat down next to her. He wanted to hold her hand to comfort her but thought she might consider it inappropriate. He feared that any sign of intimacy would distract her or drive her away from him. That was the last thing he wanted. He was wary of exposing the attraction for this woman that was growing inside of him.

"Tell me." he urged, distracting himself from his emotions.

"Do you have advanced weapons onboard?"

Phoenix stiffened while looking into her eyes. "Why do you ask?"

"Harp asked about advanced weapons as soon as we started our debriefing meeting early this morning. Then she asked to listen to our debriefing audio reports as soon as we were done. That's not the normal procedure, especially since it happened outside of her jurisdiction. Vice presidents never attend debriefing meetings."

Phoenix stood and began pacing. "Maybe you'd better start from the beginning."

"Okay." Jun took a deep breath, followed by another sip of wine. "After the Senate meeting, I saw how pissed Vice President Harp was, so I followed her."

"You followed her?" he asked, looking at her in surprise.

"Well, my father's first business was a security company." Jun admitted.

"A security company." Phoenix repeated.

"Yes, they did mostly executive protection and investigations, but he had a few armed security clients, bouncers in clubs, and things like that. The point is, I learned a lot from being around my dad's work."

"I can see that." Phoenix said, his eyebrows raised as he resumed his pacing.

"I was concerned about what Harp might do, so I placed a listening device in her bag."

Again, Phoenix stopped to stare at her, but this time he did not interrupt.

He seldom interrupted someone when they were giving vital information so as not to risk disrupting their mental flow, which could lead to them unintentionally leaving out important details.

"She was yelling at someone on the phone, talking about the weapons technology on Blood Sky that this person had told her about. She said you have better weapons than New America's military." Jun paused for a moment and gave Phoenix a curious look. "Do you and Harp have a history together?"

"What?" he asked, half in a daze as he turned to stare at her.

"No." When the realization of her meaning of possible intimacy hit him, his face contorted with disgust. "Aw, hell no!" He saw a look of relief in Jun's eyes as she turned away.

"Then she's not just racist; she really hates you."

"Why do you say that?"

"The names she was calling you and your son. At first I didn't know whom she was referring to, but she wasn't holding back at all on her racist remarks and insults. She's disgusting!"

"I see. Well, she was quite vocal years ago about her racist views with one of my team members. I made a formal complaint that would have gotten her fired, but because there wasn't enough evidence to support my claims, the case was dropped after a mild counseling session."

"What happened to the subordinate?"

"He supposedly committed suicide a few months later." Phoenix took a deep breath. "He died under suspicious circumstances the day before Harp got promoted to vice president of DHS. He supposedly hung himself with some sort of wire. I asked a contact in the police department to send me the investigation information."

"And?"

"The report said he was hung with either piano wire or something similar. The crime scene looked like a suicidal hanging staged by a novice."

"What do you think?"

"The case was out of my hands and conveniently went away after she got into office. I was also told that looking into it could cause problems for my career." He sighed. "I fought for a cause and lost. I allowed my personal fight against racism to distract me from the greater war. Her actions didn't go unnoticed, but enough of the people higher up helped to get her charges out of the spotlight. Now very few people remember what happened, and even fewer care."

He sat down to face Jun. For a moment he was entranced by her unique features, then he refocused. "Back to this conversation."

"She's afraid that even if you don't use this technology against New America, you'll sell it to the highest bidder or enemies of New America." Jun said.

"I don't intend to sell our technology." he replied. "I would sooner give it away, or trade it for something I don't have or something I need and can't get on my own."

"You would?" she asked, surprised. "To whom?"

Phoenix watched her for a moment, his expression blank. "Someone I could trust."

"Oh." Jun responded softly.

"What else did she say?"

Jun hesitated, trying to regain focus. "She didn't believe that your son was smart enough to invent anything. Then she said some more racial shit." Jun turned to him, smiling slightly. "Oh, sorry!" she said, not meaning to use profanity. "I didn't realize when we were here before that Talon was your son."

"Yes, he is." He smiled proudly.

"He's handsome and funny." Jun giggled. "Lace underwear!" He raised his eyebrows, looked at her glass of wine, then slid it away from her toward the center of the table.

"Thank you." Phoenix said.

"She has other plans to get the technology, since the Senate meeting didn't work. Whoever she was talking to on the phone already knows the plan because she didn't go into any details. If she can't get what she wants the legal way, she's going to try to force it from you. That's what I wanted to tell you." Jun finished with a sigh of relief, thankful to have delivered her message.

"This also means that she has a spy who's feeding her information about my ship." Phoenix said.

"That's why she was pushing to get you to talk about the rescue." Jun replied. Her words were slightly slurred due to the wine, but she was a lot happier and more relaxed than when she first entered his cabin. "She was pushing you to where she could justify her argument to board this ship."

"Yes, I know. The spy already told her about the technology, so she wanted to use her position to convince the Senate to make the decision that she couldn't make by herself."

"Yes." Jun said, smiling at him.

"It couldn't have been any of my crew." Phoenix said. "In fact, the hostages were the only outsiders recently who had access to the ship." he said, looking at Jun.

"Don't look at me, Captain!" Jun said, smirking. "I didn't say anything!"

"Of course it's not you, or you wouldn't have come here."

"That's right," Jun agreed, staring at her glass of wine. She looked across at him as she reached for it, like a child attempting to sneak a candy. Phoenix watched her but said nothing as she pulled the glass of wine toward her, waiting for some sign of disapproval. He gave none. After she took a few rewarding sips of the tasty beverage, she looked up at him. "Who do you think did it?"

Phoenix shook his head in confusion, his face troubled as the same question burned in his mind.

22

INFILTRATION

~

P hoenix agreed to have Jun and her two escorts and pilot stay onboard *Blood Sky* until the ship had cleared New America's jurisdiction. While she accepted a guest cabin for the night, her team felt more comfortable alternating protective watch around the *Black Arrow* helicopter, which included taking turns sleeping on portable cots inside the hangar bay just beyond the aircraft on the flight deck.

Blood Sky cruised through the night, minimizing the use of most of its unnecessary external lights. It was still in the wide canals and seas that separate the islands of New America. With the Manhattan City Harbor on the western side of York Jersey, it was more efficient for *Blood Sky* to skirt the New America islands, keeping them on the right side of the ship as it traveled southbound. Many inexperienced travelers would have chosen to head east, deeper into the Atlantic Ocean, but that would have added to their travel time and caused them to burn fuel unnecessarily. Phoenix and Athena agreed that cutting through the Florida Strait that ran between the Miami

Isles and the island of Ala-Georgia was the most efficient route.

The standard crew security patrolled the ship, one on each deck, checking in regularly with each other and the security base within the ship. None of the security teams during that evening's patrols spent much time patrolling the ship's inner levels due to the continuous presence of various elite combat personnel within the ship's hull throughout the night.

The shipping crates from Senator Gash sat in the darkness in the main cargo hold, free from wandering eyes. There was no one in the room to hear internal latches releasing inside the two crates. The lower wall of one of the crates opened, revealing a man in a fetal position.

He raised his head just enough to look around the room. An oxygen mask was strapped around his face, leaving only his eyes and strong jawline visible. Once he was certain there were no crew in the cargo hold, he slipped out of the crate. His call sign was "Quebec." He was a Black man in his late forties with the chiseled features of a man who had lived through hard times at an early age that had made him tough inside and out.

Quebec knocked on the top portion of the second crate. After a moment the bottom portion opened, revealing a thickly built Black woman. She crawled out and stretched, then turned and glared at Quebec. She removed the oxygen mask and stretched her back and legs.

Before she could speak, the door to the storage room opened. In one graceful move, she raised her sidearm, which she had kept clutched in her hand throughout her confinement, and shot the silhouette of a man in the dim lighting who had walked through the door. Two shots rang out, and the man crumpled to the floor. While her pistol had a suppressor attached to the muzzle, it was still loud enough to startle Quebec, whose back was to the door.

"What are you doing?" Quebec scolded in a whisper, "Our orders were in and out, undetected!"

"Fuck that!" Yankee snapped. "He would have seen us. You shouldn't have turned your back!"

He let out a deep frustrated sigh, then continued preparing his gear as Yankee did the same, as if the life she had just taken meant nothing to her. In truth, it did not. Once Quebec was finished, he dragged the body off to the side, out of sight.

"Quebec online." Quebec said into his hands-free transmitter.

"Yankee online." Yankee responded.

Quebec looked down at his phone, which had an image of a Korean destroyer on it, a model that appeared to be similar to *Blood Sky*.

"Let's go!" he whispered before advancing toward the exit that led to the ship's inner corridors.

They crept through the ship's lower section in a tactical manner, keeping their knees bent and their bodies low as they advanced. Quebec led the duo, stopping under metal stairs that led to an upper deck to check the digital map on his phone.

"This old ship is too tight." Yankee whispered. "We don't know how many people are on board!"

"The schematics say it has an accompaniment of two hundred and fifty, but I doubt that." he replied reading the data on his phone.

"No. It says that the ship holds two hundred and fifty. There's a difference." she said. "We didn't get any intel on the actual crew accompaniment."

"What are you saying?" Quebec asked, glancing back at his partner.

"This intel is shit! Quebec, there's no way in hell we can get through this ship without running into people no matter how many are here. In and out without a trace my ass!"

He took a final look at his phone and then glanced up and down both corridors, forced to submit to her conclusion. "You're right."

"We have to take them out."

Quebec nodded. "Yes."

"We need a second team. We should get off the ship and come back with at least two more teams."

"That's not happening. Once we're out of American waters, she has no jurisdiction for us to be here." Quebec insisted. "We get what we can find, then bounce before things get too hot."

"Okay, but anyone who gets in my way gets done!" Yankee snapped. Quebec nodded before moving back into the passageway, heading toward the ship's bow.

Falcon and Raptor entered the cargo hold, each of them carrying a box of old mechanical parts. When Raptor turned on the lights, Falcon lowered the box in her hand onto a nearby table and assumed a fighting stance once she saw the wide trail of blood that led to a pair of legs on the floor around the corner. Raptor placed his box on the table near the entrance while Falcon followed the smeared trail of blood, approaching the body with caution. She realized it was Medina, two gunshot wounds to his chest. She checked Medina's vitals with two fingers to his neck, then looked at Raptor and shook her head. Rage spread across the old man's face.

It didn't take much deduction to realize that Medina had been shot at the entrance and dragged to his current location.

Then they turned and saw the open lower section of the crates and two oxygen masks on the floor.

Shortly after Jun's arrival, a light dinner was brought up to Phoenix's quarters. Out of respect, Phoenix made sure that the door to his cabin remained open so that passersby could see that no inappropriate behavior was taking place. When she first arrived unannounced, a closed-door meeting with the captain was expected, but now that it had been made clear to the crew that Miss Li and her entourage were guests, standards were different. Although he knew very little about Jun, he felt the need to protect her reputation as well as his own.

Reputation was an important factor to Phoenix, as it encouraged respect from his crew and for this representative from a visiting nation. Reputation and respect were the foundation of everything he did publicly and everything he taught his children and his crew. To solidify his reputation further, he had Hawk stand guard outside the open door, along with Snow, who was one of the female protection crew members.

"Thank you for dinner. We came prepared to eat what we brought with us." Jun explained as she took the last bite of her meal.

"I couldn't have you do that." Phoenix replied, smiling. "Besides, whenever we make port and pick up supplies, it's tradition that we have a feast, so we can start eating all the things that will spoil first, especially if we haven't had them in a while, like fresh vegetables and fruit."

"Well, I'm grateful, and I'm sure my escorts are grateful that you set up a table for them on the flight deck, so they could eat without leaving our helicopter." She smiled while sipping her wine.

"Black Arrow." Phoenix stated.

She looked at him with surprise. "How do you know the name of the emperor's private helicopter?"

Phoenix watched her, wondering if he should give her the answer, which would only lead to more questions and reveal that Phoenix knew even more about her country than he had already stated. The truth was that Phoenix knew more about Shangri-La than any non-Asian was aware. The reason for that knowledge was intertwined in the secret itself.

"Attention all crew members," a pleasant voice sounded over the PA system. "This is Chef Athena here to announce tonight's dinner menu." Phoenix looked at Jun with an alert expression as she placed her glass of wine on the table, perplexed.

"I thought your chef's name was Miss Cookie." she said.

Phoenix gave her a stern look and held his index finger to his lips. Hawk and Snow hurried into the room on high alert, causing Jun to tense up and look around.

"Athena is my executive officer, second in command of this ship." Phoenix explained while focusing on the announcement.

"We'll be serving creamy tomato soup with Cajun hot sauce," Athena's said.

"Tomato soup, hot sauce. Code red alert with casualties." Phoenix said, deciphering the announcement for Jun's sake.

"Hot damn!" Hawk whispered angrily.

"Two stuffed eggplants," Athena continued.

"Two intruders, heavily armed," Phoenix said, staring at Jun.

"Eggplants?" Jun asked. "Does that mean they're Black?"

Phoenix looked at her, surprised. "No. I hate eggplant. It makes me nauseous. Stuffed means they're armed."

Jun was embarrassed at her correlation. She had heard the term "eggplant" as a description to men of African heritage from elderly Italian colleagues when she visited New York years prior.

Hawk and Snow drew their pistols. Jun was concerned that

they were going to point the weapons at her, believing she had allowed the intruders onto the ship. Instead, Hawk turned to face the exit while Snow rushed to check the balcony.

"How did they get on board?" Hawk asked.

"Served with one marinated artichoke heart," Athena continued hesitantly.

"Marinated, mercenaries. At least one person is confirmed dead so far," Phoenix translated, anger building in his voice.

"The balcony's clear!" Snow announced before locking the balcony door from the inside.

"See you all in the mess hall when you take your break." Athena said in closing, "Chef Athena out."

In another section of the ship, Quebec and Yankee hesitated as they listened to the announcement while holding their guns at the ready.

"They announce their meals?" Quebec asked, frowning in surprise. "That's not military."

"The report was that merchants bought this ship, so I'm not surprised." Yankee looked down each corridor and then smiled back at him. "The menu sounded pretty damn good though. Maybe I'll grab some to go on our way out."

He looked at Yankee, then up the stairs near them, knowing she was not serious but seeing no need to respond. After glancing at his watch and then the digital map, he turned to address Yankee. "We need to split up to cover more ground," he said. "You take the next level up, and I'll keep checking on this level."

"Got it."

"Check storage rooms and the designated weapons storage upstairs. Anything small enough, we take with us."

"Right. We're looking for tech that we don't recognize." Yankee confirmed.

"That's right." Quebec checked the time again. "We have another twenty-two minutes of recon before we get off this boat."

"I know." She frowned at Quebec, as if the reminder was unnecessary.

Yankee moved up the metal steps while Quebec continued down the corridor toward the ship's bow.

In the mess hall, Miss Cookie ushered crew members inside while Hacker kept watch in the hallway. The mess hall was the largest room in the ship and could hold most of the non-combatant crew members comfortably.

"It's going to be alright." Miss Cookie assured the incoming crew. She took it upon herself to keep the peace during crises. While she didn't carry a gun like Hacker, who remained at her side visually confirming everyone who entered, she kept a large kitchen knife strapped to her belt. In a worst-case scenario, her motherly instincts would allow her to defend the crew like her own family. She knew this was her best position in this type of crisis because as the ship's cook and welcome wagon, Miss Cookie was familiar with every crew member and guest on board. As she always said, "Everybody gotta eat." She smiled and ushered them into the mess hall, also making sure everyone was familiar. If they were not, one glance towards Hacker would send him into combat mode.

In the ship's berth section, the crew members who were not on duty hurried through the narrow hallways to close and lock their cabins or the cabins they were closest to, limiting where the intruders could hide.

23

RETALIATION

～

Kite immediately began locking down the medical bay with her staff. Nurse Zhang was the only other member of the medical team who was combat trained. Even though a few commandos arrived to stand guard just inside the area, Kite and Nurse Zhang wore their holstered pistols in case of a breach. Kite felt even more secure as she watched Zhang readied her large pocket knife as well as her firearm.

～

Swan stormed into *Lola*, which would be used as an auxiliary base. After two combat crew members entered, she closed all the doors, making sure that no one could enter *Lola* to steal or sabotage her. Even though the threat at that moment was on the lower levels, she followed protocol because all crew members were aware that a threat could change direction like the wind in a storm.

Warlord and Apache rushed into Phoenix's cabin, startling Jun. She had become accustomed to the man–giant, but the Latino man with the savage-looking Mohawk haircut and jaw beard caught her by surprise. The two combatants remained silent as Phoenix monitored the movements of the two assailants on two separate levels. He squinted in an attempt to discern the details of their faces, but their tactical gear made it impossible to identify them clearly.

"Reporting as ordered, Captain." Warlord announced. Phoenix had already holstered his sidearm, strapped to his thigh. He turned to Jun with a stern expression. When she looked into his eyes, she was surprised that while he looked like a man ready for battle, his eyes showed genuine concern for her.

"I'm going to need you to stay here, Jun." Phoenix said.

"But my men," Jun began.

"They'll be safe." Phoenix assured her as he turned to Hawk. "Hawk, meet Eagle on the flight deck, and help secure Black Arrow and the Shangri–La team."

"Roger that, Captain. Right away!" Hawk said, rushing out of the room.

Phoenix turned to face Snow, Warlord, and Apache. Jun had admired Phoenix's command presence during the rescue when they first met, but this time it was different. Maybe because it was his ship, his pride and joy, his home. Or maybe because she was on the ship and represented a foreign nation, so under no circumstance could he risk her being harmed. Or maybe, she hoped, it was because he cared for her and did not want her injured in any way. She grinned slightly at the thought.

"Apache, you and Snow lock yourself in here, and make sure nothing happens to Miss Li. Monitor the surveillance on the flight deck, so she can feel comfortable that her escorts are not in danger." Phoenix set the monitors to show Jun's helicopter, while other monitors showed various angles and passageways to the helicopter.

"Roger that, Captain." Apache and Snow said in unison.

"You're with me." Phoenix said to Warlord before moving out of the cabin. Apache locked the door behind them while Snow politely gestured for Jun to sit in front of the monitors at Phoenix's desk.

Manh, Jun's personal senior protector since she was a teenager, watched as Hawk approached the helicopter in full combat gear. Manh and his partner, Alvin, were equipped in high-tech battle armor designed by Shangri-La engineers to be streamlined and sleek. Hawk glanced up to see that Thai Phan, the female helicopter pilot, was seated in the cockpit, manning the onboard weaponry.

"They're going to flank the bird, and we'll post up on either side of the deck." Eagle reported to Hawk as he handed Eagle a high-powered semi-automatic rifle.

"Roger." Hawk replied as Manh approached both men with a stern expression, his gun in hand.

"I demand to be taken to our principal!" Manh ordered.

Eagle moved to answer in the same aggressive manner that he was approached, but Hawk, the negotiator of the two, stepped forward to address the concern before Eagle's temper flared.

"That's not possible right now, Manh."

"Why?"

"The intruders are making their way through the ship, believing they haven't been detected. You don't know the ship's layout, and we can't spare the manpower to escort you."

"But Jun Li—"

"Is being protected by SOCIT," Hawk interrupted. "The same team that rescued her before, per the captain's orders."

"Manh, I'm okay." Jun's calming voice said into Manh's earpiece. "I'm in the captain's quarters protected by two SOCIT members, as Hawk said."

Hawk and Eagle stared at Manh, wondering about his sudden silence, until Hawk saw the earpiece in Manh's ear.

"I can see and hear you, but they suggested I not use the public address system to inform you until the emergency is over." Jun continued.

"I understand, Jun." Manh replied as he glanced at Alvin, who had moved to stand at Manh's side in case he needed support.

"If things get out of hand, their orders are to make sure that she gets back here, and I know she'll want her full team here on deck, so Black Arrow is ready to lift off right away." Hawk said.

Manh refocused on Hawk, then Eagle. "Yes." Hawk could tell the man didn't like someone else being in control, but he had no other option. Knowing that he was in communication with Jun throughout the emergency was reassuring. "This is a solid plan." Manh said, then resumed his responsibility, alongside Alvin, to protect their only transportation off the ship.

Without another word, the four allied combatants moved to their respective positions and stood ready and alert to defend *Black Arrow*.

Quebec crept through the ship, checking every door, only to find all of them locked. He stopped and looked up and down the hall suspiciously. Why was it so quiet?

"Yankee, come in." he whispered.

"What's up?"

"Have you run into anyone yet?"

"No. Maybe they're all in the mess hall eating." she replied, annoyed that he was distracting her.

"At the same time?"

"Just because it's a big ship doesn't mean they have a big crew."

"Yeah, maybe. Avoid the bridge and the mess hall."

"Got it. I'm almost at the first weapons locker now." Even at a whisper, Yankee's voice was loud in Quebec's earpiece.

"Affirmative," Quebec said with relief. "Let me know if you find anything high tech."

"Yeah, yeah."

Morty had been moving quickly throughout the lab securing experiments ever since he first heard the PA announcement. Cans of insect repellent had their tops removed and replaced with plastic wrap throughout the lab. He set his last project on the table and then headed for the door. If there were intruders, he needed to get out of the lab and to the mess hall as soon as possible.

He opened the door, only to see a large, unfamiliar Black man in tactical gear. Morty's screech was silenced when the man slammed his hand over his mouth and pushed him back into the lab.

The assailant's eyes swept back and forth, analyzing the room. Morty felt the muzzle of a pistol pressed into his stomach, causing him to let out a muffled yelp. The pressure to his stomach was intense, an indication of how incredibly strong the intruder was. The intimidating Black man heard the helpless sound and turned his attention back to Morty.

"Scream and die!" the man hissed. "What is this room? Storage?" Morty made a series of muffled explanations before the man uncovered his mouth. The hardened stare at close range was the most intimidating thing that Morty had ever experienced.

"Th–Th–This is th–th–the la-la-la-lab." His stutter being a direct result of fear and intimidation was embarrassing.

"You're a scientist?" the man asked, his voice filled with doubt.

Morty shook his head, so close to the man's face that he could feel the heat from the man's breath. "N–n–no! I'm j–j–just an as–s–s–assistant! I-I-I c–c–c–clean up! I-I-I d–d–don't know anything!"

"Then I don't need you." the man said. Before Morty could respond, the man covered Morty's mouth again, and a single bullet ripped through his stomach.

Quebec let the body drop as he went throughout the room.

Tinted safety glasses. Bug spray. A can of black plaster. He groaned to himself. This was all useless junk! He rummaged through the laboratory, looking for something he could grab. The only thing that seemed to be of interest was a deconstructed engine, but it was useless, with the bullet holes inside each part.

He picked up a vial filled with black liquid. He opened the vial and sniffed it. It didn't smell like anything, but it looked like liquefied mud. Quebec set the vial down and then left the room. There had to be another room that had more valuable equipment.

Minutes later, Talon walked into the lab and stopped at the sight of Morty lying in the middle of the room, blood pooling around his body. He felt bile rise in his throat. Morty never carried a gun. His anxiety made his hands shake every time he held one. Morty could never be a threat to anyone.

"Son of a bitch!" Talon screamed, slamming his fist into the wall.

Phoenix and Warlord ran into the room and saw him shaking in the doorway. They looked past him and saw Morty's corpse in the center of the room.

"Did they take anything?" Phoenix touched Talon's shoulder, snapping him out of his trance. The last thing Phoenix wanted was for the Nibirium to be stolen.

Talon took a deep breath and avoided looking at Morty's body as he went to the workbench. Everything had been rearranged, but nothing seemed to be missing. "No." he said, trying to keep his emotions in check. He walked to the corner and lifted the lid off a plastic trash can. He pulled out two pistols that he had hidden in a plastic bag and a small black case. "They didn't check this either."

He handed the case to Warlord and a pistol to Phoenix. The pistols' barrels had been customized. Faint blue lights glowed along the barrel as Talon flicked the safety off. He put on the SPEX glasses and turned on the X-ray vision to look through the ship's hull. It was time for swift retaliation and vengeance.

Yankee approached the aft weapons storage room. Looking through the porthole, she saw various standard weapons and a few she did not recognize. Confidant that she was in the right place, she smiled and moved to open the door, only to find it locked. Her smile disappeared.

"Damn it!" she whispered. She quickly removed a lock-picking tool from one of her pockets.

"Did you really think we would be dumb enough to leave

our weapons locker unlocked?" Hearing the confidence of the woman behind her told Yankee everything she needed to know.

She whirled and fired. The woman was so surprised, she was unable to avoid the bullet, which penetrated her lower rib cage. As the woman staggered backward from the momentum of the bullet, Yankee charged while simultaneously unsheathing her combat knife.

The Asian woman outmaneuvered Yankee's first few strikes. The adrenaline of the fight must have numbed the pain of the gunshot, but Yankee knew exactly where she had wounded her opponent and how quickly she would lose blood. Within moments, Yankee's strength and the blood loss from the hole in the petite woman's torso tipped the scales in Yankee's favor, and she sliced the petite female across her neck. The woman staggered backward to avoid further injury, but with an insane look of sadistic glee on her face, Yankee shoved her knife into the woman's stomach and turned the blade. The woman's pain-filled scream bounced off the metal hallway like a shrieking spirit until blood filled her throat, muffling her final cry of anguish.

"Go to sleep, little girl!" Yankee whispered through gritted teeth as she turned the knife again, feeling warm blood saturate her gloved hand.

Before Yankee could enjoy watching the life drain from her enemy's eyes, another scream echoed through the hallway.

"No!" Dizzy lunged into the fight, throwing all her weight into Yankee's face. The female brute fell back from a stunning cross punch.

Dizzy shouted, enraged at seeing Nitro's body slide down the wall, bleeding from her neck, stomach, and rib cage. That momentary pause was all that Yankee needed to recover from Dizzy's bone-cracking punch. One kick sent Dizzy into the wall.

"Yo, sista, you damn near broke my jaw!" Yankee shouted, spitting blood.

"She's family," Dizzy growled. "You're dead!"

Pain mixed with fury as Dizzy charged at Yankee. The large intruder was quick and agile as she blocked and countered the first several strikes, but Dizzy was calculating and had blindingly fast reflexes. She attacked with combination after combination of boxing blows to Yankee's torso and face, throwing in a few ridge–hand strikes to keep her opponent off balance. Dizzy could tell the woman didn't have the endurance that she possessed. When Yankee landed on the floor, she looked surprised that she had been knocked down. With Yankee looking dazed, breathless, bewildered, Dizzy paused her attack, wanting her opponent to suffer.

"Fast hands, bitch!" Yankee said as she leapt to her feet with amazing control and recovery. "My turn!"

"Fuck this!" Sandman grunted. He opened fire, catching Yankee in the leg, but it merely slowed her down. Dizzy turned, not realizing that Sandman and Slyder had arrived from around the corner.

With a clear and uninterrupted line of sight to his target, Sandman shot Yankee in the other leg and in each shoulder before the charging human–rhino fell to the floor. Even though she was wounded, she yelled, enraged that she had been bested. Deacon rounded the corner and rushed to Nitro's aid while Dizzy, Sandman, and Slyder quickly disarmed Yankee while she squirmed in helpless pain on the floor.

"Time to talk, bitch!" Slyder said, kneeling on Yankee's bleeding leg while Dizzy rushed to Nitro's side. Yankee glared at Sandman and Slyder, then glanced at Nitro's body. For a moment, remorse and regret flashed in her eyes, but only for a moment.

"Fuck it!" Yankee smiled with difficulty, her cracked jaw

beginning to swell. Then she bit down on something in her mouth and went into convulsions.

"Hell no!" Sandman yelled as he and Slyder tried to pry her mouth open, but it was too late. She died within seconds, her face contorting in pain. Slyder dropped back, angry at being beaten without a fight. Dizzy watched as the foaming acid poured out of Yankee's mouth.

"Suicide pills? Who still does that?" Slyder asked, out of breath.

His hands drenched in Nitro's blood, Deacon tried everything he could to stop her bleeding, to no avail. When her body stopped moving, and the open wound slowed its blood release, Deacon stopped his desperate struggle. He checked Nitro's vitals and shook his head. Dizzy's body shook with sobs as she clung to the body of her closest friend and pseudo sister. In the midst of her grieving, Dizzy wondered how she would explain this to Nitro's cousin, Jet.

Quebec looked through the porthole in the door of the primary weapons locker and smiled at the large arsenal. As he reached into one of his pouches, he looked up at the opposite corner of the foyer to see a camera directed at the door and him. It was obvious to him that the camera was not standard for this model of warship.

"Damn!" he whispered as he grabbed his lock–picking tool. He crouched down and began picking the lock when the door suddenly clicked open and slammed into his face, knocking him backward. The largest man he had ever seen stood in the doorway holding a machete in one hand and a futuristic-looking rifle in the other.

"I was getting a few toys before I came to look for you, but

now you've come to me." the man said with a heavy Latin accent
and a sadistic smile, staring confidently at Quebec.

Quebec reached for his pistol, but the behemoth kicked it
out of his hand. Quebec dove to the side, rolling to his feet and
grabbing his knife from its sheath at the same time. The huge
man tossed his rifle into the weapons locker. Quebec winced as
the tower of muscle and girth closed the door and stood
between him and his gun.

The giant charged with a feral smile, swinging his machete.
Quebec ducked and weaved away from each swing, looking for
an opening, but the Latin Sasquatch was too massive for him to
maneuver around. Luckily, the tight hallway forced the big man
to shorten his broad swings and alternate them with lunges.

Lobo's machete lunged for Quebec's neck, but he slipped to
the side, slicing the giant's wrist with his knife. The man–beast
let out a roar like an angry grizzly bear as Quebec moved past
him, only to see a tall young man wearing goggles standing at
the end of the hallway, an augmented pistol in hand.

"Lobo, don't kill him!" the young man shouted, "We need
answers!" Quebec's newest opponent kept his aim focused on
Quebec as he raised his goggles, revealing his identity to
Quebec. Quebec wasn't sure if he should be relieved or cautious
that his secondary objective had come to him: Talon, Captain
Phoenix's son and chief scientist.

Quebec gauged the distance between him, Talon, and his
pistol, which was lying on the floor between them. Talon was
aiming at Quebec's chest. All Quebec had to do was get him to
shoot Lobo, and then he could capture or kill Talon and take the
augmented pistol from him. Although Quebec's primary orders
were to collect weapons and snatch the boy genius, he was
outgunned and out of time, so he figured that preventing the kid
from making more inventions was better than explaining how
Talon had gotten away.

"I surrender." Quebec dropped his knife and raised his hands. Talon relaxed slightly and lowered his aim to Quebec's waist.

Lobo wrapped his arm around Quebec and reached for his throat. As soon as Quebec felt the giant's fingers touch his neck, he grabbed Lobo by his hair and shirt and threw himself into a crouch, using the momentum to flip Lobo over his body. Then Quebec grabbed his knife and plunged it into Lobo's neck.

Talon froze in shock at the amount of blood spurting from Lobo's torn neck. His hands trembled as he shot at the charging intruder, but each shot whizzed past the dodging assassin. Adrenaline and fear filled Talon's body as he stepped back to put more distance between them. He clenched his finger, and a blue bolt struck his attacker's arm.

"Gah!" Quebec dropped his knife but continued charging toward Talon.

Quebec ducked below Talon's arms and punched him in the ribs with his good arm. Talon dropped his pistol as he chopped downward with his elbow. Talon drove his knee repeatedly into the man's stomach, but between blows, Quebec managed to grab a smaller knife from his belt and slam it into Talon's thigh.

Talon doubled over, clutching his leg, which gave Quebec enough time to get behind him. He pulled Talon into a head-lock, wincing as he held him with his bad arm, then he kneed Talon in the back, causing him to yell and drop lower.

Quebec reached over with his good arm and picked up Talon's augmented pistol. "Neat gun." Quebec pressed the cold barrel against Talon's ribs. "Got any more?"

"Stop!" a voice thundered from the opposite end of the corridor.

Quebec pointed Talon's pistol at the newcomer, then froze in response to a familiar sight.

"Kilo?" Quebec said with shock and slight fear as he stared at Phoenix.

"D–Dad!" Talon shouted, then quickly corrected himself. "Captain!"

For a moment Phoenix's face twisted in rage, seeing his son held captive. Then he returned to his stoic self. "Quebec. What are you doing here?" he asked, anger tainting his voice.

"You're supposed to be dead, man!" Quebec snapped, shock all over his face. "What are you doing with these pirates?"

"You were never very smart, David." Phoenix said, glaring at Quebec. "This is my ship. The people who sent you didn't even show you footage of the captain of the ship you were sent to infiltrate, did they?"

"You can't be Phoenix! That's impossible! You're Kilo; you're dead!" Quebec's eyes flashed down at Talon, then back at Phoenix, seeing the resemblance between the two.

"Why exactly are you on my ship, Quebec? Who sent you, and what are you looking for?"

Quebec's face changed with the realization that his chances of escaping the ship were gone. He was injured and was now holding the son of a former fellow combatant at gunpoint. He narrowed his eyes and pointed the pistol at Talon's neck.

"You know I can't tell you, Kilo. The mission comes first." Quebec said, trying to maintain his nerve. "You taught me that."

"Let go of him!" Phoenix ordered, his pistol aimed at Quebec's head.

"He's my ticket out of here. Shoot me, and your son dies! You know how twitchy my trigger finger can get."

Phoenix remained still. He knew that if Quebec fired, the round would go down into Talon's arteries and heart, and there would be no way to save him. Fear set in as he imagined his son dying. Phoenix made sure not to allow his greatest concern to show on his face, though.

"I'm sorry," Talon whispered. Phoenix could see that despite the pain, his son's eyes were filled with disappointment in himself. He also knew that Talon was aware that his father would make sure Quebec didn't leave the ship alive.

The sound of heavy boots on the metal floor caused Quebec to look behind him and instinctively raise his pistol toward the newcomer, Warlord. The second the pistol was away from Talon's body, Phoenix fired.

The first blue bolt of light hit Quebec's shoulder. Talon dropped to the ground, giving his father clearance to open fire. In seconds, Quebec's torso and face were shredded by the augmented ammunition.

Even before Quebec's lifeless body dropped to the floor, Phoenix was sprinting toward his only son. He hugged Talon, tears falling down his face.

"Dad, I'm sorry!" Talon sobbed. "Lobo's dead because of me."

"It's alright," Phoenix whispered. "You did the best you could."

Warlord activated his communication device. "All crew, this is Warlord. Second assailant is down. All combat units conduct a ship-wide search for any unauthorized personnel or unidentifiable objects—explosives, surveillance equipment, anything. Warlord out."

He turned to Phoenix, waiting for his next order. Phoenix pulled away from his son and activated his communication device while eyeing Quebec's corpse.

"Sandman, Phoenix." Phoenix said, his voice leveling.

"Sandman here, sir." Sandman replied.

"The other intruder. Black woman, stocky build, light-colored hair?" Phoenix's voice sounded numb, emotionless.

"Yes, sir." Sandman's tone implied a question, but he dared not ask the captain over an open channel how he was able to identify a person he had not seen.

"Phoenix out." Phoenix responded, ending the transmission. "Yankee."

"Phonetic call signs." Warlord realized while watching Phoenix.

"And he called you Kilo." Talon pointed out, struggling to keep his voice calm. "I thought 'Kilo' was just a nickname you had when you were younger."

Phoenix did not answer, his eyes fixed on Quebec's corpse.

"Who was this guy?" Warlord asked.

"We worked together a long time ago." Phoenix said, turning to look at his son. "When I was younger. Covert ops."

"Was there anything you did that was public knowledge, cuz?"

Talon was taken aback with the fact that despite all that had happened and that there were two dead bodies in their proximity, Warlord's tone was that of a conversation at the dinner table.

"Just civilian work." Phoenix said.

Talon squatted to examine the body. "We may have a problem." he said as he removed Quebec's damaged goggles, staring at the miniature camera mounted on the side.

"A camera?" Phoenix asked.

"Does it have memory?" Warlord inquired.

"I don't think it had much. It's damaged now." Talon said while examining the device.

"Which means it was probably transmitting a signal somewhere off ship." Phoenix looked at Warlord, who acted with urgency.

"Communications, this is Warlord. Jam all frequencies coming from this ship until further notice."

"Communications, copy, Commander." a young male voice responded.

"Talon, you and Hacker get on this right away. Pull all the

data you can from this one and the other one then destroy them." Phoenix ordered.

"They may have trackers on them." Talon said.

"Exactly."

"What about the bodies?" Warlord asked.

Phoenix looked at Warlord with controlled anger, then turned back to Quebec's body. "Pull all useful data, then give them an acid bath." he said before turning to walk away.

24

LEAVING NEW AMERICA

∼

Throughout the night the ship's crew worked diligently to remove all signs that there had been an attack hours prior. The science team was well versed in the process of thoroughly removing all evidence of blood and bone from crime scenes, so there was no lingering evidence. The mixture of acids, bleach, and other solvents employed was a useful cocktail for dissolving flesh and various clothing materials, which prevented evidence of any attacker from being found at a later date in case the ship was boarded.

At sunrise the *Blood Sky* crew held funeral services for Lobo, Medina, Morty, and Nitro. Jet told Phoenix that her cousin's wish was to be buried at sea, so he felt content in being able to meet that request. Medina's wife and child attended the brief funeral service, devastated and crying. Because *Blood Sky* was the home for the crew, many members had either brought their loved ones onboard to assist with non-combat duties, and others had found love amongst the crew members. When Talon called *Blood Sky* their home, he meant that active crew members raised their families on the ship. Lobo had no blood relatives to mourn his passing, but he had the SOCIT crew, who loved him as much as any family he had ever experienced. As for Morty, he was an orphan who was so excited on the day that Talon accepted him into the ranks of the science and engineering division to be his protégé. Talon could not stop staring at Morty's body, wrapped so in a specially designed burial shroud that was weighted on the bottom and had an optional window on the torso area in case the person died in a manner that made the body presentable for viewing.

Jun stood with the commanders on the upper deck to attend the services. She reflected on her day with Nitro, who had been so bubbly and full of energy when they were shopping. It was difficult to accept that she had only met her a few days earlier. All that remained were memories as Jun and the crew watched the bodies being carried over the edge of the rail, followed by a formal salute.

After the funerals, Jun and her team prepared to leave *Blood Sky*. They were impressed and appreciative that Phoenix had ordered his deck crew to fill the helicopter's fuel tanks. She mentioned that she would be sure to inform the emperor of this generous deed, as fuel of any kind was in short supply and very expensive. Before entering *Black Arrow*, Jun and her escorts bowed with respect to Phoenix and the command team.

When Manh and Alvin stepped closer to their helicopter, Jun Li intentionally stayed in position staring at Phoenix, her eyes softened and filled with despair.

"Captain." Jun called out. Phoenix remained, staring at her as the rest of his team stepped away from the chopper. She wanted to express how appreciative she was of how he protected her while avenging his crew, but she saw in his eyes that he was still numb and angry from the previous night. His expression had returned to the stone-faced warrior she met in the midst of chaos over a week ago. She felt an emotion stirring deep within for this man that found a way to balance violence and peace in a way she had not seen before. She wanted to tell him positive, encouraging words, but she wasn't sure if they would be received at this time, so she stared. That was when she saw it. The glimmer of hope deep in his gaze that made her feel that in spite of all that he had gone through, he somehow managed to show gentleness towards her in his eyes. It was just a subtle hint, but it was enough for her to hold on to. This was all she needed to confirm that they would meet again when the conditions were better. "Thank you." Was all she felt she needed to say verbally. He blinked. Then his eyes smiled ever so slightly before he blinked again. Her respectful head bow, acknowledged the acceptance that he knew what she meant. That was good enough for her to turn and boarded the helicopter with no regrets.

Once the helicopter was far enough away, Phoenix turned to his commanders on the flight deck, his face grim. "Everyone, meet me in the War Room." They followed him without comment, realizing he had something important to discuss now that Jun and her team were off the ship.

Minutes later, Phoenix was seated at the head of the board-room-style table. Also seated were Warlord, Swan, Kite, Athena, Falcon, Sandman, and Talon.

"We have a problem." Phoenix said, going straight to the point. That was never a good sign. "Jun Li came onboard to tell me that she received intel that Vice President of Homeland Security Karen Harp is making plans to get Blood Sky's technology."

"Jun told you this?" Kite asked, raising one eyebrow.

"Yes." Phoenix replied with an expression that indicated that no further details on that portion of the discussion were necessary.

"Which technology is she after?" Talon asked, worried.

"Jun wasn't able to get those details, but I think Harp wants all of it."

"But for her to get that she'd have to take—"

"The whole ship." Phoenix said. Everyone in the room expressed mixed levels of concern, frustration, and anger.

"Can she do that?" Athena asked.

"She tried in the Senate meeting by accusing us of being involved with the abduction, trying to get the Senate committee to authorize a search of Blood Sky for contraband. I'm sure that she intended to duplicate or confiscate any tech they found. Fortunately, her request was denied, at least temporarily."

"You think she sent those two last night?" Warlord asked.

Phoenix nodded. "I'm sure of it."

"Then you know she'll try again." Sandman said. "She has a reputation for not giving up and always getting what she wants."

"This I know." Phoenix replied.

"It's not like we didn't know this was coming, especially after she got the DHS position." Warlord said. "I just didn't expect it to be so soon."

"I'm sure rescuing the senators tipped our hand when we had to expose some of our tech to government officials," Phoenix noted. "Getting to them before the Navy didn't help."

"We were sailing under everyone's radar all these years, unnoticed." Warlord said. "Damn!"

"Maybe we shouldn't have done the rescue op." Falcon mumbled.

"That was not an option," Phoenix stated.

"I know, sir. But it cost Nitro and Lobo their lives. Medina too, and he wasn't even a combatant." Falcon's voice was filled with regret.

"This was why I left the government in the first place." Phoenix admitted. "Too much need for control over things that don't belong to them. And you never know who your friends are or if the same people who are loyal to you today will be loyal to you tomorrow."

"Let them come!" Talon said, glaring at the table and trying to keep himself from tearing up again. "So we can avenge our crew!"

"No," Phoenix insisted. "We're not ready for what they'll bring."

Talon looked at Warlord for support, puzzled as the giant shook his head. "But we've won every battle with every pirate who's ever come at us." Talon said.

"That's because Phoenix is a smart captain and only goes up against an opponent he knows we can beat." Warlord explained. Talon turned to Phoenix, who merely looked at him without saying a word.

"But they were tough!" Talon added. "Look at what we did to the terrorists that abducted the senators!"

"And look at what they did to Lola." Swan reminded him, an edge of frustration creeping into her voice. "We just finished putting her back together."

"We're not here to challenge anyone." Phoenix said calmly. "That's not what we're about."

"And we're not ready to go head to head with them either." Warlord reiterated.

"But we're Blood Sky!" Talon cried. "Are we just going to let them get away with killing our crew? Our family?"

The room fell silent for a moment. They saw the might of Phoenix in Talon's words, though it was driven by lack of experience. Kite looked away, concerned at what Phoenix's drive would be like without the wisdom needed to control such passion. She saw it in her younger brother. Talon was not listening or seeing the entire situation. His ego was blinding him from the truth. His guilt for his actions in the altercation against Quebec was disguised by his eagerness to right a wrong.

"Don't you understand, Axel? We've gone up against backwater pirates, not New America's military!" Kite snapped. "We've never gone up against a world power before. We're only one ship!"

"Talon," Warlord said calmly, "Me, Athena, Sandman, Proctor, and your father have been on the battlefield of military and civilian operations for a long time together. We have a good idea of how they're going to come at us."

Athena looked at Talon and tapped her eyepatch as if to say that losing an eye served as her personal reminder. "Captain Phoenix and Warlord helped write some of New America's training manuals on tactical maneuvers." she said.

"Great!" Talon sank into his chair. A moment later, he stopped pouting and straightened up in his seat. He was a commander, after all. "So, we would be going against commandos like SOCIT?"

Athena nodded. "An entire fleet of commanders who may have received the strategic training that Phoenix and Warlord taught."

"Put that with the fact that we're one ship against whatever number they can send at us, and we're not ready." Phoenix explained.

"But can she control the military?" Talon asked, still unwilling to concede the point. "She's just one person."

"She's not in charge of the military, but if she gives a good reason, she might be given a squadron of ships, which would still outgun us." Phoenix stated.

"Especially since they would *all* be military trained while only a little over half our team have received that level of training." Warlord pointed out.

"But we're combat ready." Talon insisted.

"We are essentially a merchant ship with a few teams of combat-trained mercenaries onboard." Warlord said. "We're not a military warship. We just live on one."

"Yes, and we would give them one hell of a fight before we died or got arrested." Phoenix replied.

"What do we do, Captain?" Falcon asked. "We can't just let them take Blood Sky, can we, sir?"

"Not at all." Phoenix replied. "That will never be an option. For now we'll continue our course to pick up cargo from Cuba and transport it to Brazil. Talon, have your science team prepare to break off."

"Where are we going?" Talon asked.

"You and your team are going to Thunder Island. You'll need to help with phase two."

Talon's expression turned to anticipation.

"Phase two, sir?" Sandman asked, exchanging a bewildered look with Falcon.

"I'll explain in detail another time." Phoenix said. "Like we said, we were expecting this, just not so soon. If we can stall the harpy from doing anything for a few more months while we keep moving around the ocean, then maybe we'll be ready for her when she comes."

The hopeful tone in Phoenix's voice inspired his team.

25

MORE THAN A MERCHANT

~

In an undisclosed editing room somewhere in the seedy part of York Jersey Island, Vice President Harp walked in with a sense of urgency. DHS Agent Xavier "X-ray" McClain was holding the door open for her. X-ray was a tall Black martial artist who was known for having heightened situational awareness, making him the perfect protector for his job. He was suspicious of everything and often insensitive to the greater picture, focusing mostly on the here and now of all current situations. He wore a suit and tie alongside Harp, who was radiantly dressed, as always.

"Wait for me outside, X." Harp said with a wave of her hand, not making eye contact with the large-framed protector.

"Yes, Madam Vice President." X-ray replied then closed the door. The editing technician kept his back to Harp as he worked at his computer, which was linked to several monitors.

"Were you able to recover any useful footage before the signal stopped?" Harp's voice was calm and patient, but her eyes stared at the back of the technician's head as if she was holding back violence.

"Yes but not a lot," the technician replied. "The signal had a hard time getting through all the metal in that old ship's hull."

"But you captured something?" she asked, growing impatient.

The technician pressed a few keys, then leaned back in his seat as he pointed to the large monitor on the wall in front of them.

Harp stepped forward and stood beside the technician's workstation. His lustful eyes scanned her, surprised to see her in a sexy but elegant dress that displayed her cleavage and her legs. He didn't attempt to hide his stare when she caught his gaze.

"You pulled me out of a very important fundraiser, so this had better be worth my attention." she warned. The truth of the matter was, it was her modus operandi to always be present during a public function when she gave the order for an unsanctioned operation to take place. This gave her plausible deniability and the perfect alibi if things did not go as planned or if an investigation involving a lie detector was presented.

"This is what I have so far." the technician said, refocusing on his monitors.

She watched the images of *Blood Sky's* interior from the point of view of a person in motion. In the bottom-right portion of the screen was the word "YANKEE." The view showed unusual weapons on the other side of a glass porthole.

"What type of guns are those?" Harp asked, pointing at the screen.

"I don't know. I'm not into guns unless it's in a game." The technician frowned as if she had asked a stupid question to ask him. She caught his condescending look but remained silent.

"Are you able to put screenshots of those images on a memory chip, so I can take it with me?"

"Sure, that's easy, but that's not why I called you." He looked over his shoulder at her and smiled after enjoying a second peek at her athletic figure while she stared at the screen.

"Why?" Harp asked, hope rising. "What did you find?"

"Some really cool gamer tech!" the technician said as he typed on his keyboard. Harp rolled her eyes, then pulled up a seat to sit next to him.

"Show me." she said, growing more impatient. She watched as the view on the main screen changed from Yankee to Quebec, along with the image.

"Here you go!" the technician said before playing the recording. Harp watched the main monitor as Phoenix fired multiple shots at the camera from Quebec's point of view. She jumped at the sudden barrage, seemingly headed in her direction.

"He killed him!"

"Dude," the technician said, "he didn't just kill him. He tore his shit up!"

Harp looked away from the screen, multiple options racing through her mind. "That's useful. At least now I know why my team didn't report in."

"It gets better." the technician said.

"What do you mean?"

"It's not just *that* they shot him. It's *how* they shot him."

"What do you mean?"

"Was this already edited by some gamer, like me?" the technician asked, casting a suspicious look at Harp. "Do you have someone else on your payroll?"

"No. Why?"

"Look at it again when I slow it down."

She focused on the screen as the technician played the shooting at a slower speed. Harp's eyes widened in wonder as she stared at the light-blue projectiles that fired from Phoenix's gun.

"What are those?"

"I'm not sure, but I think they're ice bullets."

"There's no such thing as an ice bullet."

"I heard they tried it a while back, but the ice was too light-weight to be accurate."

"What would be the significance of a bullet made from ice?" Harp asked, staring at the image, which was now frozen with the projectiles in motion.

"Are you kidding, dude?" The technician looked at her as if she were stupid.

She stared back at him, awaiting his answer. "Enlighten me."

"You shoot someone, and there's no exit wound, depending on the caliber and the power behind the shot. But if anyone checks later, there's also no bullet to be traced back with ballistics to any gun. It's the ultimate assassin weapon, bro!" Her face remained placid in the face of the technician's giddiness. "A bullet that dissolves after it's done its damage."

"And you're saying such a thing exists?" she asked.

"Hell no! Well, I didn't think so until I saw this. It would be the kind of thing a gamer would think of."

"A gamer?"

"Yeah, you know." The technician smirked. "Young guys like me who play interactive games and shit."

"Damn it!" Harp shouted. The son.

"What's wrong?"

"Nothing! Put all that on a memory chip too." she growled.

"You got it." The technician began working his keyboard as Harp stood up and started to pace, then stopped when a thought began to emerge.

"I need you to do one more thing."

"Sure."

"Edit some of this footage, but I don't want it to look like it was altered. Can you do that?" She smiled at him. The technician smiled back.

"You bet! Isn't that why you hired me?" He winked before taking a moment to stare at her exposed athletic legs from the slit in her fitted gown. Then he started typing again.

"Yes, it is." Harp said, giving him a seductive look.

As the technician worked, different screenshots from Quebec's footage appeared on the screen. Harp focused on the image of Talon aiming his augmented gun and wearing the SPEX goggles that he introduced during the Senate meeting.

An unmarked hunter-green civilian helicopter flew from the north over the Florida Strait off the coast of the Miami Isles, which opened into the Atlantic Ocean. The helicopter had no running lights or distinguishing marks to identify its registration code. It flew at a substantial distance from *Blood Sky* so as not to present a threat or to show up on radar. Piloting the aircraft was Theta. At her side in the passenger seat was her brother, Omega. They watched as *Blood Sky* grew smaller while heading out to the safety of the Central Ocean and international waters.

"This is as close as I can get to Blood Sky without risking being seen." Theta said with a British accent as she pulled her long strawberry-blond hair farther back from her cheek.

"It doesn't matter." Omega said, frowning. His accent was muddled between proper British and rugged Scottish, but his features were sharp and model−like, including a thick head of rich blond hair and steel-blue eyes. "Quebec and Yankee missed the pickup, and we lost the signal."

"We could have gotten closer, but the Shangri−La chopper was still on board when their signals went dark." Theta said.

"Yes, and they didn't leave until the destroyer was out of New

America's jurisdiction, so we can't touch them now without her having to challenge US politicians."

"And you know she wouldn't want that."

"Yes, Theta," Omega said, sighing in frustration. "I know that."

"What are you going to tell her?" Theta asked.

"The truth. She'll have to find another way."

"What's next?"

"Let's get out of here." Omega ordered.

As Theta veered the helicopter back toward New America air space, Omega's cell phone rang. He pulled it out and looked at the screen.

"Is that her?" Theta asked.

"Worse. It's him."

"Do you think he knows what we're doing?"

"I don't know, but I have to answer it." Omega said after switching his headset and microphone to link with his cell phone. "Alpha? Theta's online with me."

"What is your present location?" Alpha asked.

"We're in the air under her orders to pick up two of her agents."

"You're following Blood Sky?"

"Yes, Alpha."

"Why would two of her agents be near Blood Sky?" Alpha asked in a reprimanding tone.

Omega hesitated.

"I asked you a question." Alpha said.

"She told us to go in as the extraction team after they completed their mission. We were supposed to retrieve them from the water once Blood Sky was far enough away."

"Then what happened?"

"They missed their rendezvous time and are off the grid."

"Then they're dead."

"Yes." Omega replied.

"Were these agents people of color?"

"Yes, Alpha. A Black man and Black woman."

"Two of ours?" Alpha asked, frustration in his voice. Omega hesitated before answering, wondering if Alpha had guessed or was aware of the mission details.

"Yes, Alpha. Quebec and Yankee."

"Damn it! She did that on purpose."

"Why do you think that?"

"She decided they were expendable, just like she did with Phoenix years ago."

"But how could she know they wouldn't succeed?" Theta asked. "They're part of PALADIN."

"Because the ship's captain was a PALADIN agent too."

"He was?" Omega was not prepared for that answer.

"Yes." Alpha responded with a tone of regret.

"Do you want us to eliminate him?"

"No! Your orders are to stand down. Report to her that her agents never made the rendezvous and then head back."

"But the PALADIN code states that anyone who takes a PALADIN life must be hunted down and killed."

"No, it states that they are to be judged and sentenced. That is the original PALADIN code, not your interpretation of the rules, Omega!"

"Yes, Alpha." Omega pouted at being berated.

"There is more to this than you know."

"What do you mean?"

"The crew of Blood Sky has access to advanced technology. One of the crew commanders has above-average strength, and the records show that before he disappeared, the captain possessed a high IQ and a natural ability to infrequently predict the future in real time."

"You're not saying he's a hybrid, are you?" Theta asked.

"That has yet to be determined."

"But if he used to work for your government then you have access to his DNA records." Omega said.

"The captain, his cousin, and two of his children worked for the New America government." Alpha replied. "I remember their records showing anomalies that could not be explained."

"Then you checked their genome, right?"

"No longer available. Every government facility that would have stored their DNA was destroyed during your father's damn Vapor Incursion. After that such information was sealed and classified beyond my reach." Alpha spoke with regret of the calamity.

"What about one of those civilian find-your-relatives-dot-com sites?" Theta suggested, wanting to change the subject from her father's error in judgment.

"They weren't naïve enough to willingly give their DNA samples to civilian companies, so they could later be sold to the highest bidder as company property. Phoenix is smarter than that." Alpha said.

"Then how do you know about the anomalies?"

"As I said before, their test scores. High IQ and exceptional talents above all standard results. Phoenix graduated high school before he turned sixteen, and his three children each received their bachelors degrees by the age of eighteen. His son has a natural ability to solve technical problems, which contributes to his inventions. One of his daughters can identify medical conditions without a detailed invasive examination or a patient history. The other daughter can see complicated technology in her head that doesn't exist, then reproduce what she sees in design format. This works well with the son's ability to solve complicated equations. And the big guy, Warlord, is freakishly strong."

"Then you're saying they *are* hybrids." Omega said, concern in his voice.

"I'm saying this captain may be the key."

"The key to what?" Omega asked.

"Everything."

"Are we supposed to know what that means?" Omega asked. Alpha went silent for several moments. Omega waited patiently, sensing that it was in his best interest not to press any further.

"We will deal with this another way." Alpha said.

"And what about Quebec and Yankee?"

"I'll address that. For now, call her and report to her *only* what is necessary regarding Quebec and Yankee."

"Yes, Alpha." Omega replied before disconnecting. He turned to Theta, but she said nothing more.

EPILOGUE

~

Harp paced the editing room in a rage while the technician sat quietly facing his multiple screens. "Damn it! He got away!" she snapped, disconnecting her call. She paced even faster as she pondered her dilemma. "Why didn't those slants get off the ship sooner?"

She took a deep breath to calm herself and then slowed her pace. After a few moments, she smiled and turned to the still image on the big screen in front of the technician, staring at the streaking blue projectiles.

"Maybe it's not too late." Harp said, a grin emerging on her face. "We'll just have to implement your edited footage ahead of schedule." She paused to look down at the back of his head. "You don't mind do you?"

Harp turned the technician in his chair, so she could reach the memory chip. The chair's momentum caused the technician to slump backward, a thin wire wrapped around his neck and blood dripping from the open wound.

"I'm sure you don't." she said pleasantly to his corpse as she removed the memory chip from the computer.

She walked to the door and opened it. X-ray was in the corridor, ready for her orders. He noticed the technician's body slumped over in the chair but remained unfazed.

"Ma'am?"

"Make it look like an accident or a suicide, X-ray. I don't care which." She turned to look at the equipment in the room. "I think an electrical fire would be good this time. Set it to go off in about an hour, so we can get back to the fundraiser and have an alibi, just in case."

"Yes, ma'am. I'll take care of it."

"I'll be in the car." she said as she walked out of the room. X-ray entered and closed the door behind him.

With a smug expression, she pulled out her cell phone and dialed a number. "I'm going to need to borrow your best surveillance technician." she said. "No, he didn't work out. He was disrespectful." She pursed her lips before continuing. "Once I have this footage edited, we'll call an emergency meeting in about a week, so I can say that an investigation turned up new evidence." Harp paused to listen to the voice on the other end of the line.

"When they see what I have, it will be the first step to officially declaring Phoenix a renegade from the law. He will be branded a pirate, and once he's arrested or dead, his ship and all the technology on it will be mine."